WHITE FANGS
GARETH J GOULD

This is a work of fiction. Names, characters, places, and incidents either are the product of the author's imagination or are used fictitiously. Any resemblance to actual persons, living or dead, events, or locales is entirely coincidental

Text copyright © Gareth J. Gould, 2022

Map illustration by Gareth J. Gould and Michael Schafer, 2022
Front cover created in Canva

The moral rights of the author have been asserted

All rights reserved
No part of this book may be reproduced in any form by electronic or mechanical means, including information storage and retrieval systems, without the written permission of the copyright owner

Acknowledgements

With thanks to Michael Schafer, without whom my writing days would have been over not long after they had begun. Thanks to Melissa Gould, whose time spent as an alpha reader she will never get back, and above all, thanks to my wife, Lyndsey Gould, whose unwavering support is the sole reason this manuscript was dusted off and published.

White Fang and surrounding territories,
by Drenik, Advisor to the King

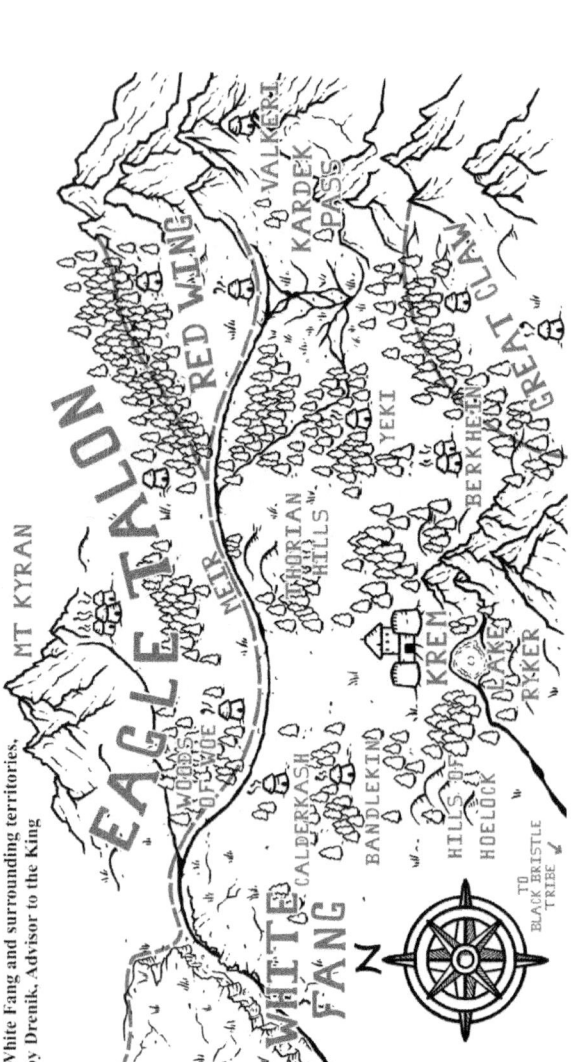

Prologue

Ever since man began to walk upright, he has invented and schemed, forever imagining himself in the likeness of a god. He grew too clever for the other animals to molest him and too powerful for the limitations of nature to hold him back. Until, at last, the only worthwhile enemy of man was himself.

Young Reshmal sat on the cold stonework contemplating this under the half-guttered hallway lights. He had done so for the last hour; such was the magnitude of the decision he was about to make. As long as man looked out for himself, he would always have enemies, and for Reshmal, his were those who stood in the way of progress. He knew that ambition was both sanctity and sin, but the world flourished on necessary evil. In nature, the weakest offspring starved, and predators killed those who were not quick enough to escape with the herd. Invariably, the natural world sought to shed itself from those who would merely hold it back. Therefore, it was only natural for man to impose his superior knowledge of order and justice upon those without – even if they themselves did not know they needed it.

Beyond the palace walls, Reshmal heard the faint ringing of the bell tower chiming the hour of midnight. It was now or never. The heavy chamber door swung open, and two bronze bound guards emerged and proceeded down the hallway, passing him by in the gloom. With the stark realisation that his moment was now upon him, he slid up the wall to his feet and stole through the doorway, adrenalin compelling him into action. Within, a small firelight cast its sombre glow across the blood-red tapestries and tarnished bronze gilded ornaments. To his surprise and fortune, the door to the emperor's bed chamber stood ajar. As silent as death he entered and brooded above the sleeping figure. Even in this gloom, Reshmal could see the deep wrinkles age had given his emperor, once a defiant conquering ruler, now a mere shell, empty of all ambition and dreams. Still, men say the emperor is immortal, placed by the Gods, and infallible in his actions – perhaps this was why his first blow caught in the bed sheets. Emperor Rundir's eyes flicked open. In the grogginess he sent word with a slave woman that he wished to speak with the king before removing his halberd and seating himself on the crumbling stone steps, running through the explanations of his actions in his head. They would be seen as mere excuses, he knew.

When the wait grew, Kalac examined his weapon. He would have to provide the halberd with a proper clean and reoil the head, but there was no damage to the haft or its leather-bound strapping. Once satisfied, he drew some dried leaves from a pouch at his side and struck a small fire to warm him through. He eyed the passers-by in what remained of the orange evening light; men and women scurried between the myriad huts executing various tasks to keep the community healthy and complacent: food in their bellies, thatched roofs over their heads, and weapons in their burly hands. Some glanced back at him, a blank expression disguising their mild disdain. It was not wars that they hated. War was a necessary part of life. The population of Neferia had exploded in recent years, and each tribe encroached into another's territory vying for one extra pasture, one extra hillock, one extra tree. And it would cost a handful of lives to protect, but defend it you must. For if you allowed them one tree, why would they not return for another? And another? No, he guilt rested upon his shoulders. Kalac felt miserable. They expected too much from the eldest son of the great tactician, whose shadow had long hidden him from the warmth of his own achievements and was impossible to step out from under. He weaved his way through the crowd, his head hung low with an unhealthy mixture of shame and resentment. What did they know of the difficulties he faced? Perhaps they would have understood had they witnessed the unfamiliar tactics these foreigners had fought with, but he knew it was not enough. He had not proven himself a competent leader even when the battles had been assured, and now he was paying the price. Cursing his accusing mind, he drew his thoughts to the foreign, Talran-designed shortsword in his left hand. The weapon was a puny affair compared to the great cleaving weapons the Neferians preferred. Even his own unusual weapon, the halberd, raided from a far southern country where it was birthed, looked far more deadly than its Talran mass-produced counterpart. And yet, he had seen the devastation it wrought in battle.

He trudged through the dirt paths between the numerous mud huts of the outer city and the weathered stone buildings of the inner part where the more valued members of the tribe resided. As he approached the decrepit palace,

1

The torn red flags with the faded white motif of the bear fang danced high either side of the wooden city gates. For the small group of battle-weary and weather-sodden warriors approaching, it was a sign of the homecoming celebrations soon to follow, and all but one would be glad to once again be within the sanctity of her crudely constructed stone walls.

For Kalac, the welcome would not be so warm.

When the gates were heaved open, Kalac saw the throng of women and children gathered about the entrance, their necks craned for a sight of their loved ones. Their wide, hope filled eyes imploring questions many would not receive an answer to: where is my lover, my brother, my father? And for every desperate plea, another hate consumed stare would fix itself on Kalac, for he should have been leading them, and therefore the after sleep, he glimpsed his attacker's features in the ill light.

'Reshmal?'

The second blow did not miss. The dagger plunged into the emperor's lungs, and Reshmal watched as he wheezed his last breaths.

Casting the weapon out of the window, the new Emperor Reshmal II, son of Rundir, raised the alarm. In the ensuing chaos, he had blamed the chamber guards for the atrocity. At least five were put to death in the exaggerated conspiracies which followed. Of Reshmal, there was no spoken suspicion, for the emperor was placed by the Gods and to speak out against him was to speak out against the Gods themselves. No man, no matter how strong their conviction, wished upon themselves that sudden, dreadful foreshortening of life.

And so man ascends to infallibility as the God Emperor, another weakened link in his battle to break the chains of mortality, another step towards that ultimate goal. Unfortunately, gods – even gods in the making – are very rarely appeased.

thought, what they despise is me.

Nursing a growing irritation, he cursed the length of time he was being made to wait and slowly returned his attention to the Talran shortsword, remembering the tower shields which had accompanied them. The foreign soldiers had fought like a single soulless machine, devoid of all honour and glory, scores of eyes all showing the same condescending glare of civilised men forced into a backward corner of the world.

Civilisation, he thought, pahh! A pox on civilisation! His father had once said that such a thing was the death of the free man, and though he rarely saw eye to eye with his father, some of his more poignant beliefs had stuck with the young Kalac as he grew. 'They would call us barbarians,' his father had said. 'And why? Are threats and abuse not commonplace around their grand cities? Are men not rutting other men's women? And yet no one is insulted in Neferia because no man wishes to stake his life on the fight to the death which could follow, and very few men cheat, both at gambling or with another's woman. Rules which deny a man his natural instinct to defend what is his makes us naught but slaves to those with influence.' His fist came down in his hand. 'Cattle! All of them! It is a mercy we are not tainted by their sins. Be wary of an item called Coin, my son, for the foreigners brand it *the root of all evil*, yet it is the one thing they worship above all else. Men called Merchants horde it, and great Bank temples are raised in its name. Why the nine gods have not seen fit to destroy them, none can say, but against their taint, we must forever be vigilant.'

Eventually, the fire crackled and died. The smouldering embers aptly reflected Kalac's seething fury. Finally, the foreign slave woman he had sent to inform the king emerged from the massive oak doors behind him.

'Marek King grants you an audience, Kalac.' Her southern accent made difficult some of the pronunciation.

'Marek King grants you an audience,' he said, kicking the smouldering ashes of the dead fire with a leather sandal. 'I don't need to be granted an audience! I sent you to *tell* him I wished to speak with him! Rouse him from his sleep if you must!' Rage twisted in his stomach with the knowledge that he had already waited nearly two hours for that old man, and he dared the slave woman to voice it. Swiftly he hefted his weapon and marched up the few disintegrating stone steps to the, perhaps, once less dilapidated entrance to the palace where he had spent many years as a child and a youth. The slave trailed behind him as he trod through the grand hall to the throne room beyond. The brooding figure, Marek, King of the White Fang tribe, sat upon his raised high-backed throne but stood as the warrior entered. It was not a greeting. The slave woman bowed deep, but Kalac did not. The slight did not go unnoticed, and the king stepped down from the stone dais. His mood, as always with Kalac, was frosty.

'Speak.'

The reply was a clatter and a rasp as the shortsword slid across the stones to halt at Marek's feet. The king stared hard at the blade before lifting it, judging its weight.

'I told you to bring back a weapon, not a damn toothpick!' He swung it through the air – a good foot from Kalac's face. 'What could they possibly do with this?'

'The sword is designed to be thrust, not swung,' said Kalac coolly.

Though Marek King feigned a lack of interest in the correction, Kalac could see the subtle annoyance in his features. Kalac smiled inwardly.

'What of the warriors?' asked Marek, tossing the blade casually aside. The sudden change in the subject had now put Kalac on the back foot.

'Ten warriors have fallen. The Talran fight very well for such a small body of men.' Kalac steeled himself for the criticism to come.

Marek raised an incredulous eyebrow. 'You ambushed a small encampment and still managed to lose ten of my men?'

Kalac's voice came strained. 'They're not simple prey, Father! They're regimented, disciplined veterans, despite how they're perceived by the soothsayer!'

Marek stared hard, his gaze as piercing as any spear. 'Are you calling the seer a liar?'

Kalac raised his hands, palm open, in a desperate attempt to compromise. 'I'm not saying the soothsayer is wrong,' he said, backtracking. In fact, though Kalac would never admit it, the seer had been right more often than he had. 'They certainly have nothing on the strength and size of our warriors, but their tactics are something I've never before witnessed. It is difficult to fight against something so different.'

Kalac hated the soothsayer and everything he stood for; no man should have the power to witness the future. Therefore, according to Kalac's bitter reasoning, he must serve some dark, repulsive god, granting him gifts for who knows what in return. His father, however, refuted Kalac's many accusations over the three years since the seer had arrived and taken his invaluable position beside the king. He treated it as mere jealousy from his eldest son, for whom battle tactics had never come easily. His father was probably right, of course; on this occasion, his reaction was inevitable.

'And I'm to trust you on tactical decisions? If you're not up to the task, boy, then I shall find someone who is!'

Kalac gritted his teeth. 'I will manage, Father. You just worry about what that seer is telling you.'

'Neklic has no part in this conversation. Tell me of their plans: why send so few and in such ragged groups?'

The very name caused a repulsive shiver to course through him, his mind conjuring up the wrinkled, stooped old figure; the polished bones of Neferian enemies stitched about his unholy rags, the face disfigured from an old accident with a brazier. An accident Kalac wished had finished the job.

'Who knows? It'll be difficult to guess if their plans are as foreign as their battle tactics. Heed me, Father. Despite their numbers, we must prepare for the worst.'

The king fell silent for the first time since he arrived at the palace, which unnerved Kalac more than his father's rage. At least his rage was something he was used to. In the awkward silence, he could hear the foreign slaves scuttling about through the dank, stone corridors with orders of wine, food, tapestries, anything their Neferian masters desired. The very palace itself was built by a slave architect using their ancestor's sweat and blood. Unfortunately, the architect proved weaker than his counterparts, and before the top levels could be completed, he had perished from an illness brought on by lack of food and sleep. The schematics died with him; subsequently, the dimensions of the upper floors had been measured by an untrained eye. Kalac smiled. Even in the flickering torchlight, it was evident that one wall was taller than the other three and the roof was slanted, causing the upper two floors to be lopsided. Marek King caught his smirk.

'Something amusing you, boy?'

Kalac's face straightened. Familiar territory again, he mused. 'No, Father.'

'Good. Neklic informed me before your arrival that the next encampment will be thirty-six strong at the Thorian Hills in three days. Head north, then follow the waters of the Meir east; their horses will no doubt need her precious sustenance.'

'Yes, Marek King,' said Kalac obediently as he turned swiftly away to shade the anger etched in the hard lines of his face. Once again, he had been ignored.

'Kalac!'

The young warrior paused at the door but did not look back.

'Bring back all of my men this time!'

Two days of travel had passed since that conversation, and Kalac thought, once again, of the mighty figure of his father. Although aged, a life dominated by wars with the other tribes had kept the bunched sinew of his body from waning, but despite his giant appearance, his fighting prowess was only moderate at best. What he excelled at was stratagems, something he had not passed on to his eldest son, though not through a lack of trying. Many proclaimed he was the greatest mind of his generation, and the people loved him, which was more than could be said for Kalac. Even now, as he strode through the shadowed landscape guided by the dark waters of the Meir, he could hear the warriors around him whispering questions about his suitability for the job. He considered spilling the guts of the nearest to threaten the others into silence, but where would that get him? The situation was one step away from mutiny as it was.

Aided by torchlight, his forty men trod through the night to the foot of a sparse wood, where he ordered the torches doused. He heard whispers of his madness, but the order was obeyed nonetheless and stilling their hanging sheaths, the warriors stalked through the trees as silent as ethereal wraiths. The scavenged weapons of various enemies upon their backs and hips were as ill-regimented as the formation in which they moved and fought. A dull glow lit the way as though the horizon had begun to accept the sun. He knew this was impossible, however, for the sun dance was not for a few hours yet. Then something caught his ears, and he called the men to a halt, his voice as faint as the wind in the trees; so subtle a few of the men failed to hear and had to be halted by the hand of the nearest warrior.

Kalac eyed the black silhouettes of the frost shrivelled trees etched on the dark blue backdrop of the winter night. Something shifted in his vision, and a branch snapped as the shadow hovered away. He slipped his halberd from his back and, alone, skulked off after the patrolling sentry. The Talran's large lumbering shield snagged on the skeletal branches, and he pulled it free with a whispered oath which hung half finished. Kalac jerked the halberd point from the back of the soldier's neck and grabbed the slumping man before quietly lowering him to the floor. Listening intently, Kalac called the others forward, and they rejoined the path of the Meir. The trees gave way to dense reeds, and the warriors crouched within them, the light now undoubtedly a man-made fire. No moon shone, but a wild glow reflected in the eyes of Kalac as he raised his head above the tall reeds. The amber light of a pair of campfires shielded within the breast of two hills outlined the hard angles of the bronze-disked armour of three dozen Talran soldiers huddling in their warmth. His ears pricked and caught the sound of one of their heathen horses lapping at the precious waters of the Meir. Dropping back below the reeds, he glanced sidelong at the orange outlines of the warriors crouched with him, each hardened of body and mind that could only come from a life devoid of luxury.

Kalac shifted his halberd across his chest and gripped it with both hands, the movement causing the reeds to ripple. His thoughts were solemn for a moment, feeling every accursed eye upon him, wishing he was his father. Neferians did not fear death, for they left it in the womb as they were thrust onto the barren soil of the birthing tent, but none could deny the sickening taste of losing good men to reckless tactics. Anger twisted within. He was a fighter, not a philosopher! Did they expect a potter to be good at sowing or a slave to be good at *anything*? He had decided to act at nightfall, knowing the tired Talran would react slower as slumber began to spin her soothing web; some of the sentries had already returned to the fires' inviting warmth, ignorant of the importance of their job this night.

It was the best plan he could come up with; it would have to do. Without another thought, he leapt into a wild charge, a wordless war cry on his retracted lips. His forty warriors rose behind him like swamp beasts in their murky leathers, their faces painted in the image of Neferian demons. Surprised shouts rent the air with a foreign tongue, then Kalac was among the enemy. His halberd axe cleft the nearest skull before the stunned man could rise. Another swing severed the arm of a soldier reaching for his tower shield. Flames blazed in Kalac's eyes, not wholly from the fire. Chaos had erupted now. A mishmash of broadswords, axes, and spears clashed against impenetrable bronze, but the disorganised Talran were no match for the encircling barbarians. Twelve soldiers tried to form a shield wall and back their way to the horses, but a Neferian lunged with a longsword, scoring a great line across a Talran's shield, who stumbled back under the blow. The warrior took several shortswords to the gut and fell, trampled by his comrades as they leapt through the staggered line. A bloody, close-quarter battle ensued for which the

Talran's fighting style was designed. Only sheer numbers kept the advantage with the Neferians. Kalac's reach left the shortswords useless, and he slammed his halberd down onto the rim of his enemy's shield. The oxhide and bronze tower hammered into the earth, and Kalac thrust over it, stabbing into the Talran's exposed face. A warrior fell beside him, and Kalac hacked off the thrusting arm of the Talran before he dragged the disorientated warrior back to his feet, returning the twin-headed axe to his hands. Then Kalac plunged back into the melee like a ravenous wolf at a feast.

The sheer weight of the Neferians made the outcome inevitable. More soldiers fell, and the shield wall routed. Many were cut down before the Talran could mount their steeds and gallop for the safety of the border. Within heartbeats, any remaining soldiers were either dead or had disappeared over the hill line.

As the battle lust faded, Kalac ordered the enemy to be stripped of all valuables as he took stock of the dead. Sixteen warriors had given their lives in the ambush, and their skulls would soon have an honorary position within the city walls to watch over it as they had in life; the Talran had lost almost thirty, and only the maggots waited for them. A traitorous thought wondered how many warriors his father would have saved. He cursed, thinking instead of the situation at hand. This was the third time a group of Talran soldiers, too few to win any decisive battle, had been found on Neferian soil. Scouts? No. Kalac was sure of it. These men were too heavily armed for scouts. Something else was going on. He knew it. Something even the Great Marek's mind could not guess at and which offered Kalac this peculiar sense of foreboding that stood his hair on end.

2

'Ho, Turesh!'

Turesh jumped from his skin and crammed the short letter into his trousers as he turned.

'Ho!' He grinned and raised his hand in a friendly gesture as the fellow warrior passed his section of the crenulated battlement. The squat wall, no more than a steep mound of rock, had been built by the slaves of a previous visionary king. It surrounded the palace and the grimy stone and mud huts of the common people in a crude fifteen-foot fortification which over time had grown thicker as the skulls of the honoured dead were layered across its front.

When Turesh was sure no one else was watching, he turned back to the letter, flattening its neatly folded creases as he read. How long had it been now? Sixteen, maybe seventeen years since Marek, King of the White Fangs, the most dominant tribe in

Neferia, had decimated the Great Claws and forced their leader to unite with them as he had so many others. This had been humiliating enough. The Elder Shaman of the Great Claw should have ordered everybody to take their own life rather than suffer defeat! But to make the situation worse, the White Fangs had robbed half of their young men to replenish the warriors the war had cost them, marching them to the White Fang capital of Krem. One of those young men had been Turesh, a frightened sixteen-year-old hunter. True, he mused, his upbringing had not been any worse than it would have been back in the Great Claws; in fact, he enjoyed it here, but always were his heartstrings crying for home.

Reaching the end of the letter, he sighed before burning it in a nearby torch.

Kalac's mind reeled with questions as he approached the throne room and pushed open the heavy studded doors, pockmarked with woodworm. Why send so few men to a hostile land? The initial answer was that Neferia was backward in the eyes of those who would call themselves civilised. Backward and simple. And as such, they assumed a few men chorused in their art of modern combat would be more than a match for outdated Neferian ways. But why would they continue to send so few after their first defeat? If the Talran emperor could devise a new strategy for warfare, why would he continue to make callous mistakes such as this? He was so lost in thought that he failed to realise the room was empty until he was halfway to the dais. A thud echoed from the coarse wood floor as Kalac stomped his foot in frustration. Now was not the time for hide and seek! Leaving the room, he trudged down the confined spiral steps to the floor below. The stones, still cold to the touch, had not yet been warmed by the shafts of morning sunlight through the slit windows. Hearing the familiar goaded shouts and extended death throes of a child's warfare, he stopped short of his brother's dormitory and knocked. The door was ajar, so he called out, 'Lekta!'

The battle in the room suddenly ceased. 'Ho, Kalac!'

The door swung inwards, and Lekta stood aside, grinning his ignorance of worries as only the young know how. The nine-year-old held an expertly crafted miniature wooden warrior in his hand. The rest were strewn across the floor and perched on tatty books behind him in a vague likeness of a city siege – if you squinted hard. No doubt the toys were a lovingly made gift for a child before they had been stolen in a raid, the crafter likely killed. Now years later, they served another child.

The warrior gazed at his brother's cheery smile, a dark contrast to how he saw the world. 'Where's Father?'

The child began to enthusiastically swing an imaginary broadsword. 'Did you kill them all, Kalac? Did you?'

'You can rest peacefully,' said Kalac, smoothly avoiding an answer. The less Lekta knew of the horrors to face him in years to come, the better, he reckoned. 'Now, where is he?'

'He's with Neklic in his ritual room.' Lekta ran across the dormitory, his spindly frame moving like one of his many wooden puppets. He pulled up a roll of parchment and let one end drop to the floor. 'Neklic helped me draw this!' He held it aloft so Kalac could get a better look. The image was a crude depiction of the palace and the surrounding grounds. So crude, it was almost like the real thing, he mused.

'Does he not scare you?'

Lekta frowned. 'Who, Neklic? No.' His attention span waning, he dropped the drawing and moved on to something else, his smile returning. 'He amuses me.'

Kalac shook his head, unable to see how amusing a man versed in the dark arts could be.

'I'm going to see Father. Enjoy yourself!'

He closed the door behind him and was about to set off for Neklic's room when the door opened again. Lekta stood there, the happy-go-lucky mood of a moment before gone.

'Does Father like me?' he said.

Kalac knelt beside him and placed a comforting hand on the child's shoulder. 'Father *loves* you. Why?'

'He shouted at me this morning.'

Kalac could not disguise his smile. 'What were you doing?'

Lekta raised his hands. 'Nothing, I swear!'

'Do not fret, Lekta. I shall have a word with him.'

The child's grin returned. 'Thank you, brother!' He spun on his heel and closed the door behind him.

Kalac smiled and shook his head before returning to the stairwell and the vital matters at hand. He had no wish to wander around Neklic's upper floor, so he asked a slave at the top to point out the room in use. He rapped on the door before entering, his defiant features disguising the repulsion of a room used for what he considered unholy worship. Neklic sat cross-legged in the centre, his hands hovering above various colours of crystals and stones. Occasionally he would twitch, the bones stitched in the lower recesses of his robe scoring the wood beneath him, and he would whisper something inaudible. Marek King sat atop a dusty stack of stolen leather-bound books, his eyes fixed almost spellbound on his soothsayer, the only light from a flickering candle in his hand.

'Father?' said Kalac eventually.

Marek twisted his neck, and his eyes narrowed. 'Shhh!' he whispered. 'Not now, boy.'

Neklic began to twitch more violently.

'Valkeri will fall... six days... Kardek Pass... eight days,' he whispered as though fighting for every breath.

Marek King took on a keen edge, his passage to the future now open. 'What of their numbers?'

'Eighty soldiers... Valkeri will burn... soldiers trudge through the ashes of its people.'

Marek exploded. 'I shall muster one hundred and twenty warriors and set off for Valkeri tomorrow at dawn. Defensive tactics will have to be written on the way-'

'Valkeri will burn... too few days... too great a distance... Valkeri will fall.'

Marek King was stunned into silence for a moment. Valkeri was the closest White Fang outpost to the Talran border. A mountain top settlement home to two hundred people, and, according to his soothsayer, in six days, all would perish. Then a glint shone in his eyes.

'What of Kardek? That is the same mountain range.'

'Something blocks the vision... Another seer... You will arrive before the Talran... they will descend into the pass... something blocks the vision... must not fall in!'

'And victory, seer?'

'Another seer blocks the vision....'

Then Neklic fell head-first into his stones and passed out. Marek stood up, his face a mask of indecision. Kalac stepped forwards.

'Wake him! Find out more!'

Marek turned on him. 'Don't you think I would if I could? He always does this. He could be out for hours, maybe even until tomorrow. Time we simply do not have!'

'Then let me go in your stead. I have seen how the Talran fight. Do not underestimate them! You don't know how quickly they could turn this battle!'

Marek King rose to his full, daunting height. 'It'll turn out better if I go! How many warriors did you bring back this time from your escapade, Kalac? Not the number I sent you with, I bet!'

'Twenty-four,' mumbled Kalac.

'I sent you with forty! That's the third

ambush in which you have managed to lose nearly a score of my men! *Who*, Kalac, is ambushing *who*?'

'Their tactics are unfamiliar, Father! How many more times?'

'Pahh! If only you could conjure up a tactical decision as quickly as you make your excuses! What difference does it make how they fight? They all need to be thrown from Neferian soil! And that's precisely why *I* need to sort this mess out!'

Kalac turned away in anger. Once again, the stubborn fool would not listen.

He heard Marek call out behind him. 'Did you know our Talran envoy came back this morning? What was left of him.'

Kalac was still bitter. Why had his father not seen fit for him to go? Had he not achieved three victories already? He could not watch Marek leave at dawn, for he knew his people would not just treat his father as a king but as a hero as he emerged from the palace for the Dance of Journeys, and Kalac would be left feeling sick with envy. The young prince pushed the thought from his mind. He would not be there, so none of it mattered. Even so, a deep-rooted mixture of jealousy and guilt still dwelt within him. Time to drown that envy, he told himself. Kalac strode past a myriad of darkened, stubby huts. Frost glittered on the stones between the muck which held them together, and dotted between the buildings, darker still, were the mud huts of a growing population running out of space.

He arrived at one much larger than the rest, perhaps one of only a handful still lit this late at night. The wine huts were ugly but sweet sirens calling Kalac into troubled waters, for it was inappropriate for royalty to be seen drunk, especially in front of commoners. Hauling back the goatskin flap, Kalac felt the warmth of the braziers as he stepped into the hut where dented mugs of crimson wine traded hands freely. People sat in a circle on the earth like a pack of animals in their horde of pelts, cowhide barding, and goatskin boots laced with hare fur, enjoying the dancers and the beat of the drums. Off to the side, people gambled away their possessions on the roll of the bone die. After filling his mug from a wine barrel, he sat to one side and listened to half a dozen men who had braved the cold in their warrior leathers and were now trying their luck with the dice.

'Ho, stranger!' one of them said with a grin. 'You'll find it hard to drink with a scarf that far up your face!' The men around him gawped and smiled.

'I'll manage,' said Kalac coldly, lowering

the furred hat further over his face, its fluffy raccoon tail wrapped within his scarf.

'Suit yourself,' said the warrior, returning to the game.

The wine barrels emptied as the night wore on, and people grew louder in their jests and slurred speech. Items had traded hands like obsessive whores, and the air stunk with belches and spilt wine. The mood was jubilant, and Kalac relaxed, allowing the alcohol to take control. Lifting the scarf, he took another mouth full of wine before tugging it back into place. The strange act had drawn people's attention, but he no longer cared. The warrior who had greeted him earlier stumbled over to sit with him, and a few of his friends followed.

'Ho again, stranger. Wondered if you'd fancy a game with the die?'

Kalac thought for a moment and then nodded.

'Glad to hear it,' said the warrior, laying the bone die on the floor between them. 'And what will you be playing for?'

Kalac scanned the warrior's person and noted the ornate handle of a small carved dagger sticking from his scabbard belt, clearly a token from a successful gambling night.

'The dagger.'

The warrior laughed in good humour. 'A keen eye. And I shall play for your fur coat.'

Kalac picked up the die. There would be four rolls, he knew. Firstly, he would need to roll a three or more to attack his opponent. If successful, the warrior would need to roll a four or more to defend his item. Then their roles would reverse.

Kalac rolled the die, and all eyes craned to look at the dark spots.

Three.

The warrior smiled. 'Only just, my friend.' He placed the dagger between them and grabbed the die to roll his defence.

Two.

The warrior shrugged as Kalac took up the blade. 'It was never mine anyway.' He plucked up the die again and rolled his attack, his smile returning almost instantly.

Six.

Kalac reluctantly doffed his coat and placed it in the no man's land between them. The warrior stared at the hard leathers underneath.

'A fighting man, I see.'

Kalac ignored him and picked up the die. He rolled it around his fingers, feeling every irregularity in the bone. Then he rolled. A single spot glared back at him from the floor.

One.

The warrior smiled mockingly as he slung the coat onto his back. 'Looks like I'll not be going home cold tonight. Another game?

Perhaps I should play you for that scarf and see who you really are.'

The light-hearted jest cut through Kalac's relaxed mood, and the warrior placed a hand on his shoulder as he moved to get up.

'I meant no offence, stranger.'

Kalac shot him a dagger gaze, and as the hand loosened, he stood and left the hut. Outside, the fresh cold air made his world spin, the end of his nose became numb, and his ears felt strange. Then the top of his stomach suddenly felt like the bottom, and he retched but swallowed it. One step at a time, he thought. The journey back to the palace felt much longer, but fortunately, he could not feel the cold anymore.

'Psst!'

Kalac stopped before turning to the sound, unable to do two things simultaneously. A figure hid within the shadows at the side of a mud hut. A slender arm covered in the dirty rags of a robe reached out and beckoned him over.

'Come, Kalac.'

Kalac felt the bile rise in his throat. Only one type of woman could have known who he was though his face was hidden by scarf and darkness.

'Keep your voice down, witch!'

The woman sauntered from the shadows,

bones stitched into her long bedraggled garment, her face perhaps beautiful if not for the jagged scars across her lips. Her voice was low, but her face stern. 'Be warned, sire. Avoid Kardek. It is a place of death.'

Fuelled by hatred, Kalac's drunken rage was great. 'Hold your tongue, vermin!' he slurred, 'We White Fangs are warriors! Men die; cities crumble; only the great gods are immortal! Death will come, but only a coward runs from it! Such men are not made to last!'

The soothsayer shook her head. 'You misunderstand me, sire-'

'No! I understand you well enough!' He reached down for his dagger, the effort causing him to stumble. As he recovered, blade in hand, the seer had vanished into the night.

Turesh stood guard at the gates, and looking up at the multitude of white specks which made up the stars, he wondered about his insignificance. Would it really matter if he lived or died tonight? The answer he had come to believe was no. He breathed into his cold hands and looked around at the darkened huts imagining the people within sleeping under their rugs and fur blankets. The duty of Gate Watcher had come sooner than he had thought, mainly because no one else wanted to stand out at night in the freezing cold, and now that the responsibility was his, he was about to abuse it. The replacement guard would not be long, probably just beginning to rouse from his slumber, he mused. No one else walked this night. The only sounds were from the distant wine huts. He turned swiftly and unbolted the small side door before stepping out into the moonlit glade. His highly tuned ears caught the stealthy sounds of a fox prowling the shadows for rabbit burrows, and he instinctively loosened an axe from a strap about his waist. Moving forwards with a mixture of haste and caution, as only a hunter knows how, he crested a steep rise and stalked down into the ditch behind where a lone rider waited, hidden from the city.

Turesh slipped a letter from his trousers, scrawled in his own barely legible hand. A nervous tension weighted his arms as he handed it over. 'Make sure it gets delivered.'

The masked rider stared for a moment as though offended by the implications of his comment. Then he merely nodded and swung his horse away into the darkness. Turesh wasted no time in watching him go and instead trekked back through the glade, the moon casting a silver light on the grinning skulls layering the city wall, which gazed from hollowed sockets. Turesh did not believe in such hocus-pocus. In the village of his youth, he learnt that the spirit travelled to the stars after death, and only a pile of old bones remained behind. Still, he could not shake the feeling they were trying to frown upon him. Maybe one of them had even raided that village and killed his father...

Tearing such thoughts from his mind, he pushed his way through the gate door and bolted it shut after him. Now he would wait for the replacement, for, at dawn, the ageing Great Claw hunter was to leave for Kardek. He thought once more of the stars and hoped with all his heart that he would not be meeting them soon.

After four days of gruelling travel, Marek King lay amongst a pile of feathered cushions and pillows in one of the grandest huts the little settlement of Yeki had to offer. Its usual resident, a wealthy merchant, had been honoured to have the legendary tactician as a guest, and together they had swigged fine wine all evening. Still three days from Kardek, Marek was careful not to get drunk, which was more than could be said for the merchant who would no doubt be nursing a terrible hangover come the morn. Now, with his drinking partner snoozing face down in his rugs, empty goblet still in hand, Marek enjoyed the stillness of the tiny settlement, far from the ruckus of Krem, where four thousand people lived almost on top of one another, vying for space. Thinking of home caused him to think of Kalac, and he sighed, though not from disappointment. Kalac never did have the best start in life – his mother, the beloved Vaye, died in childbirth. Without a mother's love, the child had grown bitter and resentful. He had hoped that the blessing of a second soulmate, the beautiful Lynaea, would give him the stability and love he required. The young Kalac grew close to Lynaea, almost forgetting his birth mother. Still, he remained wild and boisterous, his talents better suited to fighting men rather than leading them. Marek would never allow Kalac to become king without him first showing sufficient signs of leadership. Sorrow touched him then. He knew Kalac was desperate to win his favour, and Marek could only blame his son's shortcomings on himself. Perhaps if he had been a better parent, things might have turned out differently...

Then had come Lekta, and Marek had sworn to do better. The twisted hands of fate, however, had other plans. Barely two years after Lekta's birth, Lynaea had caught a hackling illness from which she never recovered. Her death had been long and arduous, and Marek had been devastated and vowed never to love again. Despite this, the young Lekta was growing into all that Kalac was not. At the tender age of nine, he was already showing signs of sound tactical decisions when Marek would sneak in a lesson with the boy's toy soldiers. He was a sly little rascal as well! A cunning that would serve his people when the lad was older. Even so, he would be no fighter, Marek knew. In battle, his warriors would stand with the deadly Kalac, but Lekta's cunning mind would be what kept them alive as a whole. Marek smiled then. When it was time for him to step down as king, the pair would bounce off each other's strengths and weaknesses and put their old man to shame.

The joy in his heart suddenly made him sleepy. Though both his soulmates had gone, they had left him with two sons he would never change for the world.

Three days later, Marek King sat astride his grey gelding, watching his men scurry about in their haste to complete his orders. Over a week of hard travel had left the king with a sense of weariness; he had allowed his men as much sleep as possible, but Marek himself had been up with his advisors the past few nights planning the assault of the pass. Kardek now fell away before him and rose up on either side like stone giants; a mere fifteen men would fill the width of the pass, but more than four hundred could be squeezed in from end to end. Marek glanced up at his skilled slingers nestled on the snowy precipices on either side of the canyon. The rest of his men were waiting in the tree line just beyond the valley exit. He pulled his gelding around and trotted up the steep cliff path overlooking the gorge, stopping every now and again to ensure his slingers had a suitable view of the canyon floor. The enemy would march into the pass blissfully unaware of the trap which lay in wait. As the enemy regiment squeezed into the valley, the slingers would rise along the rear half of the pass raining fist-sized stones into their tight formations. With the slingers at the rear hounding Reshmal's every step, they would quickly press forwards and be forced out of their lines. Then, as they emerged from the valley, the warriors would charge in among them, their numbers overpowering, hacking down the jagged lines of the Talran. Unfamiliar tactics or not, he mused, they would all be dead by day's end.

Marek King allowed his mind to wander as he waited, shifting his attention from his freezing hands and face. Of all the petty tribes vying for supremacy from which he could choose an enemy, he had never expected it to be a neighbouring kingdom. Partly because an enormous mountain range lay between them, and any army would be forced to walk its treacherous path. But also because there was little value in Neferia for those who enjoyed polished walls and lavish feasts on gold-adorned banquet tables.

A movement caught his eye, and he watched a lone horseman gallop through the dry canyon, shielded from the worst of the snow, and then up the cliff path towards him. The rider's speech came quickly as he approached.

'The Talran are marching from Valkeri, Marek King. They'll be here soon!'

'And we'll be ready,' said the king. 'What of Valkeri? Did you see anything on your ride?'

The rider shook his head. 'Not much, my king, but wisps of smoke can be seen from the ridge and soot coats the snow.'

Marek's mood darkened. Of course, Neklic's word was the truth, but he had been wishing the seer wrong on this occasion.

'Return to your position!' he said, unable to contain his anger. The scout wheeled his horse away with a word of respect for his king, but Marek did not hear; nine hundred yards away, the first of the Talran were entering the pass, their harsh bronze helms and coated ox-hide shields glistened in the sunlight. Leading the regiment was a flag bearer hoisting high the pale cross sewn onto a bright blue background, a colour impossible by any Neferian dye. What caught the ageing king's eyes most, though, were the ragged brown burn holes in the stretched linen caused, he guessed, by falling ash: Valkeri ash.

'Remember your orders,' he shouted before turning his horse from the cliff edge and galloping down the path to the rest of the men waiting amongst the snow-covered trees. An advisor graciously nodded as he approached. 'The warriors await your order, Marek King.'

Marek nodded and turned to address the men, shivering in their hard leathers and fur-lined cloaks. 'We wait until the first score emerges. Charge as I do. Do not give chase into the pass. Leave them for the slingers; our greater numbers are our advantage.'

From high in the saddle of the gelding, Marek could see just over the ridge of the pass as it sloped away and gave an involuntary shudder as he eyed the wall of tower shields filling its width. Regimented and organised, these foes were far more deadly than the rabble warriors of the Neferian tribes he was used to. He knew then that the information from his son had been invaluable. Had he chosen to fight them head-on, they would have all surely perished. The warriors grew restless around him, unable to see their foe but able now to hear the rhythmic beat of their march.

'Wait for the order,' he whispered, and the advisors quietly relayed the message to those out of earshot.

Suddenly the air was still, and no more were the sounds of marching; the Talran had halted in the canyon. The scream of a man amidst his death throes shattered the silence, and Marek threw a fist into his saddle in undisguised rage. Someone had loosed too soon! Now the whole plan was in jeopardy!

More screams rent the air, but they sounded as if originating from *outside* the valley. Marek's hair stood on end as he realised a Talran cavalry regiment must have already crossed the valley before they arrived! Now it was sweeping around the pass, hacking down the slingers before they slung a single stone. When this was confirmed a moment later as the horsemen charged down the cliff path, lances levelled, Marek knew it had all gone wrong.

'Hold your ground!' he shouted. 'Stay within the trees!'

'Soldiers at the rear!' he heard someone shout, and he whirled around to see a regiment pressing through the trees, the uneven ground and the boughs breaking up their formation. 'Aim for the gaps!' he ordered as he eased the gelding through the trees and hefted his spear from atop the saddle bags. He drew close to the enemy line, and the horse instinctively reared, its hooves pounding on a shield, forcing the wielder back. Marek's spear struck down over a soldier's guard into their bare face; another jab lanced an exposed forearm. Then the gelding shuddered as a shortsword caught a foreleg. It reared and turned to bolt, instinct taking over, but the uneven ground caused it to stumble awkwardly. Marek firmly grabbed the reins and rubbed soothingly at its flank, using every effort of his iron will to bring the beast back under control. As he whirled the gelding around, he saw that his men had given ground under the sheer rhythmic block and counterthrust efficiency of the Talran. Warriors had started to fall back onto open soil and were swiftly impaled by the levelled lances of the horsemen who were being fed more victims with each passing moment.

'The cavalry's butchering us!' he heard an advisor say. 'Fall back to the pass!'

'No!' shouted Marek at the top of his lungs lest the advisor caused a rout, 'To fall back is death! The other regiment is within!'

'And to stay here is death!' said the advisor.

'Then we must push through!'

Marek dug his heels into the gelding and charged through the trees. His spear caught on some branches and was torn from his hand. Loosening his feet from the stirrups, he crashed through the Talran shields and slid off as the horse fell. His foot kicked out, snapping a leg as he drew his two shortswords and struck like a snake. Warriors followed in his wake, desperate to protect their king. Marek parried a stabbing sword aside with one blade and removed the arm with the other. He felt something slice at his ribs, and he spun, plunging his sword deep into the neck of a Talran. Lunging forward, he crashed into a shield and sent its wielder sprawling before cutting down the foe beside him in the shield wall. Something else plunged into his side, and his legs buckled. He glanced up and tasted his first defeat as the shortsword split his skull.

Less than a quarter mile up the mountain pass and within the confines of his lavishly decorated tent, Emperor Reshmal II stirred the contents of his soup bowl. Though he was not out on the battlefield, his stomach was tight with nerves. He needed a decisive victory here, not only to bolster the confidence of his troops early in the conquest but to cripple Neferia's chances of resisting. He had known for some time that the White Fangs were the largest tribe in this swamp-ridden country, and it was no secret that their leader was widely regarded by the native barbarians as one of the greatest tactical minds of his generation. A decisive victory here would set an example of modern military might.

He noticed the quartermaster and his chef glancing nervously at one another by the tent flaps; he knew both would blame the other if the soup caused him displeasure. Reshmal placed the soup spoon down on his favoured oak table. Both items had travelled as far as he and made the tent feel less like a whore's hovel.

'The soup is fine,' he said at last.

Both men breathed a sigh of relief, but Reshmal looked beyond them as the camp filled with shouts and cheers. The tent flaps parted, and two of his soldiers staggered in, weighed heavily by their burden. Shuffling to the centre of the tent, they stood to attention as best they could, and Reshmal eyed his prize sagging between them both.

'Have the rest of his men fled?' asked the emperor.

'No, sir,' replied one. 'They fought to the last and have all been dispatched.'

Reshmal nodded and scanned the large drooping figure of Marek, former King of the

White Fangs, hanging by the arms between his men. One of the soldiers dragged the giant's head up by the hair. Dry blood encrusted Marek's face from his cleft skull, but his dead eyes still shone with defiance. He looked more like a warrior than a thinker, mused Reshmal, but if this was the best Neferia had to offer, then they posed the emperor little threat. Like him, the rest of the barbarians would fall before Talran might. Reshmal waved the soldiers away, and they dragged the once proud king from the tent. He looked towards his chef.

'Now that the day is done,' he said. 'I think I shall enjoy my soup.'

3

Kalac had waited days for any news of victory. It had been nearly two weeks since his father had left for Kardek with his one hundred and twenty warriors, they were not expected back yet, but Kalac was surprised his father had not sent a report back ahead of them. Did his father really despise him so much as to send nothing at all?

Finally, on the mid-afternoon of the sixth day, the scout he had sent to gain word of White Fang accomplishments had returned. He hoped that Marek's tactics had not proven too useful so that he could rub his father's nose in it upon his return.

The scout had been admitted into Kalac's chamber and knelt on one knee before him, his face sombre, his eyes always averted. Kalac could sense something was wrong and a lump formed in his throat.

'Kalac King,' said the scout and the former

prince wished to hear no more. He left the room and wandered almost involuntarily to the only place he knew no one else would be. His bedroom was not large by his standards, but it was comforting, and the former prince sat at the bedside, his head in his hands. He wondered why he could shed tears for the old fool, yet they had done nothing but bicker throughout his life. His shoulders shook as he sobbed, knowing full well it was not true. Throughout Kalac's life, his father had tried to teach him the error of his ways. To study and reason with tactics; to listen and give thought to other people's opinions rather than callously dismissing them; to understand not only the needs of yourself but the needs of others, especially your friends and foes. The list was endless. He had clung to him as a shipwrecked sailor clings to a rock in a violent storm. Sure, it was uncomfortable, and he quickly grew tired of the company, but it was something on which he could always depend.

And now the mighty figure of Marek was gone. He had not even wished his father farewell on the jubilant day the king had left Krem.

Later that eve, Kalac had called for the scout to be returned to him, and he had stood from the throne and apologised for his swift dismissal earlier, putting it down to his tiredness. He could see from the scout's expression that the lie was not believed, but the man merely nodded before divulging the rest of his knowledge of the incident.

Part way through, Neklic had arrived; he stood to the side and listened to the news, occasionally interjecting with questions Kalac's reeling mind would not have thought to ask.

'Where are the regiments heading now?' he asked.

The scout turned to the ragged, old figure that was Neklic. 'North, sir. They've grown tired of trying to negotiate the marshlands and turned north towards the small Red Wing tribe, but more regiments are traversing the mountain pass daily.'

'That's to be expected in an invasion,' said Neklic bluntly. 'There are sixty thousand free people in Neferia. It will take more than three regiments to bring her under their sway.'

The scout stood dumbstruck for an instant before the seer's absolute calmness. Kalac was in no mood to question Neklic; perhaps the soothsayer knew something comforting about the future, or maybe he did not want to instil panic in the tribe. Either way, the scout turned back to his king, seemingly more at ease. 'The pass is held by a small force; no more than a dozen men. Furthermore, Kalac

King, upon scouring the nearby wood, I found a survivor. The only one. He is wounded and has caught a fever, but between his meandering thoughts, he disclosed a name: Turesh. I have no idea if it's his or a name he remembers for some other reason.'

'Where is this man now?'

'He's being treated in the healing hut, my lord.'

Kalac nodded. 'If that's everything, you are dismissed.'

The scout bowed low and turned away, leaving Kalac to slump into the hard padded throne. Suddenly everything seemed to catch up with him. His father was dead, and soon, the White Fangs, tens of thousands of people in the jostling city and settlements of the tribe, would be looking to him for leadership and asking questions once again. His first task was, no doubt, the protection of the Fangs.

'Have you told the child yet?'

Kalac's deep thoughts drew away, turning his red-rimmed eyes to the seer.

'Your brother?' said Neklic.

Kalac shook his head.

'Then I believe it's about time you did, Kalac King.'

An angry retort made it to the end of Kalac's tongue before he let it slide. The seer had done nothing but help in his time of need, and how did he repay him? Hate. Pure and simple. He stood and, without another word, left the chamber. Thoughts of how he would break the news to Lekta crawled sluggishly through his head, and then he was outside his brother's dormitory, his mind still blank. The scratching of a quill from within suggested Lekta was drawing something for he could not write. Even Kalac could not; few adults could. He knocked and entered to see Lekta lying on his stomach, scrawling meaningless shapes onto a piece of parchment. The child looked up and beamed, a smile which would be shattered in a few moments.

'Have you had news from Father?' It was a question Lekta had asked every day for the last few days.

'I have.'

The child leapt up. 'Yay! When is he coming back?'

Kalac swallowed hard. He was not good at painting pretty pictures around things, so he just came straight out with it. 'He's not.'

Lekta frowned. 'What do you mean he's not?'

Kalac sighed. 'Father... fell... in battle. He will not be coming home.'

The child stared hard, unflinching. They were just words, harmless enough, but the words held meaning, and after Lekta had deciphered them, he began to cry.

'I want to talk to Father again,' he said between sobs.

So do I, Kalac mused. *I would ask him to go through his many strategies again, only this time, I would really try to understand.*

A knock drew his attention to the door, and a slim bald head popped from behind it, which the king recognised as one of his father's advisors. 'I'm sorry to interrupt, Kalac King, but we really must talk of battle plans and perhaps a Dance of the Dead.'

Kalac shook his head. 'I'm in no mood to learn of tactics, advisor. Draw up what you must.'

'I have already taken the liberty of discussing plans with Neklic and sent word to the other settlements, but you must ultimately have the final say, and so you must learn. My name is Rhek. Call me to the study when you are ready, my lord.'

The face disappeared, and Kalac followed him out into the corridor. 'Advisor!'

The senior figure turned. 'Yes, Kalac King?'

'Spread the tragic news to the tribe and send horsemen to the settlements bearing the grim message. Then issue a Dance of the Dead for tonight. I shall take the vows of leadership afterwards.'

The advisor bowed low. 'As you wish, lord.'

* * *

That day had been the longest Kalac had ever known. He had no dreams of being king; all his aspirations had lain with humbling his father as he had done to Kalac on so many occasions. Now his dreams lay shattered, and realisation dawned of the pettiness of them all, as a man understands the warmth of the sun once darkness descends.

And darkness *had* descended. The Neferians were at war with the border kingdom of Talran. Nineteen hundred warriors were under his command, and yet he was in no fit state to command them. Slaves scurried about the palace preparing the late feast, which traditionally followed the sending. As Kalac made his way outside, music had already begun to disturb the silence of the night.

The deerskin drums pounded with an emotional beat, and many chanted along with the Song of the Dead. Most of the city's four thousand occupants had turned out, sitting in a wide circle twenty rows deep around an enormous central fire that billowed smoke mixed with incense. Those that had been chosen were dancing within the circle, their feathered costumes splaying as they twirled. Many were children, for only they were blessed with the unending reserves of energy required to dance for so long. One such child was Lekta, who held his hands to the sky upon the final lines of the hymn to show the lost spirits the way to the gods, for they had been unable to retrieve the fallen bodies and those souls still attached would become phantoms twisted in their loathing of the living.

After a brief pause in the music, where the guests helped themselves to the various cooked portions of beef, hare, and duck, the wind instruments chirped for the beginning of the Hymn of the Gods, who, in the end, decide the fates of mortal souls.

Kalac sat at the back of the crowd, contemplating the limited choices he had. He was ill-equipped for such a role, and everyone in the crowd knew it. And yet, if he did not take up the position, would the great name of Marek be slandered because of it? A few people nearby had noticed him, and mutterings of his arrival spread quickly around the circle.

Kalac had made himself officially known as the wine began to flow to celebrate the departed. The drums beat for another hymn, but the young warrior waved them quiet as he stepped into the circle and scores of eyes cast their doubts upon him. The dancers skipped off to the side, allowing Kalac centre stage.

'You all know why I'm here,' he said, his

voice hard. 'The rights of my father have passed to me. His right of leadership is now my right of leadership, but as tradition holds, any who wish to challenge that right may do so now.'

His eyes scanned the beady eyes of the circle. Most seemed willing to give him a chance, but he could see the undisguised malice in the eyes of others. All had heard of his fighting prowess, and he knew none wished to face him, so it came as a shock when, as he was almost outside the circle, the challenge was voiced.

'I oppose, cur!'

Kalac whirled, his eagle's gaze picking out the middle-aged figure long before he stood. 'Your name?' Kalac's tone was even and calm; if there was any doubt in him, no man knew.

The brooding figure stepped over the heads of the others and strode into the circle, the fire casting shadows in the hard grooves of his face.

'I am Girak.' He turned to address the crowd. 'A leatherworker by trade and a warrior in time of need. I see no greater need than now, for I can make tactical decisions far better than this young pup.' He waved a dismissive hand in Kalac's direction. 'All those who know me know I should lead now that Marek is dead!'

Nods and murmurs of approval came from

small pockets within the crowd; most notable were the votes from several horse herders and one blacksmith, key roles which held significant weight in society. The newcomer needed more support than the current leader to issue a challenge. With the rest of the crowd remaining silent, undecided or unwilling to commit to a side, it was enough to grant his rival a chance.

Kalac eyed Girak's hard features as he turned back to face him, and a traitorous thought saw him falling to his blade. Perhaps the White Fangs would have more success with Girak, and the son of Marek could fade from history as the king that never was. The grizzled man unsheathed his shortsword from the worn scabbard about his waist, a great contrast to his honed blade, which shone like the stars in the firelight. And off to the side, Kalac heard the gasp and saw the distraught face of a child who had just realised the magnitude of the situation; a child who would be alone in this harsh world should Kalac fall. The would-be king saw a disturbing future where Lekta's ragged, muddy blanket beat about him in a gale as he lay on the cold earth, alone, wet, and hungry. A former child prince, now an outcast. What were the odds of survival for such a child? The image saddened Kalac but, more importantly, steeled his resolve.

'Come, pup!' said Girak.

Kalac hesitated for only a moment. He had not expected a fight during Neferia's invasion and had come without his halberd, but he did have the ornate dagger he had won with a cast of the bone die. He drew it from his belt and struck like an enraged panther, his lithe movements giving the shortsword no chance to bite. As the gap grew between them again and they circled to one side of the fire, a crimson line had been drawn on the big man's cheek.

Then Girak attacked like a savage bear, his speed belied by his hulking strength. Even Kalac, swift of hand and foot, was forced to parry the swing. Still, the sword slid from the tiny blade and bit into his fingers. Girak followed it with a shoulder charge which sent Kalac spinning to the floor. Kalac rolled Girak's downward thrust aside, flinging red ash from the fire into his eyes. Then the young warrior leapt as a desperate jackal leaps, the dagger point bursting a gelatine eye and lodging in Girak's skull. As the big man toppled like a tree, Kalac glanced at his bloody hand and cursed. One of his fingers was cut to the bone. Clenching his fist around the dagger hilt, he unsheathed it from Girak's eye, drawing up the bloody shortsword in his other hand. He stood stock before his people, dark eyes simmering like coals, adrenaline and pain fuelling his hatred for betrayal.

'Anyone else?' he shouted.

As fearful eyes averted from him, he stormed from the circle, leadership his... for now.

Kalac winced as he flexed his finger, the animal hair stitches stretching the inflamed skin around the wound. Rhek looked over at him from the other side of the study's pillowed rug on which they sat. A shaft of dawn light through the window illuminated a dozen wooden blocks between them, a crude letter carved into each. They had been placed at various points on the rug with the two blocks at the extremities less than an arm span apart.

'It didn't go as planned, I take it?'

Kalac shook his head. 'But it could have been worse.' Then after a moment, he said, 'Lekta didn't seem to like it. He followed me after I left the dance and asked me why I killed him.'

Rhek sighed. 'Children shouldn't see these things. What did you tell him?'

Kalac stared at the stitches, shame flushing his face. 'I snapped. Told him that's how it is, and if he liked all his toys, then he'd shut up!

He is a prince only as long as I am alive! I regret it now, of course. I always swore I would never shout at Lekta as Father did, but he's too young to be told everything.'

The advisor nodded. 'I fear that's the only way the young can still smile at the world.' He picked up a block with the letter 'H' upon it. 'Horsemen, lord. Now, where would you like them?'

The battlefield was complete with books for hillocks and pieces of parchment denoting wooded areas with thinly drawn lines for the rivers. The whole charade reminded Kalac of the days his father had tried to teach him tactics with the toy warriors, which now belonged to Lekta.

'Remember, son,' his father had said, 'your warriors are like pieces of a puzzle. Only with your pieces in the right places will you succeed.' Kalac could not have cared less about any puzzle, and he soon became bored of pussyfooting around and charged his warriors in. He would constantly lose; his father just seemed to have warriors *everywhere*.

He spent the following days indulging Rhek, but by week's end, he still felt as though all the better strategies were eluding him, and the old advisor had made it painfully clear to him that this was to take a long time.

'How long have you been fighting, Kalac King?' he had asked.

'Since I was fourteen,' he said, without hesitation. 'I helped my father take a province in the south. I can still recall my first taste of death even now.'

Rhek nodded. 'I remember that day. You were clumsy with a sword, but now you are a twelve-year veteran, a renowned fighter whose experience makes your reactions almost instinctive. My point being, only after years of experience can a man become a veteran in any art, especially at strategy.'

Turesh swam in hazy dreams, unable to determine reality from imagination. He saw Kalac enter and crouch beside the rug on which he lay, the agonising screams of the others within the hut drowning out what he had to say. Then the mud walls disappeared, and Kalac grew wider and older; the mighty figure of Marek stared down at him and thrust a pair of axes into his hands.

'Don't let me down, lad!'

'I won't, my lord!' said Turesh mechanically. He turned and saw Kardek before him, but there was no sign of the enemy yet. A warrior standing alongside nudged Turesh as he shivered in the cold. He whirled to bark an insult at him but halted aghast. The warrior's scalp was hanging from his head. The mutilated figure turned and winked at him with an empty socket. The cold chill of terror stood Turesh's hair on end.

'Mother of Mercy!' he said as he backed into another warrior who was desperately pushing in his guts, his hands covered in dark venous gore. Another, the skin shredded from his face, was spitting out his broken teeth.

'Be strong, warrior.'

Turesh spun to the young woman who had just spoken. She wore a long horsehide dress spattered with crimson, a healer no doubt, but apart from being in a wood, there was nothing unusual about her.

'You're… You're not dead?' he said.

The woman turned to another who had appeared beside her as if by magic. 'He's hallucinating again.'

The sky darkened, and mud walls seamlessly rose from the earth. Turesh rolled over on the rug. 'What are you doing to me?'

There was a cool sensation as one of the women touched him. 'Applying a salve. It should draw out the fever.'

Her soft touch made him relax, and his eyes closed. He was unaware of any time passing at all. Then he awoke with a start. Half of the Great Claw village was burning, and tents were disintegrating in flames, his father already dead. The remnants of the tribe had been forced back into the Elder Shaman's stone hut, but the young Turesh had decided to hide in a barn with his soulmate, Resha. Fear gripped him as the flaming thatch began to throw embers into the dry haystacks where they were hiding.

'Come!' he said as he took Resha's hand and catapulted himself through the locked barn doors.

The enemy had been outside, and a strong arm grabbed him.

'You're to come with us, boy!' said a gruff White Fang.

'No!' said Turesh, and he spun to catch the hand of his soulmate, but mighty hands pulled him back. 'Resha!'

His heart had broken then, tears filling his eyes as he was bundled onto the back of a cart. Someone followed him up and stood over him. 'Better to live for us than to die with the rest of your tribe,' he heard, then a pommel struck him in the face, and he fell unconscious.

But the tribe shamefully surrendered, and Resha still lived...

His eyelids opened, and his arms felt weak, but mercifully, the darkened hut was not swimming or on fire for the first time in days. A healer came to him and placed a cool palm on his forehead for a moment. Satisfied, she stood.

'I'll call Kalac King,' she said, but before Turesh could question her meaning, she had left the healing house. He sat and gripped his pounding head, the moaning injured about him doing little to help. His eyes caught one of them, a man who had joined Kalac on his first meeting with the Talran almost three weeks ago. He was as pale as an otherworldly spirit with an arm lopped off at the elbow, a fatal injury until recently; experimental balms and bandages had reduced his possibility of the dreaded gangrene. Other warriors within the hut had been wounded in that same skirmish. The prince was a whirlwind of death in battle, but his lack of plans left the healers with many patients.

And now Kalac was king, he thought, which meant Marek had not made it...

The hut flap tugged back, and Kalac entered, Neklic stumbling in behind. The king came close and crouched beside him while the seer stood nearby.

'What's your name, warrior?' asked Kalac.

'Turesh, my lord.'

The king nodded. 'Can you remember what happened, Turesh?'

'Too well. It was an ambush, Kalac King.'

Kalac took a deep breath as though fighting an urge to leave this wretched place. 'Tell me from the beginning. How was it my father and one hundred and nineteen men managed to be ambushed?'

So Turesh told him everything he could remember about the dreaded moment the cavalry had ridden from the cliff path and a second regiment had attacked the rear.

'The regiment in the pass had been a decoy?' asked Kalac, 'They did not rush in?'

'No, lord.'

Kalac shot a dagger gaze at the soothsayer, who ever so subtly flinched before his composure set in.

'I tried to warn your father, Kalac. I did not have all of the facts.' Neklic turned his dark eyes on Turesh and, perhaps to change the subject, he asked, 'How was it only you managed to survive?'

Turesh shook his head. 'I had no idea it was only me. I remember falling in the mayhem to a great clobber that knocked me senseless, and my blade was skewered in the neck of a man whom I must have pulled down with me, for he lay on top of me. As the Talran line swept past, I was stood on and booted, and somewhere I must have passed out.

'It was a massacre, wasn't it?' His king gave a remorseful nod. 'Then I'm glad I didn't see it.'

Kalac sighed with what seemed genuine

relief. 'Rest and get well, Turesh, for we could do with you back with the warriors.'

Kalac and his subordinate left the healing hut, and once in the darkness outside, Neklic turned to the king. 'You think there's something suspicious about Turesh?'

Kalac thought for a moment, letting the joyous sounds from the distant wine huts fill his ears. 'I did. His tale seems a reasonable one. The man was knocked unconscious and fell among the dead. Assuming the Talran check the dead as we do, it's not unlikely they would miss him in so many fallen. No doubt he's a lucky man, but lucky does not make you disloyal.' He eyed Neklic. 'You, on the other hand….'

The attack was only half meant, but Neklic did not seem to realise. 'I told you, Kalac King, another seer blocked the vision who would have also viewed the event, perhaps the part I was missing.'

Kalac fell silent; the sounds of the night seemed to drown in his thoughts. A hazy recollection filled his mind of the female soothsayer who had confronted him that night in his drunken state. She, too, had known about the battle of Kardek, but he did not know if he had the stomach to visit a seer's hut in the dark, where the cruel gods preyed on their oblivious subjects.

'I'll see you tomorrow, witch,' he whispered.

Neklic partially heard him. 'Sorry, lord?'

Kalac moved to clap him on the shoulder but feigned at the last moment. 'Never mind, Neklic. Enjoy yourself.'

With that, Kalac stalked off to the palace for a scarf and his father's cheapest fur coat.

4

Kalac awoke the following morning with his throat as dry as the desert sands and a sickly taste to his mouth though his head was fine. He pushed his legs from the assortment of warm animal hides and sat up, his feet cold on the stones. Ordering a slave to fetch a pail of water, he waited until her return, then filled the crude tin bowl by his bedside before swiftly washing and dressing. As he left his chamber, he met Rhek, who had just come up from the floors below.

'Good morning, my lord. I'm glad you are awake. I thought you might like to know that Neklic conducted another ritual last night while you were,' he made an exaggerated attempt to clear his throat, 'otherwise engaged.'

'What did he find?' Kalac made no attempt to hide his impatience – the female seer would not bring herself to justice.

Rhek shifted uneasily. 'To be honest, lord, I think he's going blind. Not in our sense of the word, of course, but in his. His visions are blocked, and all he can gather is the obvious: the Red Wings have been decimated by the armies of the Talran. He says they have doubled back south to cross the shaded region of the Meir out of sight and back into White Fang territory.'

Kalac shook his head. 'No. Reshmal is too wise for such a risky tactic. They will not be able to spot our warriors in the tree line. Surely he would expect us to attack as they struggled across the river. We already have a group of warriors shadowing them, I presume?'

Rhek nodded. 'As soon as I heard that Marek had fallen, I scrambled half of the remaining warriors from here and most of the northern border guard to keep track of the enemy from across the Meir. A thousand in all. Our priority is to stop them from crossing back into our territory.'

Kalac nodded firmly. 'Then he will be planning something else.'

Rhek gesticulated over his king's shoulder, his eyes wide like he had seen a ghost, and twisting around, Kalac saw the aged, almost corpse-like figure of Neklic shambling through the corridor. The soothsayer's brazier-blistered face only added to this effect. He caught them both staring.

'A problem, my lord, and Rhek?'

The advisor shook his head and gave a look of innocence, but Kalac was not one for niceties. The world had never been nice to him.

'Your advice is bitter, seer. I'm not about to put total trust in your diminishing sight. Not after it killed my father. Your dark gods have been amply fed!'

Neklic looked bewildered. 'I do not understand, Kalac King. What dark gods do you speak of?'

'Enough!' said Kalac. 'You don't have total control over your future-sight, and that is that. The Talran will cross downriver where the flow eases.'

Rhek interjected. 'How do you know this, lord?'

'Because!' he said, then realising he had alienated everyone, continued at a more level tone, 'because you cannot survive twelve battle-filled years without knowledge of the obvious. Stretch the men into groups along the southern side of the Meir. It must be defended at all costs. Tell them to dig trenches, defensive mounds, and anything else deemed necessary to halt the Talran from crossing the river. The emperor will have nowhere else to go but Eagle Talon soil. Let them deal with this problem as they have with us for the last three decades, with fire and steel and cold dark hatred.'

Rhek nodded in agreement and then looked sidelong at Neklic, who seemed indifferent. 'Anything to add, seer?'

Neklic shook his head and eyed Kalac. 'Other than to ask what it will take for you to trust me, lord?'

Kalac shrugged, losing all patience with the conversation. 'The sun to shine at night.' He budged past them both.

Neklic caught the ridiculing tone and replied with his own. 'I shall order the sun dance for tonight then, my lord.'

Kalac reached the end of the corridor and paused briefly behind the door as the conversation drifted to him.

Neklic's voice came first: 'What do you make of him? Is it wise to trust what he says?'

'Without his father around, he's more open to admitting what he doesn't know, and with your recent troubles, I think we are right to trust in his instinct.'

'Then I shall send a rider with the orders immediately.'

Making his way out of the palace, Kalac moved through the city with the efficiency of a lion tracking its prey, asking everyone he met in his wanderings: bakers, skinners, tanners, healers; most knew nothing, but eventually, he tracked her to a goatskin tent on the outskirts of the city. Bile rose in his throat as he sighted the place. His father had placed too much trust in the whimsical abilities of Neklic, and all it had taken to send him to the gods was a traitorous seer hampering his guide. He loosened the sword Girak had gifted him. If he had not been drunk and had killed the witch that night, perhaps his father would have still been alive. Loathing turned to hate as he rushed through the tent flap, desperate not to make the same mistake twice. He glimpsed her briefly before the world exploded in a cloud of dust. Kalac hit the floor, sword tumbling from his hand. His eyes stung, his throat burning with every wheezing breath.

'Your gods shall not feed on another son of Neferia!' Gritting his teeth, he pushed himself to his knees, but his arms tingled and did not feel his own, shaking with great effort to hold him up.

The witch woman knelt before him. 'Please, lord, it's just the effects of numbing herbs and bitter spices. I don't wish you harm, but you must listen. I didn't feel the presence of anyone else when I walked the future. Even if Neklic had been there, surely *I* would have been blinded if your seer is half as powerful as he claims. I did not kill your father.'

Kalac spat on the mud floor and blinked at the itching in his eyes, then suddenly he looked up, eyes bloodshot with the pain. 'I should have known you would foresee my coming! Go on then! Who is it? Enlighten me!'

The seer seemed to recoil from the bear-like endurance and ferocity of the crippled king. Kalac noted her hesitancy.

'I don't know, but you must believe me, sire, when I say I wish to help you.'

'Help me?' He choked. 'I don't feel like you're helping me now!'

The woman strutted across the dingy tent, void of any real luxuries, not even a hide for the floor. She grabbed a crude copper jug from one side of the dark room and brought it before him. 'It is water. Drink, my lord.'

Kalac hesitated for only a second; she could have killed him a dozen times by now, he figured. After he washed the spices from his throat, he splashed the water over his face and rubbed his eyes. Eventually, he asked, 'What is it you want?'

'I wish to serve you in place of Neklic. If he is blinded, then he is of no use to you.'

Kalac pushed himself to his feet, embarrassed at his foolhardy charge straight into the witch's trap. Had he forgotten everything Rhek had tried to teach him? All he wanted to do now was leave. He was not about to put his trust in any seer. 'Forget it! Witchcraft had a hand in my father's death; I shall have help from none of it!'

He stumbled out, leaving the sword behind.

Kalac was angry at himself, and with nowhere else to go, he returned to the palace and locked himself in his chamber in an attempt to hide his disgrace. He, King of the White Fangs, had been humiliated and humbled by a lowly witch woman. If word of his recklessness was to grace the ears of those less favourable to him, they could twist Krem's myriad of doubters into opposition of the young king. Regardless of whether she was the sole cause of Marek's death or not, she needed to understand the price of treachery. He unlocked his door and called for a warrior; the slaves did not dawdle to chance his wrath and scurried away to find the nearest.

When one was brought before him, Kalac was supine on the rugs of his bedding, staring up at the blackened stone which formed the ceiling. His eyes did not waver. 'Do you know of a seer's tent on the city's southern outskirts?' The tone was monotonous and lacked any emotion at all; only a man seething with so much disjointed hate can conceive no expression with which to do it justice. The warrior picked his words carefully.

'It shall not take me long to find, my lord.'

'Good. Wait until dark, then burn it to the ground. I want the watchmen on the walls to feel its warmth tonight. Kill any that emerge.'

The warrior bowed his head. 'As you say, so shall it be, Kalac King.'

Once the warrior had rushed away, Kalac began to imagine the flames licking at the dark sky and smiled. So what if she knew of the future? By night's end, her tent would be a smouldering wreck. Rising from his bed, he stalked down to the study and sent word for Rhek, hoping that listening to his tactical knowledge would draw his mind from the earlier embarrassment. It did. Almost.

That night he received word of the tent's destruction. Whatever was in it must have been highly flammable, for eyewitness accounts said the place erupted into a fireball. No one emerged or would even have had time to escape. Kalac slept soundly that night, and over the next few days, he took to studying with Rhek. Slowly they began to formulate a plan to retaliate against the invaders.

'How sure are you this will work?' asked Kalac, his mind still reeling with the numbers.

The advisor shook his weary head. 'Nothing in life is certain, my lord, but if this small group of men,' he moved the representative block across the battlefield, 'can make it to

Kardek, they can block the pass with tree trunks and large rocks. The rest of the Talran soldiers will be forced to march around the mountains.' More blocks moved. 'That journey will take them two months, at least! The war could be over even before they arrive.'

Kalac nodded. 'How defended is the pass?'

'The latest scout report suggests only a small force – to guard their supply line more than anything else.'

'Then pick a good advisor and have him select four dozen keen men. I want them out by tomorrow morn. It'll take them a week to arrive.'

'I understand, my lord. I shall see to it personally.'

As Rhek bowed his head and left the room, Kalac looked back at the wooden blocks scattered across the animal hide. He found himself considering his options even before the battle had begun.

A knock drew his attention to the door. 'Forget something?'

The door opened a crack, and Neklic sidled in. Kalac's face fell into scorn. 'Oh, it's you.'

'I have some bad news, sire.'

Kalac waited, and the silence grew. 'Well? Out with it, man!'

'I have just received word from a messenger that one of the groups along the Meir crossed the river a few nights ago. Some drowned by tripping in the dark waters as they crossed, and many more were slaughtered when they reached the opposite bank. The subsequent rout left three in every five.'

Kalac's rage exploded as he leapt, booting a mound of books at his seer. 'Who gave that order?'

Neklic seemed to shrink before him. 'I believe they took it upon themselves, my lord.'

Kalac hefted a book and threw it at the wall to release his pent-up anger. It had almost no effect.

'Leave the room, Neklic!' he said, 'before you never leave!'

The soothsayer disappeared, and the young warrior seethed in silence. Disobedience was hard to swallow. His people were indifferent about him at best, and news like this would quickly sully his name. His days of leadership would be over before they even had a chance to begin! He sighed, realising the only choice left. His father had led from the city, his words as though the gods had spoken them, but Kalac did not possess such skills, and so, his decision made, he called for a grey, gathered his necessary possessions and left the palace as swiftly as he could.

It was not swift enough.

'My lord!' said Neklic, 'I heard the call for

the horse. Where are you riding in such dire times?'

'I go where I please, Neklic! I shall lead my men from the front.'

'That is not advised, sire. Not so soon after your father's death.' The seer trailed after him until Kalac slammed the heavy palace doors into his face.

Outside, a simmering sky of fire heralded the sunset. As the grey gelding was brought to Kalac, he dumped his belongings unceremoniously into his saddlebags, mounted the horse and heeled it into a trot across the quietening city.

'Ho, Kalac King!' said the gate watcher as he approached.

Kalac could hardly recognise the warrior living with delirium and fever not more than two weeks before. 'Ho, Turesh! Gate watch, eh?'

Turesh unbolted the gates and hauled one aside. 'Only for tonight though, lord. I have been listed for Kardek again tomorrow.' He gave a cynical smile.

Kalac caught it. 'You feel troubled by that?'

Turesh shook his head. 'Nah, a fight's a fight. It matters little where it is.'

Kalac smiled and gave what he hoped was an understanding nod, for anger still bubbled beneath. Then he spurred his horse through the open gate but caught a whisper in the wind. The sound of his name came again louder. Kalac reared the horse and wheeled it into the direction of the voice, halberd leaping instinctively into his free hand. Turesh must have heard the ghostly whispers, for he, too, stepped through the gate to have a look. His curiosity turned to caution as the horse reared, and he loosed the twin axes from his belt strap. Their eyes peered into the murky darkness, and in reply, the seer woman stalked from the shadows of the wall mounted upon an old mountain pony.

'It's but a seer, lord,' said Turesh, his interest subsiding faster than a landslide. 'Their images come from a derangement of the brain and are mostly nonsense. Would you have me kill her?'

The soothsayer's voice came full of arrogant fury. 'Come and try your luck, knave!'

Turesh made to move but halted begrudgingly at his king's wishes.

'I don't know how many lives you have, witch,' said Kalac, 'but you should stop bumping into me.'

The woman gave a mirthless smile. 'The last time, it was you who sought me.'

Kalac clenched his teeth as his bottled anger burst. 'Damn it, witch! I don't wish to play games!'

'And that's not why I have come. You are destined for the warriors defending the Meir. I wish to join you. The journey is long, and you look like you could use the company.'

Turesh glanced at his king. 'My lord?'

Kalac did not respond immediately, his mind weighing up the choice. She had proven her abilities numerous times, despite what Turesh had claimed, though mostly to humble Kalac. Perhaps she would have her uses, he thought, and as he did so, he wondered if his father had felt the same of Neklic before the seer's blindness.

'Return to the gate, Turesh, and may fortune favour you.' Kalac turned his horse to the muddy path and glanced back at the pony-riding woman, his mood cold. 'But I travel alone. I refuse to make the same mistake my father did.'

The witch woman's face grew bitter with rejection, but Kalac spurred his horse on before any more words could be spoken.

The torchlight flittered through the woods like a golden spirit, disappearing briefly behind darkened boughs. For the lone woman tailing it, it was an easy task. Her pony could not hope to match the speed of Kalac's grey, but then it did not have to, as the woods were treacherous to travel at any great speed in the night. This knowledge, however, did not fill her with comfort as she tugged her furs tighter around her. The winter night was cold, and the frost had stretched its icy fingers across the ground. She would have liked to have been somewhere less open to the elements, but sooner or later, the king would need her, for she alone knew the truth.

Onwards her pony stumbled, deeper into the depths of the wood, and when Kalac finally halted for the night, she hung back in the trees some fifty yards away. Iskel was no fool. A man harbouring all of the pent-up rage life had to throw at him was a predator in the darkness, unpredictable and wild. We have much in common, she mused.

The soothsayer was wrong about one thing, Kalac reflected as he sat in a clearing under the boughs of a birch tree and watched the moon winking through the branches; the journey was not long enough! By his reckoning, it was ten years too short. He had wanted to bring Rhek to aid in his strategies, but he knew the old advisor would be invaluable in defending the city, should it come to that. Therefore, he would have to rely on the advisors already in the field. Kalac sighed. It would be an embarrassing few weeks if they were not as understanding as

Rhek.

His ears pricked to a noise in the stillness, which he had heard underneath him all evening, but now it was far off to the side: horse's hooves, two pairs, galloping hard. Casting a swift glance at the darkened tree line, he took his halberd and darted off through the woodland to intercept the noise. At first, he thought it to be a messenger relaying some urgent information, but the break-neck pace with which the horseman was moving did not slow. Kalac's eyes narrowed in suspicion. Swivelling the weapon to the hook on the reverse side of the axe, he leapt into a clearing as the masked horseman swerved past, fur coat billowing behind like a black phantom's tail. Kalac swung the long halberd up, caught the rider's feathered undergarment and wrenched him from the saddle. He fell hard and reared like a venomous snake, sword rasping out in the dark. Kalac lanced his halberd at the silhouette before his enemy could get close, sticking him in the shoulder. He heard the blade fall, and he twisted the spear end as he yanked it free and thrust it through the leg of his foe as he turned to run. Then Kalac leapt upon him like a hungry lion, knees on his chest and hands round his throat. The horse had long since bolted. Whatever it had been, it was not a white fang grey.

'Who are you?' he shouted, barely able to resist wringing the rider's scrawny neck. 'Why are you riding in White Fang lands?' He reached up with one hand and tore off the rider's mask.

The man's bloodshot eyes glared cold hard hatred. 'Slaver!' He choked, then spat in Kalac's face. 'Let the gods judge you!' His hand jerked up, and Kalac felt something bite into his side. Kalac roared, dug his thumbs into the rider's neck and savagely twisted. The neck snapped, and the head lolled back. Collapsing beside the corpse, he saw the bloodied dagger in its hand and moaned at the throbbing in his side, scrunching his eyes shut against the pain. When he opened them again, the witch woman stood above him, her stern expression lending her a curious sense of impartiality considering what had taken place between them. Kalac groaned.

'Have you come to rub salt in my eyes again, witch?'

The woman undid the lower half of her robe to reveal a grotty goatskin bag which she pulled something from, and knelt beside Kalac. Her poking fingers caused harsh words to escape his accusing tongue, but quickly the pain seemed to fade. He was about to haul himself to a sitting position when the seer's arm crossed his chest to bar his rise.

'It's just numbed you, you oaf! It's not healed you. Take care. I shall examine you by torchlight once we have left the clearing.' She glanced around as if expecting more riders to gallop from the trees, then crouched before wrapping one of Kalac's arms about her neck and lifting. Her king, however, seemed occupied by the rider's fur coat and was too heavy for her to lift alone.

'Leave him!' she said. 'You have plenty of coats!'

'I'm not after the coat, wench! This was likely a scout for another tribe, and though most messages are conveyed by word of mouth... ah-ha!' He tugged a folded parchment from a pocket and pushed himself up with his good side. 'Let us get that torch.'

As they reached the tethered grey, Kalac, aided by the seer, lowered himself to the ground and watched the woman scurry off to her pony, which she led into the clearing, before returning with a tinderbox and torch. Striking flint and pyrite, she ignited the doused hide wrapped around one end of the torchwood before stabbing its base into the earth. Doffing Kalac's fur cloak and leather jerkin, she rolled him onto his side and prodded around the wound.

Kalac felt none of it; the numbing herbs were so potent he could no longer feel his toes.

Nonetheless, he watched her every movement with suspicion.

'Your wound isn't deep,' said the seer eventually, 'but the blade has grazed your pelvic bone. I've done all I can. Time has always been a greater healer than me.'

Kalac shrugged, redressed, and turned his attention to the note, noticing the care and attention with which it had been folded. Opening it, he glanced fleetingly at the scribbled mess. The witch's head craned over his shoulder, and he heard her disappointed sigh as she moved away. 'Just words to me. As far as I'm concerned, it would have made as much sense if it was written in symbols.'

In truth, Kalac also saw them as no more than random squiggles on the page. He had been hoping for a map or diagram denoting something structurally important or tactically significant, which would have confirmed his suspicions without ever having to read a single word. As things stood, though, he could make out the shapes of only a handful of words dotted over the page, nowhere near enough to form an understanding of the sentences. Irritated by his shortcomings, he threw it carelessly to one side in a bid to forget it.

'Anything interesting?' asked Iskel as she took a last listen to the darkness before settling down for some rest.

'Not that I could make out.'

Kalac sat still for a while, enjoying the silence of the night. His wound began to itch, but he ignored the urge to scratch. He began to wonder why the witch-woman had chosen to help him. What did she hope to gain from such an act? Friendship? Forgiveness? No, Kalac reasoned, though many hold these things dear, nobody is ever willing to fight for them; fame, respect, and any kind of betterment to improve the way they lived were the sorts of things he knew people fought for regularly. He glanced at the woman huddled up in her mangy robe under a nearby tree; the hands poking out of her long sleeves suggested she was in her late twenties, but her scarred face, creased from frowning too much at life, hinted at an age closer to forty. Kalac wondered which betterment she was hoping for. The witch adjusted her position and caught him staring, which made Kalac feel awkward, though he had no idea why, so he gave a scornful laugh. 'How is your tent doing, seer?'

The insult was only half meant, and the reply was listless. 'I have no riches you can take from me. I slept on the cold dirt within my tent; I can sleep on the cold dirt without.'

'Really? You'll think differently when the

rains come.'

'Why do you taunt me so?'

Kalac started. He had been expecting some form of a sardonic comment, but instead, the question was so sincere it had almost pierced his emotional veil. He changed the subject. 'What of the Meir? Can it be defended?'

'Anything is possible.' She said sleepily, her eyes closed.

Kalac's anger rose, but he bit it back. 'I know that. Tell me of the future; for now, I expect the worst.'

The woman rolled over, turning her back to him. 'I can't.'

Kalac's voice was suddenly firm. 'You can't, or you won't?'

The seer turned, her moonlit face staring into his. 'When I said I wanted to help you, I meant it, but in this, I cannot. A seer can see many futures, and until you decide how you will defend the Meir, any may yet come to pass.'

Kalac nodded slowly. 'Then tell me when I make my decision.'

The woman rolled over once more, and in the deadened silence, an owl hooted somewhere in the branches above.

'It won't do you any good, you know?' she said without looking around. 'Once I see it in the certain future, it cannot be changed. That's the thing about certainty; it will always happen.'

'Is that a trick of your dark gods? You can tell me I'm going to die, but no matter where I run, I will always die.'

'There are no gods involved with this, Kalac, other than to say I was placed on this earth with this gift they, in their infinite wisdom, decided to give me. The bones we wear help us commune with the spirits for whom time has lost all meaning as they travel freely and endlessly across it. They're not the bones of those we have slaughtered or eaten or any other foolish stories men tell around campfires.' The woman's shoulders seemed to sag. 'Instead of trying to understand, people just brand it evil.'

'Well, what of you, seer? Why is it you could see me coming and change the outcome?'

'It's a gift all seers have,' she said nonchalantly. 'Now, let me get some rest. We still have a five-day ride ahead of us.' Snuggling into her robe, she was still.

Odd, reflected Kalac in the silence, how two soothsayers could be so different; the witch seemed to constantly delve into her own future, and yet Neklic seemed only to mention the war in his. Perhaps between periods of unconsciousness, he only ever had time for his king…

After a while, he heard the woman's breathing deepen as she drifted off to sleep. Kalac, though, could not sleep. His head was crammed with the decisions he may have to make upon his arrival at the Meir. Decisions which would have to be right the first time, for he would get no second chances. Six hundred men would be defending the river, hundreds of lives that he would not have cared for only a month before. Now his head swam with basic offensive tactics, defensive positions, counterattacks, pincers, and flanking movements. So much he had learnt, and yet so much left to learn. He was well out of his depth, he knew. He would never voice it, but he felt like a child forced to complete a man's job. As a distraction from berating himself further, he reached for the mysterious note again, willing it to part with its many secrets. He was about to discard it again when he recognised the name scrawled across the bottom.

Turesh.

5

Kalac limped about in maddened fury; the herbs had worn off and a stabbing pain renewed in his side, fuelling his annoyance further. 'I can't believe I let the bastard live! I should have slit his throat the moment I laid eyes on him! He was a Great Claw once, and I bet you a fur coat that rider was too!'

'It can't be him, Kalac!'

He turned on the seated witch with a snarl. 'That's Kalac King to you!'

'Think about it for one heartbeat!' she snapped. 'If the note was so incriminating, why write his name on the bottom?'

Kalac spun away, restless with his thoughts, and then he shook his head. 'It all makes too much sense to be wrong! The invasion began upon my father's death! That can't be a coincidence; it takes months to plan these things! My father died because that imbecile told the Talran exactly what my father was planning, and in return, he was spared!'

'And how exactly would he tell them? The riders? Kalac, he was with your father the whole time! Surely one pair of eyes would have noticed him missing!'

'Anybody who would have seen him has since been killed! Besides, the Great Claws are a vassal tribe. Written messages to them are not forbidden just as long as they are proofread for traitorous wordage.' Kalac stabbed a finger into the palm of his hand. 'We have official channels for this! Why do it any other way?'

'I'm not saying he has nothing to hide. Everyone harbours secrets.'

Kalac hefted his halberd from amongst the dried leaves used to clean it and suddenly thrust it towards the witch like an accusing finger. 'You're not above suspicion either! You saw what was to happen at Kardek, so *you* could have blinded Neklic and sent the messages yourself!'

The seer was, at first, stunned by Kalac's change of tack, then suddenly, she leapt to her feet in defiant rage. 'Listen to yourself, Kalac! I knew about Kardek, yes! I tried to warn you, but you were too damn *drunk*!'

Kalac's last remnant of composure cracked, and he struck out. Bark chips burst everywhere, and the halberd shaft vibrated as the spearhead embedded into the trunk beside the seer. He stood ridged for a moment, his teeth clenched, his breath hissing between them.

'I'm just tired, Kalac King,' pleaded the woman.

It was then that Kalac sighted the undisguised fear in the soothsayer's face, and the shame of his wild outburst hit him full on. It was an ice bath on a cold day; it was a burst river turning his home to sediment, and it was all he could do to slump to the floor at her feet. Perhaps it is not the seer, he thought; perhaps it is not Turesh. If it was not, then somebody elsewhere was taking him for a fool. Had Girak killed his father for a stab at leadership? Or was he just clutching at straws now? Had it all just been one big coincidence all along? His head swam with exhaustion, and almost before he could lay it against the nearby trunk, he blacked out.

The following three days had been wet but passed without incident, and Kalac's bored mind roamed far and wide, searching for answers he did not possess. On the morning of the fourth day, with the rain easing and their food supplies dwindling, Kalac roamed the woods, checking the traps he had set the previous night.

Returning with two rabbits, he began to skin them and place chunks of meat into a forged cooking pot which he had fished out of one of his saddlebags. Then, with the newly born sun just beginning to pierce the trees, he filled it with his water bag and hung it from his makeshift pot hanger over the cooking fire. He was thankful for the slight distraction, for his subconscious mind had begun to weave absurd tales of treasonous plots which, upon waking, he could not shake. His grim mood had worsened thanks to the continuous drizzle from which the leafless canopy above scarcely provided shelter. Despite his cloak, the thin layer of wool beneath his leathers had absorbed some of the rain, irritating the wound in his side. As such, he and his companion had barely exchanged words other than the occasional forced pleasantry. He glanced over at the woman who was still asleep on the damp earth. A bird sang somewhere overhead, and suddenly he, too, felt sleepy as the long days of travel caught up with him. He pushed his back against a tree and closed his eyes to rest them.

Kalac's eyes flicked open and scanned his surroundings, for a moment forgetting where he was. The witch woman was stirring the contents of the cooking pot with his knife, the ringing as it hit the sides had been the noise which had awakened him. Kalac shifted from the awkward position he had slumped into whilst sleeping, and the seer looked over.

'The soup is almost done,' she said.

Kalac's eyes widened with surprise. 'Soup? How did you manage to make soup?'

'Magic.' And the woman gave a wry grin.

Kalac's face became suddenly stern. 'Of that, I have no doubt.'

The seer gave a shrill laugh. 'I have herbs and spices aplenty, and you already threw the rabbit bones in with it. I can easily conjure up a thick broth.'

As the double meaning sank in, Kalac smiled, and the tension within him eased slightly, though he could not shake his troubles.

'We are still two days ride from the Meir, and I have no idea if we will arrive before Reshmal decides to cross the river.'

'We will. This, at least, is certain. Reshmal is having trouble with his supply route. The small wheels on the carts of his baggage train are not designed for the rocky, dirt-ridden paths of Neferia, and he dares not commit hungry men to combat.'

Kalac nodded slowly, his relief overshadowed by a further question. 'Why are you helping me, woman? For what purpose?'

The seer stirred the soup for a short while,

and Kalac began to doubt she had heard him, but then came the soft reply: 'You are my king. What else would you have me do?' The question was designed to be rhetorical, for she quickly changed the subject. 'The soup is ready. I have a couple of copper bowls in one of my saddlebags. I shall fetch them.'

As the woman moved away, Kalac sighed. He was not happy with the avoidance of a proper answer, but for now, he was thankful for any help he could get.

Two days later, the witch woman, mounted atop her laden pony, sat on top of a hill on the edge of the White Fang camp. A chill wind blew in from the north, turning the rain to sleet and causing flurries of snowflakes to dance in the bitter-cold air. Pulling up the fur-lined hood on her robe, Iskel knew her reception, like the weather, would be frosty. Her heart was beating hard in her chest, though externally, she was calm. A voice in the back of her mind told her to return to Krem, avoid any confrontations with the warriors, and live alone in peace.

Peace? She chided herself. When have you ever known peace? You were a worthless nobody living in your makeshift shanty town outside the city walls with the sorry beggars and the ugly whores, gathering scraps of food and fending your tent from hungry men and animals alike on a regular basis. This is your chance to do something worthwhile! Besides, you have seen what is to come. Only death and deceit await you back in the capital.

Taking a deep breath to calm her nerves, she carefully spurred her pony down the slippery hillside and towards the camp.

Her mountain pony became increasingly irritable as they left the relative shelter of the trees and were hammered by freezing gusts. Any other time, she would have led the animal back into the woods and cared for her until the winds settled, but now the seer felt safer on her sturdy mount than she would have had she walked in on her own two feet.

A guard spotted Iskel approaching and moved to intercept her, eyeing the bones stitched within the robe.

'Very rare to see a soothsayer wandering around. What business have you here?'

'It's imperative that I speak with your advisor.'

The guard raised an inquisitive eyebrow. 'Why?'

'It's a personal matter,' lied the seer. 'Now, will you escort me or not?'

The guard paused for a moment, then reluctantly nodded.

Being a woman had its advantages, Iskel

knew. Had she been a man, there would have been far more questioning, and she would have likely been turned away, but there was much less suspicion surrounding a lone woman.

Slowly, they navigated through the maze of hundreds of scattered tents and warriors preparing for the long days of battle ahead. All eyes were upon her as she passed by. Nearly every man here, she knew, was a veteran of some sort, whether it was fighting insurrections, the surrounding tribes, or keeping the Talran at bay in the months past. She returned the gazes of a few and saw the battle scars etched on their stern faces and muscular arms. Their lust-filled eyes told of the distance between them and their lovers back home.

Suddenly a handful of warriors stepped into the witch woman's path, and she reined in her pony, stroking the irritable beast's mane to calm her. A couple of them laughed at the sight of the short, stout animal. One of them stepped forward, ogling her curves, his salivating mouth opened, and an undisguised desire for flesh gleamed in his one good eye.

'Dangerous out here for a woman such as yourself,' he said.

The seer's gaze turned icy cold. 'And I suppose you'll be the one to protect me?'

'Why, of course,' said one eye, licking his lips. 'I only ask for a small price in return for such a good deed.'

Iskel straightened her back and stared down at the man.

'It'll be too short, over far too quickly, and I'll be disappointed.'

The warriors around one-eye laughed with genuine humour at her rebuke. Her escort waved her through, and she heeded her pony past the group. One of them clapped the now sheepish one-eye on the back.

'She knows you well, old friend!' he said, causing more peals of laughter from his comrades.

At length, the seer approached a large tent at the far end of the camp. Dismounting, she thanked the guard, tethered her pony to a sturdy cross beam with the other mounts and pushed her way through the tent flap.

'I understand your concerns, Koren, but I'm here now. I can assure you I have total control of the situation.'

The tall, wiry man who had just spoken broke his gaze from the barrel-chested giant before him and stared hard at her. The seer recognised him from public speeches as the old king's most trusted adviser, Drenik. He was fortunate, she knew, for he had been sent to oversee a border dispute in the west only a fortnight before Marek and his elite met their end at Kardek. Had Drenik been available, he would have surely been with them.

'Do I know you?' he said, his tone calm and calculated.

The witch woman bowed her head in genuine respect. 'No, Great Advisor, but I seek an audience with you.' She flicked her gaze to the giant. 'A private one.'

Drenik returned his gaze to the barrel-chested warrior. 'Are we done here, Koren?'

Koren nodded, bowed, and swiftly left the tent without uttering another word, though he stared suspiciously at the woman as he passed.

With the giant's departure, Drenik's shoulders sagged, and the tension inside him seemed to ease. He turned to the seer, and his eyes, set within an aged and weary face, gazed over the many bones stitched upon her dark, wet robe. 'It's not every day I have a soothsayer wander into my camp. Perhaps, if the gods will it, you can offer me some good news.'

'I am Iskel, Advisor, and I bring word of Kalac King's imminent arrival. He is less than a day's ride from camp.'

Drenik swore softly. 'What in the gods' names is he doing here?'

'He intends to lead his men from the front as many a warrior king has done before him. He demands a tent fit for his status,' she glared at the advisor and decided to risk a small lie, 'and one for his seer.'

Drenik's eyes narrowed. 'Kalac said that, did he? That sounds... most unlike him. I have never known him to be sympathetic towards your kind.' He stared at her, weighing up the odds of both choices in his mind. 'Very well,' he said at last. 'I'll try to break it gently to the men. Then have your tents constructed.' He was silent for a moment, and then he sighed. 'I came directly after hearing about the debacle a week ago. The men were in a right sorry state. I told them I would take command, which put many of them at ease. Now I'm to tell them otherwise.' He shook his head. 'I'm cold, and I'm tired. Please tell me there is some good news.'

Iskel remained silent for a while, hesitant as to how much knowledge she should part with. Reaching a conclusion, she said, 'Kalac was not responsible for the mess here, though many would happily accuse him of such things.'

Drenik raised a curious eyebrow, but the seer shook her head.

'That is Kalac's story to tell,' she said, 'but you will understand it soon enough.'

* * *

Kalac's dreams were haunted. He saw himself as a child in a room full of men, all talking of war. Partway through their conversation, one of the men began to speak a different language which Kalac did not recognise. Then another joined in, and another, until soon everyone was talking in a foreign tongue. Suddenly one of them turned to him.

'What say you, Kalac?'

The child mumbled and stuttered, a fear gripping him, stopping any words from escaping his throat. Something was expected of him, though he had no idea what to say. Then they began to laugh and belittle him.

Kalac awoke. Something nudged him. He rolled over and saw a huge beast looming above him. But there was no alarm. The seer's pony was chomping at the grass beside him, occasionally bumping its head against him as it tore at the undergrowth. The witch woman muttered an apology and led the pony away before continuing to tighten the saddle and pack everything into the many saddlebags which burdened the beast.

The seer had spoken more since the ice breaker around the fire, but it was always idle chatter, so the woman had remained a dark enigma. Much like the events surrounding his father's death, he mused. Though as the days wore on, his dreams became more and more about his feeling of ineptitude than traitorous activity.

Then the witch woman had left, galloping ahead to warn the camp of the king's arrival. Kalac recalled Neklic informing him of the ridiculous advance across the Meir and the subsequent rout which followed. The first thing he needed to do when he reached the camp, he decided, was to find out who issued that command and relieve them of their duties. This, he hoped, would instil some confidence in him. Then he would need the labelled maps which Rhek had drawn up, located in his saddlebags, along with the counsel of whichever advisors were in the camp to assemble a battle plan.

Two nights later, as the winter weather firmly settled in, Kalac crested a hill and saw the dark outlines of a myriad of tents stretching on into the darkness. No torches lit his path lest the enemy see them from across the Meir. As he approached, he saw the witch woman was waiting for him, and she led him without a word through the night to a freshly erected tent. With a word of thanks, Kalac dismounted wearily and pushed the rawhide tent flap aside. A brazier was already burning, and the warm air hit him as soon as he stepped in, it stank of the tannin process used to prepare the skins, but Kalac did not care. He lay down on the many furred hides furnishing the floor, and after a few pleasant moments with nothing more than the crackle of a dull brazier, the witch woman pulled back the flap and stepped in.

'Is there anything you need, Kalac King?' she asked, 'for I'm frightfully tired myself.'

Kalac's eyes remained closed. He was enjoying the comfort of the soft floor, a great contrast to the wet, stony ground and the jarring horse riding of the past week. He stretched his back out on the rugs.

'Who is currently in charge of the camp?' he asked.

'Advisor Drenik, my lord.'

The familiar name caused a sense of relief to wash over him. Drenik had been his father's advisor for as long as he could remember. He visited the palace often as Kalac grew up – so often his father had seen fit to grant him living quarters – and the young boy eventually took to him like an uncle. Kalac sighed. The last time he had seen Drenik, he had stood beside his father, tall and proud, days before he was sent west to deal with a border dispute. How proud would he be, he wondered, standing beside the great man's son?

Kalac sat up, working his stiff shoulders. 'Send for the old advisor before you retire. I wish to get to the bottom of last week's mess.'

The seer nodded. 'I had the men construct a smaller tent for me further down the bank. I don't trust them to keep their hands to themselves whilst I'm here. I'll be there if you need anything else from me. Send word for Iskel.'

With that, she gave an unconvincing bow and backed out of the tent, leaving Kalac a few more precious moments with the warmth of the brazier. He sighed away his tension and, getting to his feet, strode out to his grey and emptied his saddlebags before returning the contents to his tent. Rummaging through the stuff, he pulled aside and unravelled a map of the river and the rough positions of the men along it. Rhek was a poor drawer, but the map would serve its purpose. Hunkering down beside the fire, he began to study.

Koren seethed with rage as he watched his comrades reluctantly erect the king's tent in the sleet and snow. Under a makeshift awning, a few of the camp's tanners were finishing the preparation of the hides and skins that had taken all afternoon to gather as the warriors set to work constructing the frame. Kalac deserved nothing less than to be cast out from the tribe, thought the giant, for he would yet be their downfall. He looked away and shook his head. He thought he had gotten this message across to Advisor Drenik when he requested that Koren join him in his tent earlier that morning. Drenik, as always, had been calm and composed, and Koren could not tell whether the old man was offering help or hindrance.

'Your previous advisor, the young Ricken, was killed in the failure to cross the Meir, I take it?' asked the Great Advisor.

Koren kept his head low as the old advisor spoke; his body was wrought with equal measures of rage and shame. He merely nodded.

'Well, as you are aware,' said Drenik, a firm edge to his voice, 'I have taken command over these last few days. Now I seek to know what happened.'

Koren remained silent for a moment, inwardly cursing his part in the events leading up to the river crossing. He sighed. *What is done is done; it cannot be undone.*

'The day before the... *incident,* a messenger rode into camp informing Advisor Ricken of Kalac King's want to push across the Meir and send them running back to Talran. He went on to say Kalac had received news that most of the enemy had been injured in the battle of Kardek, and a speedy assail across the river would leave them vulnerable to superior White Fang strength.' Koren shook his head.

'It was all lies. What was Kalac thinking?'

The giant glanced up at Drenik for a clue as to an answer. The advisor's expression remained passive.

'What happened?' asked Drenik.

So Koren told him of young Ricken's deep-seated hatred for Kalac and his unwillingness to commit any of his men to his reckless acts without first seeing the evidence for himself. 'This was sound reasoning in hindsight,' he admitted, 'but many of the men knew the real reason for his disobedience: Ricken wanted the challenge. Of course, he could not leave his men leaderless and ride back to Krem with the Talran just across the water, so he was to ignore all messages from the city in the hope that Kalac himself would ride out with his usual fury and then Ricken would get his challenge.'

'And what of Reshmal during this time?' asked Drenik.

'Ricken swore he would not let the Talran cross the river, but if the enemy were as injured as Kalac believed, they wouldn't try it anyway.'

Drenik nodded conservatively. 'So what changed?'

Koren's head almost slumped into his lap. 'Such flagrant abuse of challenge rules was absurd; he had no majority support back in

Krem. I rounded on Ricken, accusing him of betrayal. Nearly half of the men in the camp stood with me. Not because they liked Kalac but because he was king, and kings needed to be obeyed.' The giant sighed. 'So we tried to cross the river, and Ricken was last seen floating down the Meir with an arrow in his gut.'

An uneasy silence grew between them, then Drenik spoke: 'I can see this has taken a heavy toll on you, Koren. Do you blame yourself?'

Koren's rage rose to the surface.

'No,' said the giant, baring his teeth, 'I blame that vile Kalac for everything that has happened here! His words are poison!'

Drenik remained silent, and Koren realised the potential consequences of his outburst. 'I'm sorry, Great Advisor.'

Drenik shook his head. 'I understand your concerns, Koren, but I'm here now. I can assure you I have total control of the situation.'

Then the seer woman entered, and the giant left. Koren knew she would be trouble the moment he laid eyes on her, for he had seen the frown lines on her face. Born, he figured, from scowling at those she issued ill omens and curses upon.

He had been right.

Koren had spent the rest of the morning training with the men, then Drenik had emerged from his tent with some ill news: Kalac was coming. The announcement came as a bitter blow to everyone, and the old advisor assured the warriors that the king would have counsel from him and his many years of experience under Marek. Koren was not convinced. The advisors back in Krem, he guessed, must have surely thought the same thing.

Back in the present, the giant shook his head sadly and walked away from the construction work. At least the tannin process will make the tent smell like shit when Kalac arrives, he mused. The thought made him smile, and he returned to his tent in a lighter mood.

Hollow clay balls were stacked in one corner of the tent, and the rest of the space was dedicated to turning animal fat into usable oil. Many furs and hides lined the walls and floor, and Koren, himself, wore furred garments under his leathers, for no brazier adorned his room. The giant's eyes adjusted to the gloom, and he continued to work on his new project, remembering the time as a child when he would carelessly burn the oil just to see the destructive power of Airc, the capricious fire god. Koren shivered at the recollection of his terrible accident.

'Never again.' He whispered.

Later, as dusk descended and made the room

too dark to work in, Koren left the tent and wandered to the river's edge, where he washed his face in the icy waters. A second smaller tent had now been erected downstream to house Kalac's loathsome seer. The clouds parted briefly, and the waxing moon shone through; its ghostly reflection rippled on the cold, black surface of the river. Then it was gone again. Koren glanced across the Meir. Just out of sight, the Talran forces lay in wait for their supply lines to finally catch up with their military's swift advancement into Neferia. Not for the first time, the giant wondered how the Talran emperor had defeated five lesser tribes in as many weeks. He must have sacrificed no end to his foreign deities to claim such victories. But the gods were fickle, Koren knew, and Reshmal had not yet faced the might of Neferia's own savage gods.

Suddenly the seer emerged from her tent and passed him by without a word. Koren eyed her suspiciously as she wandered through the camp, and he decided to follow at a distance. Many of the men had retired to their tents, leaving only the perimeter watch to grin and bear the weather. One such warrior nodded his respect to Koren as he walked by, but the giant was staring at a horseman riding at this instant into camp. The seer greeted him, and Koren's stomach twisted. It was the vile Kalac, the man who would send scores of warriors to their deaths on a mere whim.

As the soothsayer moved further into camp, urging her king to follow, Koren did too. They reached the king's tent, and he waited until the seer left. She passed him by, and they exchanged glances for a heartbeat. Koren shivered. He had seen fire in her eyes.

Then Kalac appeared, collecting his belongings from his saddlebags before returning to his tent once more. Koren advanced. The veteran warrior was once a loyal man, serving as he had under the old king for nearly two decades and building a stalwart reputation among the men. Now that loyalty was in tatters, and all that remained was the mutual trust for his comrades. If he was to save just one of their lives from another tragedy, then tonight, king or no king, Kalac would die.

6

Dragging the map closer to the brazier, Kalac strained to see what simple worded notes Rhek had written next to each group. Two groups would defend the bank, forcing the enemy back into the slippery silt of the river, two more would hold slings and lob rocks at those crossing the Meir, and a fifth would be held in reserve. At present, the groups were stretched along this portion of the river with no way of knowing where the Talran would try to wade. Kalac scratched his head. What would his father's next step have been?

Something moved off to the side, and he looked up. His blood froze icy in his veins as he caught sight of a massive shadow lengthening across the far tent wall. From the inside! He leapt to his feet and spun straight into a meaty fist. The world blackened for a heartbeat. He collapsed back into the brazier and fell onto the spilt embers. Instinctively he rolled aside as the rest of the brazier was kicked to the floor, scattering burning coal across the tent. Kalac leapt up as the flames roared around him. His eagle eyes scanned the leather-clad giant before him even as he swayed from the savage haymaker. Kalac's reply was a snake strike to the giant's jaw. The massive warrior did not flinch. Kalac reeled back into the rugged tent flap, wide-eyed and working his stinging hand. The tent flap was open, but he would never use it; like his father, he would never sully his family name with cowardice. The giant smirked, his gap-toothed grin yellow in the firelight. Then came his reply. Kalac batted aside the fist. He grabbed the warrior's forearm and twisted savagely. He tried to listen for the crack but a wall of knuckles connected with his face. Kalac fell into the wooden tent frame, and a piece of it snapped. Blinded by blood, he felt iron fingers clamp around his neck. Then he was lifted from the floor. Instinctively Kalac clawed at the thumb crushing his windpipe, his legs kicking out.

The giant roared. 'I trusted you, and you betrayed us all!'

Kalac's vision flickered like the flames of a dying fire. He heard the sound of splintering wood, then he fell through the tent flap as the roof caved in.

Kalac choked and wheezed as new life filled his lungs. As he dragged his legs clear of the ruins and stumbled to his feet, the giant still lost inside, he wiped the blood from his eyes. A small crowd had gathered about him, masks of confusion all too blatant on their faces. Were they really as oblivious as their faces suggested, or were they only confused as to why he still lived?

Rage twisted beneath, his muscles knotted, his teeth clenched, and his temples pulsed. If he were to be a dead man, he would die fighting! His gaze locked with the warrior in front. Then a moaning turned many eyes to the burning ruins of the tent where the giant tore through the scorched goatskin and staggered out. Both his arms were blistered red and a shoulder lacerated, his jerkin hung loose, and on his face was a pain which far surpassed the physical, a pain which had endured the decades, like a man reliving a nightmare. The men rushed around their fallen hero, stripping the smouldering fur and baked leather from his shoulders and coaxing him to the water's edge, but a few remained before Kalac, and one leaned in so that the king could smell the rotting meat between his teeth.

'Lot of men 'round 'ere don't like you. 'specially after your suicide request. But ol' Koren over there.' He gestured to the giant just disappearing into the shadows of the Meir's steep bank. 'He wouldn't listen to reason. Said a king had to be obeyed; t'was treason otherwise. Well, what could anyone say? He's something of a legend, and men follow him like sheep.' The man pitifully shook his head. 'Look at him now. For a man not used to defeat, the rout hit him `ard. Hit us all `ard, but him `specially.'

Kalac's rage seethed beneath his skin, but his voice remained even. 'I ordered no such crossing. Any man who did so held to his own fate.'

The warrior's eyes remained accusing, but an edge of uncertainty had begun to settle.

'What in the gods' names?' The old advisor shoved his way through the men. 'Back to your tents! All of you! And someone put that fire out!'

The crowd began to slowly disperse. Kalac spun and watched, with eyes of molten hate, as the warriors walked away. How easy it would be to hang their traitorous hides, he thought, and to Airc with the consequences! Perhaps a tyrant king was necessary in such harsh times. Suddenly one of the warriors fell, blood gushing from an open wound in his neck. Kalac thought he was dreaming. Then more arrows whizzed by, and shouts began to rend the air. Realisation dawned. The Talran were firing from the darkness of the opposite bank, guided by the firelight. He turned to the maddened chaos around him. An arrow skimmed his right cheek as he shouted, 'Douse the tent, you oafs!'

Turesh crouched in the woods and watched the waning moon as it breasted the distant mountains – his would-be destination – but before him rested another task. Beyond the spike-trunked barricades ahead was the small White Fang settlement of Yeki, now resident to at least seventy Talran. Of course, a skirt around the settlement was all that was called for, but somebody in higher command had grown soft. Many of the villagers had been slaughtered like cattle, but some, mainly women and children coming of age, according to the scout, were imprisoned in a large hut to the rear and destined for slavery. Turesh rolled his eyes. At least until some bright spark set his sights on their release, he thought. Looking sidelong at the other warriors, he knew by the anxious looks on their faces they were thinking the same as he: four dozen against nearly four scores. A head-on assault was out of the question.

'Gather round men,' said the rumbling voice of Garlock, the designated leader and advisor to the king, and who the men would blame for any unnecessary loss of life in this ridiculous venture. With his mighty frame, he reached up and broke a low-hanging branch from a tree before he began to etch crude shapes into the frozen soil, the warriors straining to see them in the low light of the moon, for no torch could be struck this close to the settlement. The rough shape of Yeki was a semi-circle with the stable, where the women and children were held, situated along its straight edge. Two openings on the curved side completed his sketch, then Garlock proceeded to cover it with rough arrows, and afterwards, his meaty finger retraced them as he explained. 'I counted twelve guards. The rest are no doubt celebrating their petty victory by drinking themselves into a stupor with our wine or sleeping soundly, having gorged themselves silly on our grain stores. We cannot afford to alert them, so two of you, Sayker and Turesh, will remove the guards on the southern entrance and skulk hut to hut around the settlement. When you free the villagers, have them trace in reverse the path you took. There may or may not be a guard inside with them, so be prepared. Are we clear on the plan?'

Turesh nodded sombrely. Of all the warriors he could have chosen, he thought, he had to choose me. Doffing his travel pack and stashing it under the bough of a fallen tree, he took a sidelong glance at Sayker, a lean and agile young man, but like all youths, he was foolhardy and I. In true fashion, Sayker opened his big mouth.

'And you'll just be sitting on your arse, I presume?' he said.

Garlock's face grew as red as the fire in his eyes. 'Every extra man increases our risk of discovery! I have told you the plan! If anything unpleasant should happen, I shall see to it that you get the support you deserve! Now shut your mouth and get going!'

Turesh swallowed hard. Sayker had obviously embarrassed Garlock. How much support would he deem deserving now? A knot twisted in Turesh's stomach. He knew Garlock well enough to know he would harbour a grudge against Sayker. Turesh would not have minded had he not been going with him.

Kalac watched the dishevelled line of men swiftly hauling pots, buckets and anything else that could hold water from the Meir to the raging tent. Kalac saw a pot pass to one man, who was then hit by an arrow. As he fell, the pot rolled across the dirt, spilling its contents to the ground. Another man immediately took his place, retrieved the pot and passed it on to start its journey back to the Meir again.

Once the fire had subsided and the Talran ceased loosing arrows blindly, Drenik had taken stock of the casualties before asking Kalac to join him in his tent. The command had been worded as diplomatic as the old advisor could manage, but Kalac knew there was little choice in the matter, and once the heavy tent flap had fallen behind them, Drenik dropped the guise.

'I worry about you, boy. What are you doing here?' His words were sincere, and no hidden malicious undertone lay in his empathetic voice. 'I've taken leadership here since that terrible... incident the other week, and since I have, the men haven't been able to thank me enough.'

Kalac could not look the old man in the eye. He sat himself on the wide circular rug at the centre of the tent upon which stood the brazier. The fire warmed his skin, but it did not brighten his past.

'I didn't give that order,' said Kalac softly, suddenly a lost and lonely child again in front of Drenik. The old advisor sighed and moved to sit before his new king. Kalac could not bear the repressive silence between them. 'I just wish there was a way to-'

'You don't need to persuade me, boy,' said Drenik, 'and it pains me that you think you do. You may be many things, Kalac, but a liar isn't one of them. If you say you had no involvement in that butchery, then you didn't. The problem comes,' he jerked his thumb over his shoulder, 'in persuading that rabble out there.'

For the first time since his arrival in camp, Kalac looked the ageing advisor in the eyes – and he fell into them, remembering the days of his youth.

As his father's most trusted advisor, Drenik was always around – so much so that Marek had ordered half of the third floor to be remodelled as the advisor's living quarters. Not only was Drenik involved in all matters of defence, his duties even extended to the protection of the young Kalac and his mother on royal visits to the various vassal tribes. During his younger years, Kalac hated the ageing advisor, seeing him as merely intrusive and condescending in his corrections. But Drenik had befriended his mother, Lynaea, and though this was nothing special, for his mother found it easy to make friends, when she died the night Lekta was born, the young Kalac had clung to her old friends as if through them he could still feel her warmth.

Kalac had learnt much from the advice of Drenik over the years, and the advisor had become somewhat of a guardian while his father was away sorting tribal disputes. Then three years ago, the shrivelled half-faced seer had taken pride of place in the palace. Perhaps, thought Kalac, that was one of the reasons he hated Neklic so much...

The old advisor leaned across the brazier and gave Kalac's shoulder a friendly shake. 'If you're struggling with leadership, then allow me to take some of that burden from you.'

Kalac cast his gaze into the fire. 'What do you suggest?'

Drenik leaned back. 'Let us discuss your tactics, and when a plan is drawn, allow me to address the men. They might accept it more coming from me.'

Kalac nodded, seeing no other way. Tactical decisions had to be obeyed, especially during a time of war. 'Did my father ever have difficulty getting his voice heard when he first became king?'

Drenik did not answer immediately. He stared into the simmering brazier, and Kalac saw a darkness in his eyes. 'When your father was young, he was a ruthlessly ambitious leader. He conquered and slew with ruthless efficiency, and, though the other leaders berated him and accused him of being a lucky fool, he was appointed as an advisor to the old king.' Drenik laughed. 'Funny, how the better your strategy, the luckier you become.' He waved the comment away, 'Anyway, the old king was hated, and those who would challenge him were suspiciously killed before it could take place. Revolts were commonplace, and your father had ample opportunity to prove his worth. And prove it he did. Almost overnight, he became Marek the Merciless. It took a young woman by the name of Vaye, your birth mother, to finally placate him, and Marek began to grow in popularity. By the end of the year, he had killed the king he had served so well and brought a sense of peace to the White Fangs that had hitherto been unknown. Even the tribes he was forced to conquer he did not destroy.'

The old advisor's eyes brightened, and he glanced up at Kalac. 'Marek's word was like that of the gods long before people gave their respect freely. You are nothing like your father, boy. And for that, I'm grateful. You must carve your own path through life, for no other will do it for you.' Drenik leaned forward over the brazier, and Kalac guessed it was the heat and smoke which caused the old man's eyes to mist. 'Your father has paved the way, and you must not let the tribe slip back into anarchy. I refuse to see all that we have fought for come to naught.'

'I will not let that happen, Drenik.'

The Great Advisor stood and cleared his

throat. 'Good. What you need now is a decisive victory, and we shall discuss this over the coming days. In the meantime, you will have to share the tent of your seer until we can get another erected for you.' He paused in his thought. 'I trust she will aid our cause.'

Kalac shook his head. 'I'll have no help from her. Not after my ill-informed father rode to his death on the whim of his seer.'

Drenik sighed. 'You always did have a loathing for Neklic.'

Kalac's voice came firmly. 'I don't wish to discuss it.'

'Very well,' said the advisor. 'Then I shall press no further, but a good king uses all his available resources.'

Before he could be persuaded further, Kalac rose and walked to the tent flap. Drenik called out to him.

'Take care, Kalac. If you didn't send that message into camp, then someone has clearly taken a dislike to you.'

Kalac hefted up the flap. 'That list is longer than I care to imagine,' he said before stepping out into the cold, unforgiving darkness.

Kalac kept to the darkest shadows as he weaved his way through the myriad of tents to the seer's quarters, half expecting another attempt at his life. As he passed the healing tent, he could hear from within the morbid moans of the dying, and though Talran arrows had caused their mortal wounds, it had happened because the White Fangs had been fighting themselves. The words of the old advisor resounded in his head. *You must not let the tribe slip back into anarchy.* Had Drenik's grim prediction already begun?

When Kalac eventually arrived at the seer's tent, he was not surprised to see light emanating from within. He had guessed she would have known of his coming, and he lifted the tent flap before ducking in.

The room was dim and chill. Naught but a solitary candle flickering in the draught of the tent flap fought the shadows of the dark; even the brazier had been snuffed out. Rugs lay sprawled across one half of the tent. The other side lay bare but for a few copper pots, a goatskin bag, and various stones and crystals. Among these possessions sat the seer, her dark eyes reflecting the flickering candlelight.

'I have been advised to sleep in your tent tonight,' said Kalac, to break the silence more than anything.

'I know,' said the witch woman, and even though Kalac was prepared for it, he shuddered. The seer waved an outstretched hand towards the opposite side of the tent. 'I have piled up the rugs that used to furnish the floor. I prefer to sleep on the bare earth, so you may use them.'

Kalac gave his thanks, kicked off his muddy boots, and lay among the soft rugs with his back to the tent wall. The seer began rummaging around inside her goatskin bag, but Kalac paid it no mind. His was filled with destruction and turmoil; the savage sounds of steel, the banshee wails of the near dead, and the wild flames burning Krem to cinders. If Reshmal did not have his wicked way, then his own people would cause this! He cursed and quickly dismissed the thought. Drenik had been right. He needed to use all his available resources. The men needed a show of competence, and *he* needed a stalwart victory, now more than ever.

Kalac's gaze darted across the room. The seer sat cross-legged on the dirt and had begun to place crystals and stones in a semi-circle around her, the single candle flame glinting from them like the many eyes of a demon. He swallowed hard, and the seer suddenly halted and looked up. In the silence that followed, Kalac sighed.

'You know what I'm about to say, do you not?'

Iskel sat rigidly, her voice stern. 'I would have you say it anyway.'

Kalac hesitated, then reluctantly swallowed his pride. 'I require your aid. I need you to *see* for me.' The words poured like tar from his tongue, and with them came the question of how his smote soul would be damned and delivered into the greedy hands of the dark gods to whom, with this one act, he would now be bound.

The witch woman smirked. 'Was that really so difficult?'

Kalac's anger flashed for a moment and then was instantly forgotten. He sat and gaped in silence at the peculiar scene. The seer's eyes spun in their sockets to reveal the whites, and, above the various crystals and stones, her hovering hands spasmed and jerked as though resisting unseen entities tugging upon them. The lone candle flame flickered violently as if its sacred light was no longer enough to keep the creeping darkness at bay. Kalac reached out for a fur blanket and tugged it tightly around his shoulders. Even so, he shivered.

When nothing else happened, and the wait grew, so, too, did Kalac's impatience. He was expecting a description of the future when the visions came, but so far, the seer had said nothing. Her eyes made Kalac uneasy, for he had never seen Neklic's eyes rotate inside his skull during rituals, and, though his experience was limited, he began to wonder if something was not quite right with this one. Kalac's dry mouth parted but the words locked in his throat. He dared not speak lest the ritual was broken. Then, almost in answer, the soothsayer collapsed, and the candle blew out.

Kalac lit the brazier by his side, and as its warm glow filled the tent, he slipped from his fur blanket to check on the prone figure of the witch woman. Her eyes were closed, but as he reached across for the pulse in her neck, her hand sprung up and batted his away.

'I am well!' she said, her tone partway between drowsy and annoyed.

Kalac could barely disguise his relief. 'What did you see? Where will they try to cross?'

'One question at a time,' said Iskel as she rubbed her forehead and pushed herself to a seated position. 'Emperor Reshmal is a cunning one. He will try to cross in two places at two different times. The first will be east, where the woodlands encroach on the river. He will expect that you already have an encampment positioned there and that the rest of your warriors will arrive by day's end to repel the crossing. During this time, as you move east, he and the rest of his men will march west to cross where a ford has allowed the river to freeze. He will not be expecting much resistance.'

'When is this?'

'Two nights away, when the Great God Xaer

does not raise the moon and all is cloaked in darkness. The regiment in the east will be carrying torches to make themselves known. He expects a new king, overeager for victory, and easy to fool.'

Kalac fell silent for a moment. Drenik was just across the camp. If he raced there now, they could formulate a strategy. And then what? Drenik would speak it as though his own, and the men would still believe their king to be an invalid. Besides, the old advisor had convinced him to use the seer in the first place, and therefore he would likely just act upon that information. He recalled the crude sketches of Rhek's general combat strategy, sadly lost in the tent blaze. Now was the time to put it into action. Fortune had always favoured the brave.

Kalac composed himself. 'I shall send a group east. The rest shall follow me west.'

'I know. This is for certain,' said Iskel, and Kalac was unsure whether this should fill him with confidence or not. He stood up and moved to lie within the comforts of his side of the tent.

'Then let us leave it at that,' he said. 'Too much knowledge is dangerous.'

The witch gave a look of confusion. 'You don't wish to know if I have seen you die?'

Kalac rolled away from her, feigning

ignorance. 'If I cannot change it, why does it matter?'

'I suppose.'

'I shall speak to the men in the morn,' said Kalac, 'and try to persuade them to follow me into battle.'

Only the crackling of the coals broke the silence for a while, and then Kalac heard the seer clear away her stones and stifle the brazier before lying on the hard earth. She must have lain for a time thinking of the events she had foreseen, he thought, for eventually she whispered: 'You will not persuade them, my king.'

Bethrin sat cuddled up to her mother in the darkness, listening to the quiet sobs and pleas around her. She was scared now because the grown-ups were scared. A thin trickle of moonlight through a small hole in the thatched roof of the stable gave faint outlines to the terrified faces, and Bethrin closed her eyes, squeezing her mother tightly. As she did so, she felt her mother shiver.

'We can't stay here,' said her mother to the room at large.

'What choice do we have?' said another woman.

Bethrin felt her mother's breathing deepen and her voice sounded harder. 'We always have a choice.' Her hand came up and stroked Bethrin's face. 'I, for one, am not going to sit idly by whilst my daughter is dragged into a life of servitude, or worse....' She covered the girl's ears so the rest was inaudible.

When her mother's hands came away, Bethrin heard another ask: 'What do you suggest?'

'Merkel,' a large woman shifted in the darkness as her mother continued, 'you are the strongest of us. When the guard next opens the door with the slop he calls food, hit him with anything you can find – your fist if you have to – and we shall make a run for it. The woods are only a few hundred paces from the settlement. Surely, we can make it.'

Turesh crouched behind a large rock, his eagle stare scanning the two soldiers standing watch on the gate, waiting for his opening. He prayed for the waning moon to disappear behind the broken clouds, plunging the place into total darkness long enough for him to strike. It was not to be. But a few moments later, he did get his chance, though not in the way he had intended.

One of the soldiers, a tall, lean man, gestured to the other and strolled off towards the rock where Turesh was hiding. At first, he thought he had been spotted, and he shifted deeper into the bushes behind him, but the ignorant guard moved to stand almost on top of him, hitched up his braccae and began to urinate into the bush. Turesh waited until the Talran had relaxed into the welcome relief an emptying bladder brings and then leapt up through the warm yellow stream, striking like a cobra in the grass, his axe splitting the guard's skull. The soldier's bladder continued to empty as Turesh stepped over the corpse and peered, once again, over the rock. He saw the other guard drop momentarily to his knees before pitching over, blood gushing from an open neck wound. The young Sayker stood over him like a man basking in victory. Turesh cursed the idiocy of the youth and ran to the gates, dragging Sayker down behind the nearest hut. The young warrior's nose wrinkled at the hunter's pungent stench, and Turesh returned a dagger glance.

Sayker gave a wry grin and indicated a further guard stalking amongst the huts. He was about to move off in pursuit when Turesh threw an arm out to hold him back. The hard earth would leave few tracks, he knew, but there were other ways a hunter could track his prey. Ordering Sayker to remain where he was, Turesh skulked off into the shadows of the nearby huts, for the clouds were clearing, and the moon was becoming brighter. In its white light, the old hunter could see the numerous black stains of chewing tobacco clustered together as their previous owners had been before them. The guards were obviously growing complacent. Further east and shielded by the mountains, the Talran endured much milder winters than their Neferian counterparts, their skin not so adapted to the freezing conditions.

Prowling deeper into the settlement, Turesh noticed one of the guards crouched behind a hut, tinder burning within his helmet, creating a small fire which he leaned over for warmth. A few of his companions had joined him, concealing the fire's light with their bodies. No doubt to stop a commanding officer from witnessing their stupidity rather than the enemy, Turesh considered. This left only a few men he deemed hazardous to their rescue attempt, and these would need to be eliminated. Moving back to where Sayker impatiently waited, he explained the situation and that he believed the best chance they had was to split up and take the guards down simultaneously to reduce the risk of one discovering the others. With that, the pair separated, and Turesh could not help but wonder whether he had made the right decision leaving Sayker with a task of his own. He knew the youth was no pushover, but whether he could dispatch his enemies quietly and unobserved remained a cause for concern.

The first guard caused Turesh no trouble, standing as he was, his face close to a tent wall out of the chill wind. Turesh could not help but feel empathy from one sentry to another, though his task took precedence. The second proved more alert, marching along his patrol route as his superiors expected. He was a young, lean man and, Turesh considered, probably not been a guard long enough to grow as daring as the others. The ageing hunter crouched in a shadowed recess, watching as the guard disappeared between two huts. The youngster did not chew tobacco, but he did have a heavy left marching step which broke the frozen ground beneath every footfall. This Turesh had deciphered while he waited for the monotonous route to be circled again. When the guard passed, the hunter's meaty hands emerged from the shadows, gripping the Talran and twisting so savagely that the bronze helm spun from the younger man's head. As with the last, the body did not hit the ground. Instead, Turesh dragged it into the shadows and laid it on the earth before pricking his ears for any nearby movements. None were audible, though he could hear the low hum of loud conversations taking place within the wine hut. He moved alongside the dwelling for a better view of the stable across a central clearing that had held dances and celebrations on better days. He watched, heart in his throat, as Sayker emerged from the shadows into the moonlight and approached the large structure. There was no other way, Turesh knew. As the young man gripped the heavy locking bar, the older warrior made to run over just as golden light stretched out from the wine hut. Sayker froze like a rabbit eyeing a fox, and Turesh pulled himself back, listening to the muffled sounds of rowdy men just behind the goatskin wall. The hunter's eyes were wide, his breathing slow and deliberate. He heard somebody stumble outside and retch, then his peers began to moan about the cold. Someone dragged him back in, and the thick tent flap fell back over the doorway. Turesh let out a quiet sigh of relief and turned his attention back to Sayker, who had already wretched off the locking bar. The young warrior swung open the door, and a massive rock caved in his skull. A burly Neferian woman stepped over Sayker's body, horrified by what she had done. But the others either did not notice or did not care; the huge woman was shoved from the doorway in a stampede of frantic women. Turesh watched in horror. Mothers tried desperately to shield their daughters, pulling them close as they ran.

A few women took a tumble, and sharp screams rent the air as one was trampled by the rest. Turesh cursed. A soldier ducked out of the tent next to him straight into the hunter's headbutt. The Talran hit the dirt hard, but Turesh was already running across the settlement.

'This way!' he shouted, trying to lead them to the unguarded gates as angry foreign shouts split the air. More tent flaps opened, and half-dressed men scrambled out with whatever weapons had laid at hand as they awoke. The hunter's axes leapt into his hands. Parrying the nearest Talran shortsword, he booted its wielder back into the others emerging from the same tent. To fight them all on his own was suicide, he knew. He just needed to buy them as much time as he could.

Jeshar's heart caught in his throat as the woman's guttural scream echoed across the settlement and into the nearby wood, where he stood shaded by the trees. He knew Garlock had heard it too, for he stood right beside him, though the leader did not respond. Jeshar rounded on him.

'So this is it, is it? You're just going to stand there and listen to them die, the women and children too?' His teeth clenched, and his finger struck out menacingly. 'This was your idea in the first place! And now everybody is going to suffer because one person said something you didn't like!'

Garlock raised himself to his full height, and his eyes burned red with fire. 'Know your place, warrior!'

Jeshar took a deep breath to calm himself. Garlock was a big man, and Jeshar did not wish to fight him. 'I hope you feel better for it.' He turned away as angry foreign shouts split the air. Jeshar saw now that the others were restless. They liked it no more than he, but none of them wished to face the leader's wrath. Tense moments passed in which he hoped Garlock's lightning rage would subside and he would start to see things clearly. Then a child's innocent scream ripped through the silence, punctuated by a mother's wail of despair. The eyes of the waiting warriors cast their guilt on Garlock, and his emotional armour cracked.

'Okay,' he said at last. 'We'll draw their attention from the women and children.'

'You have a plan?' asked one of the men.

Garlock drew his great notched cleaver from the cow-hide sheath on his back. 'You got a better idea?' He turned to the rest of the men. 'We can't fight them all. Once the women and children are clear, we lose the Talran in the woods. Meet me at the creek to the east when the moon is highest. Understood?'

Garlock's lips curled into a snarl. Bellowing a wordless war cry, he and his men powered through the undergrowth to the battle-marred settlement.

Bethrin ran beside her parent, her mother's body shielding her from the free-for-all shoving of the desperate and the deadly swords of the Talran. Her mother guided her and covered her eyes so she could not see the worst of the atrocities, though she could still hear their screams. Never had she known her mother to run so fast, not even when her father had become stuck in the winter marsh that time. This edifying knowledge brought with it an increased sense of fear. Not for the first time, she wondered whether she would die here.

Suddenly her mother's hand fell away, and she saw how close she was to the gates. They could not have been more than two hundred yards away. She could see the outlines of warriors hounding the disordered Talran lines in a desperate attempt to keep the way clear. The first of the women had already made it out of the settlement, and she smiled, turning to her mother with a renewed sense of hope. Her face fell. Her mother had fallen some way back, and Bethrin scrambled back to be beside her. All thoughts of freedom gone.

'Mother!' Bethrin grabbed at her outstretched hand.

'Please go...' came her breathless beg, and she threw her daughter's hand away with the remainder of her strength. Tears flowed freely from the little girl's eyes. In desperation, she clutched at her hand again, tighter this time.

'Mother!'

Bethrin shook her mother's arm, but she was still, and there came no reply.

A Talran soldier marched into them, knocking the girl to the mud and stomping on the still figure beside her with a heavy leather boot as he passed. Bethrin screamed with empty despair. Another followed and halted short, his eyes transfixing her. He took a step towards her, but so transfixed was he that he stumbled over the corpse in front of him. His hand snaked out, and she booted him away, scrambling back on all fours. At that moment, a giant hulk of a warrior reared up behind the soldier forcing a great notched cleaver through his skull. The Talran corpse fell over her mother's, and the giant turned to tackle another foe. He was beginning to get overwhelmed. Another warrior joined him, and Bethrin recognised the voice of the man who had led them through the settlement as he shouted to his companion. Quickly the giant responded, and the other warrior fell back, lifting Bethrin with a strong arm.

'Come,' he said. 'We're out of time.'

Bethrin was half-carried by the warrior as they ran for the gate. She could see now that the Talran were no longer disorganised and had formed the formidable shield walls they had used to take Yeki. They were nigh on invulnerable in such a formation, and the Neferians were just beginning to realise it.

As the warriors withdrew, Bethrin was jostled about in a fear-induced daze of screams and swords before being carried into the wood, where she hid in the long grass beside the warrior to whom the women and children no doubt owed their lives. He crouched, tense and poised to strike, a bloody axe in either hand. The Talran marched by, and Bethrin's hands began to tremble as her adrenalin passed. She glanced over at the warrior, who remained still for a little while longer. She saw now that a sword had taken him in the face; the savage gash extended down the length of his cheek, and blood dripped to the grass. He was lucky it had not taken his eye, she thought. The warrior caught her looking.

'Let us move.'

He grabbed her by the hand and led her deeper into the wood before cutting across to the east. By the time the moon had reached its zenith, the pair had entered a clearing by a creek and Bethrin was reunited with her aunt. She was both relieved to be alive and devastated that barely a third of the women and children had made it. Tears misted her vision as she thought again of her mother, but she was pulled from such harrowing thoughts by a commotion brewing amongst the warriors.

Their leader, Garlock, had not returned.

Turesh tried to ignore the tingling gash below his right eye; the blood seeping from the wound had begun to dry and encrust his cheek, making it difficult to move those muscles. At least, he hoped that was all it was.

The ageing hunter sat away from the others on a large rock near the border of the wood, scanning the ring of seated women and warriors as they sang the Song of the Dead, their eyes fixed on the children dancing around the fire in the centre. Even without the steady beat of the drums or the elaborate costumes of Krem, Turesh could feel the power radiating from the dancers. All of the souls lost today would be drawn here, he knew, and then released to begin their journey to the stars.

As the old hunter flicked his gaze back to the

woods, he thought again of the perilous journey facing the women and children. In the morning, they were to travel south to Berkhein, where the strength of the vast village would protect them from the onslaught of the Talran raiders. Though Turesh regretted it, he was sending them alone, for he could not spare the men. If he could not shore up Kardek against the waves of foreign invaders, he reasoned, then in the coming days, nowhere would be safe...

Not even Berkhein.

Not even Krem.

His gaze settled on the small girl he had carried through the woods, now joining the other children in raising their hands to the skies as the adults recited the names of those lost. His mood grew grim as his mind snapped back to the moment he had met her.

He had just warned Garlock of his exposed position. The rest of the men were falling back to the gates, but the big man had refused to budge.

'Go!' the burly warrior shouted. 'The men are meeting in the creek to the east!'

Even then, Turesh had known of Garlock's fate, and by the look in the big man's eyes, Garlock had known it too.

Turning away, he saw the girl.

'Come,' he had said. 'We're out of time.'

He hauled her upright and almost carried her under one arm as, around him, the warriors retreated. The more experienced soldiers had organised themselves by now, and he had skirted around the huts to avoid their formidable shield walls.

Suddenly a soldier had emerged from a nearby hut, hastily tying on his scabbard. As he spotted the pair, he drew his sword and lunged at the warrior. Hampered by the girl, Turesh had tried to parry the blow with his free arm. Off balance and twisting unnaturally, the blade raked his cheekbone before he batted it aside. Blood had sprayed across his face, but the ageing hunter recovered quickly, his axe cleaving the soldier's wrist in a savage reply. In searing pain and almost blinded by a crimson mist, he had run on with the child in tow.

He smiled suddenly, recalling Jeshar's remark as he winced upon seeing the wound.

'How close did you come to dying for that child, Turesh? And for why?'

The old hunter had shrugged. 'Perhaps she'll grow up to inherit a stable and offer me a fine horse.'

Jeshar had laughed with genuine humour. 'She is just as likely to grow up and inherit the task of cleaning out the stables. What will she offer you then,' he teased, 'ringworm?'

The night wore on, the hymn died, and the participants hunkered down close to the fire, drawing their blankets tightly around them. Turesh remained on watch. The moon punched through the clouds turning the sleeping tribesmen to white stone. The small girl snuggled into the arms of an old woman and unconsciously kicked out at one of the large stones surrounding the fire.

Turesh shook his head as he recalled the terrible rage which overcame him as he reached the creek, guided by a blazing beacon of light. He riled into the warriors for the ridiculous position of the fire and disappeared into the woods, returning moments later with a handful of large stones. After standing them around the flames to contain the light, he sent warriors into the wood to scout for enemy activity and to retrieve their stashed travel packs. Some of the bags had been discovered and stolen by the Talran. Turesh had been one of the unlucky few – his blanket, water skin, dried meats and fruit all gone. He was grateful, though, for the change in the men. They were less lost since he had temporarily shouldered Garlock's responsibilities.

He sighed and stood from the large rock on which he had been seated all night. Stretching his legs, he moved to lie closer to the dying remnants of the fire, kicking Jeshar as he walked past. The young warrior groaned.

'Get up!' whispered Turesh, 'It's your turn as sentry.' The hunter reached out and snatched the blanket from him. 'I'm borrowing this too.'

The ageing hunter squeezed in amongst the women and children and laid his back on the cold earth, staring up at the mystical stars. The un-winking orbs dominated the clear winter night almost as much as the waning moon, causing Turesh to feel as though the gods were gazing upon him. He wondered what more they had in store for him, but before he could speculate, the mistress of slumber had kissed him.

Turesh's eyes flicked open. The moon had barely moved across the sky, a glowing ember drifted lazily above his head, and someone nearby was talking in their sleep. He should have been calm, but a deep foreboding in the pit of his stomach threatened to unman him. The usual ambient noises of the wood's nocturnal inhabitants were gone, the air still and treacle thick.

Then, off to the far right, a rasping sound, like steel on rock. It stopped, only to resume again a few heartbeats later. Turesh pulled the blanket back and crept towards the shadowed tree line, listening intently. The intermittent sound grew steadily until he could make out a heavy thud in the silence between rasps. Then a giant figure shambled into the creek's clearing, and Turesh's jaw dropped. The gruesome figure which had emerged limped forward on one good leg, and after every troubling step, he dragged his great notched cleaver another foot across the floor. The giant's torso was a network of bloody lacerations, the skin of his face hung crimson from his chin like a rooster's wattle, and his trailing leg was hideously broken.

'You... you should've heard the hymn,' said Turesh as a thousand drummers beat at the heart in his chest.

The figure, which had once been called Garlock, halted and cocked his head towards the hunter before shambling towards him. Turesh, shaken to his core, stepped back and tripped over a sleeping warrior...

And sat bolt upright in the clearing, the blanket falling from him as he did so, his heart pounding in his chest. The moon had barely moved across the sky, a glowing ember drifted lazily above his head, and someone nearby was talking in their sleep, but no disfigured giant stood before him. His eyes scanned the blackened tree line, and his ears strained for anything other than the sounds of the crickets and the occasional owl. Nothing. Besides a strange feeling of déjà vu, everything was as expected.

He stood, unable to shake his fear of the unknown. Was he being haunted? He slipped the axes from his waist, though he doubted their effectiveness, and advanced cautiously on the shadowed thicket.

'Garlock?' he whispered as he crept deeper into the wood. 'Garlock, are you there?' With no reply, Turesh returned to the creek to sit on a stump by the water's edge. He glanced back regularly to where Garlock had entered the clearing in his nightmare. He certainly felt as though he was being haunted. Though part of him still refused to believe it, it had happened twice now in as many weeks. Both times after a bloody battle; before that, he had never experienced them at all. A thought struck him: am I cursed?

7

As the new day dawned, Kalac began to put his plans into motion, walking amongst the tents and awaking the warriors, who shouted and cursed as he passed. Then he stood upon the silt and glanced across to the opposite bank. The Talran tents were few and erected some way short of the Meir, rendering them out of reach of the Neferian slingers. Kalac had once heard the Talran dislocated their drawing shoulders to make room for extra muscle, and as such, their military housed some of the best archers in the known world. Of course, no Neferian would willingly break their sword arm to be better with a bow! He watched as the last of the Talran tents were disassembled, the column moving east. It was a cunning plan, and no doubt the rest had travelled west under the cover of darkness.

Once all the men had scrambled from their tents, eager to give someone a thrashing for such a rude awakening, Kalac briefly told them the Talran emperor's strategy and explained the workings of his own, conscious of their lack of time for him.

From the crowd came a heckle. Kalac did not have to look to know who it was. 'You 'specting us to just believe you after the orders you gave last time? We can see they are 'eading east. Look for yourself!' He pointed to the far bank.

Kalac shook his head. 'It's but a ploy!' he roared. 'Who would be so stupid as to move when the enemy can see you so clearly?'

'I was on sentry before sunrise,' said another, 'and Speech is right, 'I saw their torches stretch east before disappearing into the woods. Perhaps it's merely a double bluff.'

Kalac scanned the men and saw, to a lesser degree, a similar thought on other faces. A thought which suggested they no longer knew who was in command. He tried to explain away their doubt.

'The tragic orders each man among you received a few weeks ago were somehow skewed. Whether the messenger was waylaid by the Talran or the message was misheard somewhere along the chain of command is anyone's guess, but the orders were not mine. I have been working alongside my father's advisors, and I assure you they would not have let me issue them.'

'Your assurances are not enough, Kalac!' said another voice. 'Your skill – or lack thereof – in leadership is hardly a secret. Tribesmen have been complaining to your father for years.'

'Most of us `ave already reached a decision,' said Speech. 'We shall repel these invaders ourselves!'

With that, the warrior strode away, the crowd stretching out behind him as one in six followed in his wake. Kalac felt his anger bubble up beneath his skin, the call to kill the deserters on his lips, but doubt made him bite his tongue. How would he be seen in such an act? As the righteous or the wrongdoer? The sting of betrayal was like a freshly opened wound, and with the events of the last few weeks, his mind had almost reached breaking point. His rage, as always, erupted on those that did not deserve it.

'Those still loyal to the White Fangs pack what little you have! I want to be at this frozen ford by sunset tomorrow! Now go!'

As the men dispersed, Kalac turned to the water's edge, its placidity doing nothing to calm the mayhem in his mind. The decision to trust the witch had been enormous and one which he hoped was right, for if he was wrong, there would be no way back for him.

'What have you done, Kalac?' said a voice over his shoulder, and he turned to see Drenik trudging down the bank towards him. The advisor's nominally calm exterior was straining to hold back the anger within. 'What have you said? And where are they off?'

Kalac did not glance round; he could guess where the old advisor was pointing. 'Deserters. They are no longer White Fang.'

'What?' Drenik made to storm after them.

'Leave them!'

The old advisor shook his head in disbelief. 'Well, somebody has to talk sense into them!' He spun to a passing warrior and bellowed his orders to bring the renegades back. Then he stuck an accusing finger toward Kalac. 'Now you listen to me, boy. Control yourself! Do you forget that the Talran are just across the river, or do you plan to alienate all of your warriors and greet the enemy with open arms?' Drenik took a deep breath and sighed. 'Why, Kalac? Just tell me why you didn't come to me as I asked?'

Sadness touched Kalac then, but he did not wish to discuss it, so he looked away.

'Come,' pressed the advisor, 'I want to know.'

Kalac riled at him. 'Because *I* wanted this victory! I wanted the men to know I could be trusted! I will not live beneath another shadow!' He sighed and looked away, his anger evaporating like mist in the sunlight. 'I already live beneath one.'

Drenik stood silently for a moment, his eyes staring at nothing. Then he said: 'It doesn't matter, Kalac. Do you think Marek ignored the advice of everyone around him so that he alone could be responsible for the achievements of the White Fangs?'

'But his was the voice to which they listened.'

'Your father worked tirelessly for decades to build that respect. Don't expect it to just transfer to you along with his title.' Drenik looked for any sign of the renegades' return, and when none was forthcoming, he slid his arm around Kalac's shoulders. 'Come,' he said, ushering him towards his tent. 'Tell me of this plan of yours.'

Koren was furious. How could Drenik have allowed this to happen?

He had spent the better part of the morning at the healing tent, where the healers had applied a thick layer of soothing lotions to his burns. He had closed his eyes as their soft, caressing hands had rubbed in oils and massaged his tight muscles, and he wondered if this was what the Talran experienced inside their many fabled bath houses. But since then, he had heard nothing but bad news.

Somehow Marek's incompetent son had managed to lose over one hundred men in a single morning! Koren had been stunned with astonishment. Of course, he had enquired about the manner of the disagreement which led to the warriors' departure. Unsurprisingly, it involved the rodent that the men called Speech; his odd voice was a side effect from the day a horse kicked him in the mouth. Spat half his teeth out that morning, mused Koren; it must have been half of his brain cells too! The emperor's troop movement had been ludicrous and far too dim for Reshmal's renowned tactical mind. Koren's anger boiled. He was hoping the Neferians were stupid... and clearly, he was right.

Even so, one hundred men? What was Kalac playing at? Could he not have been more diplomatic, or did he plan to repel the invaders by sheer strength of will? And where had Drenik been during this time? Who exactly was in command?

Koren's mind was in a whirl as he stormed into the Great Advisor's tent. The sight of Kalac seated on the far side of the brazier only served to solidify his resolve. He rounded on Drenik.

'Great Advisor, in the honour and memory of the late, great Marek, I request that you strip this pup of command!'

Drenik was silent for a moment.

'And what makes you think that a mere advisor outranks a king?'

'A mere...?' Koren was knocked almost speechless. 'You are the Great Advisor!'

'An honorary title at best.'

The giant stood stock still, his gaze fixed on the king. He wanted to issue the challenge, but he knew it was a foolish idea. Who would support his claim to the throne? Sure, any one of the warriors outside, but these were hardly tanners, bakers, or stable masters. Without valued members of society, he had no hope of persuading the citizens of Krem. Not to mention other tribesmen would have more support than him. But something had to be done!

Drenik must have caught the glint in his eyes, for he stood and placed one hand on the giant's tense shoulder. 'Let us get one thing clear, Koren.' His voice was even, and his words made all the more threatening because of it. 'Your attempt on Kalac's life yesterday was an undisguised act of treason. Calling for capital punishment, however, against one of the White Fang's most decorated and revered warriors would likely, in the current climate, cause a rebellion. This, Koren, is the only reason you still live.' The advisor extended his hand towards the brazier. 'Now be seated. We were just about to discuss the king's strategy, and any constructive ideas or criticisms you may have will be highly valued.'

With the advisor's warning issued, Koren begrudgingly sat opposite Kalac, the charcoal brazier between them. The giant eyed the malevolent flames, his anxiety somewhat relieved by their metal cage. Drenik joined the pair, and Kalac started to talk at length about Rhek's battle tactics, Drenik's own plans and what the seer had told him regarding the emperor's movements and the frozen ford.

'And the seer told you this last night?' asked the Great Advisor, and Kalac nodded. 'How curious. A sentry informed me of enemy movement last night, and I ran out to see the torches drifting east. I felt there was something strange about it even then. A tightly packed, organised force should have been clear to see in the torchlight. It seemed as though the torchbearers were walking on their own. From what the seer said, they may very well have been.' He glanced across at Koren, who had sat in silence the entire time. 'Would you like to add anything before we travel west to find this ford?'

The question hung in the air. Koren had wanted to jump down Kalac's throat and tear his plan apart, but he had been surprised by the simple yet effective use of the men. The young king had clearly taken heed of Advisor Rhek, and the old man had taught him well.

'Do you trust this seer, Great One?' he asked at last.

Drenik remained impassive. 'The evidence we have suggests she is telling the truth.'

'That's not what I asked.'

'Perhaps,' said Drenik, 'you are directing that question at the wrong person.'

Koren flicked his gaze through the heat haze of the brazier to the young king. 'Is she trustworthy?'

Koren noted Kalac's hesitation before it was coolly masked with a jest: 'As trustworthy as I am.'

But what else did they have to go on? Stretched thin as they were, they could stop no one. Koren tried to picture the ford. It could not be too many spans wide, the soft shifting silt gradually building up over the years. Add to this the fact that it was frozen, the river trickling through channels in the ice, and you had one precarious crossing. He could think of no place better to test his new toy.

Koren stood to leave, but Kalac, misunderstanding, tried to wave him back down.

'I didn't mean to offend you, Koren. I'm sceptical of the witch also, but so far, she has proven her worth.'

Koren sighed. 'You didn't offend me, Kalac. Had you done so, you would have known. I merely wish to retrieve something from my tent.'

With that, the giant left and crossed the hard earth before scooping up a clay ball from his tent and returning to the advisor's. He stopped short of the tent flap as a conversation came to him from within.

'... but can I trust him not to stab me in the back at any break in the battle?' came the voice of Kalac.

'He's an honest man with stalwart integrity. And though not every king would consider them virtues, he will always give you the undisguised truth. You will find him no sycophant.'

'How can you like a man you threatened when he first walked in?'

'He looked as though he was about to do something foolish. I had to act. I don't wish to see either of you harmed, not when there is an enemy across the river into which you can sink your blades. Just give him another chance, Kalac. He may surprise you.'

'That's what worries me.'

The conversation immediately ceased as Koren hauled back the tent flap and stepped into the room. Both men stared at him as he entered, and the giant stood in mock confusion.

'Not interrupting anything, am I?'

'Not at all,' said Drenik with practised ease.

'Good,' said Koren.

He passed the clay ball to Drenik, who examined it before handing it to Kalac.

'Don't hold it near the fire!' shouted Koren, his voice filled with irrational fear.

The outburst had clearly unnerved Kalac, for he moved it further from the brazier before giving it a delicate shake. Liquid contents sloshed about within.

'What is it?' he asked.

'Something I concocted myself.' And the giant gave a mirthless grin.

Fideon had been a bitter man ever since his wife had left him. The wound was still red and raw, the empty void left within him filled with hate. Then the belittling emperor had made it worse. Reshmal had seen fit to leave him with barely half a regiment to guard Kardek Pass. Not only that, but then he had the nerve to give him standard rations like the rest of the soldiers beneath him. *Beneath him* being the key phrase. Fideon deserved a proper man's provisions! He had resolved the situation by shrewdly taking a slice of cured ham and a few dried raisins from each soldier's rations and adding them to his own before distributing the rest among the men. Any comments from those below him were quickly addressed by the false fact that Reshmal had thinned the food stocks to make sure they stretched the length of his occupation campaign. The men seemed to begrudgingly accept this, and all was well until three nights later. Fideon had descended from the watchtower to find those already relieved from duty crowding the only place protected from the buffeting winds, the shack which Reshmal had ordered constructed, he believed, to protect *him* from the wind. To add to the insult, they had even taken up all the positions around the camp's only fire! Fideon had grown angry then. Why should he be relegated away from the fire on such a cold night? Why should he have to squeeze in with the common rabble at all? Surely his noble bloodline deserved something more? He had made a show of their lack of kindling and sent some of the men out gathering, ignoring the odd looks of such a command given the time of day. The rest he had placed back on duty, effectively doubling the number of necessary guards because 'Reshmal had ordered it.' He was getting good at pinning things on his dubious emperor. The very same emperor who, he was sure, had murdered his own father to claim the throne.

Now, the morning after his spiteful decision,

Fideon could see the weariness in the eyes of his men as they sat on the rocky earth or leaned on their ox-hide shields. He began to worry that if Reshmal ever returned to Kardek Pass and saw such a sight, he would relieve Fideon from his position and send him home in disgrace. That was, of course, until the baggage train had snaked its way through the pass and into the wild countryside. He had scorned it from his post atop the watchtower. Seeing the ample food and fresh blankets destined for the men at the front renewed his resentment of his own meagre rations. He was lost in his scornful thoughts when a shout drew his attention to his lead sentry positioned in the woods to the west, where the barbarian king had fallen only weeks earlier. Fideon craned his neck, but he could not spot the sentry. The senior officer leaned over the watchtower rail, his finger pointing to unlucky individuals. He had not bothered to learn any of their names. 'You, you, and you.' He gestured. 'Go and see what's bothering the lead sentry.'

The small group wearily made their way into the surrounding woods, and Fideon was furious at their apparent lack of enthusiasm. He would need to make a show of respect. His words should be treated as though Reshmal's own! He bit his bottom lip, holding in his rage until the scouts returned. Long minutes passed, and his seething fury ebbed away, replaced by hollow sadness as his thoughts were inexorably drawn to his beautiful wife. Perhaps, he chided himself, you should not have bedded her sister.

A rock rolled from the tree line, bouncing across the uneven ground, leaving a trail of crimson behind it. Sunlight caught the rock, and Fideon frowned as it glistened. Then with stark horror, he realised it was a bronze helmeted head!

'Up, you lazy whoresons!' he shouted. 'We can all sleep when we're dead!'

The soldiers, disciplined as they were, fanned out and formed four shield walls of four before the western tree line. A further four hung back, drawing their bows, and Fideon notched an arrow to his bow from the safety of his wooden tower. His men knew he was deadly with such a weapon, and no sooner had the first barbarian emerged from the wood a black shafted arrow had been sheathed in his breast. Fideon had heard of the stupidity of these degenerate barbarians: they would throw themselves blindly onto the shield wall and be swiftly dispatched by Talran organisation and discipline. Another Neferian hesitantly stepped out before vanishing back into the undergrowth. Fideon cursed, his anger rising. He had loosed, thinking the mindless savage would run. Now they had one less arrow in the limited stockpile Reshmal had granted them. He calmed himself and stood stock for another few heartbeats, an arrow notched, his lead eye sighting down the blackened shaft. Nothing moved. Fideon felt the hairs rise on the back of his neck. Was he being played for a fool? He lowered his bow, and a movement caused him to glance to his right. The shack was on fire! The barbarians were flanking them!

'From the north!' he shouted.

Fideon shifted position and loosed into the sudden charge of Neferians, taking one in the neck. Then the warriors were upon the bowmen, and without shields, they were mercilessly slaughtered. More barbarians emerged from the south and west. Soon the Talran soldiers were surrounded, and they tried to fall in, back to back, shields raised, but the strength and speed of their opponents made it almost impossible, and those who managed were too few to make a difference.

Fideon managed to loose only a single deadly shaft during this time before he heard someone climbing the ladder behind him. He whipped his bow out as he turned, but the Neferian ducked beneath it as he scrambled onto the tower deck. Fideon stood on the warrior's right hand before kicking the sword from his grip. The warrior replied with a left hook to the knee, and Fideon buckled under the pain. As he hit the deck, the Neferian jumped on top of him. With his one good leg, Fideon booted him off and used the rail to haul himself onto his feet. The warrior jumped up and stormed towards him. In a quick burst of speed, the Talran leapt back, shoving the warrior through the rail. The crack as the Neferian hit the floor caused even Fideon to wince. Then, as he scanned the tower deck, he cursed. Most of his arrows had slid from his quiver and rolled off the tower when he was squirming around on the deck. He dropped onto his good knee and reached for the nearest black shaft. His eyes widened as he glanced through the decking boards; the tower legs were on fire! Even now, he could see them splitting!

Dropping his bow, Fideon hobbled to the ladders, and the weight shift caused a damaged leg to split. The whole tower leaned over. He slid across the deck and plunged heavily into the rail. It snapped, and he slipped from the side. Time seemed to slow. He thought once again of his wife's sister, who had blackmailed him into bedding her so his wife would not discover his terrible secret of infertility. A tear formed in his eye. He knew now he had made a horrible mistake.

'I love you,' he whispered.

And fell from her graces forever.

Ripping his axes from a severed Talran neck, Turesh straightened and cast his gaze over the area just as a second leg of the watchtower splintered. The entire structure groaned as it crashed through the roof of the blazing shack, then all was still but the fires. He was surprised by how easy leadership had come to him; how easy it was to turn the Talran's own arrogant, misguided superiority against them. Still, only twenty-three warriors remained out of the forty-eight who had set out more than seven days ago, but they were veterans now, each one sharp-eyed and hardened from his experience. He was proud of every one of them and made sure they knew it.

Splitting the group up between Jeshar and himself, they set about hacking down trees and levering boulders into the pass. The day's work was hard, and he knew every man would sleep well.

All but one.

Turesh had been both shocked and upset by the accident. One of the warriors in his team had had his legs crushed under one of the boulders. Pinned and unable to move as the rest of the group strained to get the rock off of him, he had bled profusely and died before the boulder could be shifted. In a fit of rage, Turesh had booted the damn thing then, almost breaking his foot in the process. He had got to know the man well this tough last week. When those around him were dying he had stood for them, fought for them, bled for them, only to die by accident when all that remained to do was block a stupid pass and go home. The gods were obviously ironic.

Later he had ordered a small pyre for cremating those who had fallen during the battle for the pass – their skulls collected for transportation back to Krem. Since every warrior was accounted for, there was no need for lost souls to hear the Hymn of the Dead, which was just as well as Turesh had heard it enough this last week.

Now, the men lay on the hard earth under their blankets, the glowing embers of the hollowed-out shack keeping them warm. Turesh lay under his blanket, taken from a fallen warrior's travel pack, and gazed up at the malevolent stars. Garlock was up there now, leading the other lost warriors in a trail of shooting stars across the night sky. At least, he hoped that was where Garlock was. The nightmare a couple of nights ago still caused him doubt. Why had he done it? Why did Garlock risk his life – nay – forfeit his life for those women and children he hitherto had not met? Blocking Kardek was of vital importance to the continued existence of the Neferian way of life. The significance of such a task had been emphasised by Advisor Rhek himself, and yet the big man had decided to risk it all. He would never know what Garlock had truly been thinking, and, to Turesh's surprise, the thought saddened him.

The man beside him rolled over in his sleep dragging Turesh from his sombre thoughts. Each of the men was sleeping soundly tonight, safe in the knowledge that they were returning home tomorrow.

Home...

The word echoed around the ageing hunter's mind, and one woman filled his every thought. The same scene played through his head like it always had, seeing again how she looked the day he was taken from Greno, his true home. Her gorgeous auburn hair; dark, lustful eyes; and beautiful smile. His heart hung heavy.

'Resha,' he whispered to the night.

8

The pitch darkness brought a sense of confinement. Eight hundred soldiers lay in wait on the bank of the Meir, and among them, Emperor Reshmal of the Talran felt the freezing fog on his face and smiled. Even as a renowned tactician, he had trouble keeping track of his men in the night, but this did not daunt him, for the gods were on his side. They must be, he reasoned, for they have blessed me with a fog that will be Neferia's downfall. In such conditions, the barbarians would cease to see his men until they rode hard from the mists, barbed spears in their hands and ancient battle cries on their spit-flecked lips. Losing their tribal king meant chaos would surely ensue, especially if his informant was correct and poor tactical decisions were being issued by the eldest son. Victory, therefore, was assured, and with the toppling of the largest tribe in the lands, a firm foothold could be ascertained, bringing his dream of conquest ever closer.

Yes, on the blessings of the gods, tonight would be a good night. Feeling for his lump of flint, he struck steel and lit a wooden spill before transferring the flame to a low-burning oil lamp, screened on one side by a dark shade. In its dull light, he trod carefully to the swelled river's edge and cast its light across the ford. A thin film of water rushed across furrows and fractures in the ice and on into the thawed river beyond, making firm footing unlikely. He scanned the frozen surface again. The ford was wide enough for seven men or three horses, but Reshmal did not wish to take any unnecessary risks; regiments five men wide, he decided, or two horses abreast. He quietly called for his senior officer, whose horse snorted in the frosty air as it approached to traverse the frozen ford. The lead officer took up the lamp, and slow, timid steps saw the horse on into the mists. The firelight faded from view and a few anxious moments passed before the call drifted back of his safe crossing. A second lamp was hastily lit to guide the men onto the ice, and then the emperor ordered the vanguard to advance across, out of step, lest their marching shake apart the ice.

Reshmal considered his plan for crippling the barbarian's loosely termed military as the column filed past and disappeared into the fog. Upon crossing, he would need to march east and assault the warriors as they lay wrapped up, revelling in their swift repel of the decoy crossing. The fog would only aid in their stealthy approach.

His train of thought was interrupted as the column halted, and one man slipped, bringing down the man behind as he fell, his face erupting in a crimson spray as it struck the ice.

'Drag those men up!' Reshmal hissed across the ford, 'And keep moving!'

Another man fell, cracking his head on the ice before pitching into the swell. This time Reshmal had caught sight of the flung stone, which had shattered the soldier's shinbone. Only now did he hear the deadened clashes of steel on steel from somewhere within the fog.

'Shields up!' he shouted, hauling his own from his back to a chorus of men following suit. No sooner had he done so, a volley of stones materialised from the fog and pelted shields and cuirasses. Few men were killed, for the hardened Talran regiment had weathered much worse. Another volley thudded against the bronze and ox-hide of Reshmal's shield, the distinct sound of shattering pottery lost to the shouts of panicked men. Reshmal could now see the fighting as it emerged from the mists. His men were being forced back, and as the rows bunched up, many were thrown into the Meir's icy waters. The emperor bellowed for his archers just as a giant of a warrior stepped from the veil, one cleave of his broadsword stretching the entire span of the ford. As the soldiers gave back under his heavy blows, a gap appeared between the opposing armies, and Reshmal saw shooting stars fall around him, one splintered from his shield. Then flames streaked across the ice, engulfing many writhing bodies within them. The emperor's shield caught, and in a heartbeat, a wall of fire was strapped to his forearm. Shaking the thing from his arm, he saw in front of him only flames; everyone trapped on the other side was lost. A stone whizzed through it, knocking Reshmal's helmet from his head as he turned to bellow the order for a retreat back to the bank. His archers had already lined themselves along it, and instinctively the soldiers stood behind, ready to step in when the skirmish came to an end. Reshmal knew, however, that the fires would blaze for a few hours yet; he had smelt the liquid splashed onto his arm from the impact with his shield – animal oil. He knew the White Fangs would use every moment he wasted preparing for another attack. The eldest son had not been as foolhardy as he had predicted, and with the freezing fog, he could not tell how many warriors were waiting for him on the opposite bank. Nor would he be able to unless the mists cleared in the morning. He cursed. Even half as many men as his would seriously jeopardise the invasion, for he could ill afford to wait for reinforcements.

He glanced into the darkness over his shoulder. A scout had informed him earlier of another tribe raising defences against him further west. He had dismissed the man, branding his information useless, for he had no plans other than to cross the river. Now though, it seemed like the better option. *The gods must hate me! How could they have led me to such false hopes? Am I not a devoted follower?* As despair threatened to overwhelm him another devious thought entered his cunning mind, and he smiled without mirth. *The gods must work in mysterious ways*, he thought, *for, on the brink of defeat, they have bestowed upon me the wits to turn the tide.* He offered them a prayer of thanks and promised them a show of his worth.

Soon the White Fangs would have nothing left to fight for, and then, hardy or not, the barbarians would crumble.

Koren stood a way back, outside the circle of men surrounding the raging pyre. His fear of the flame was only partly to blame for the shame he now felt. He clasped his hands behind his back, trying to appear respectful to the fallen but desperately struggling to forget the events in the final moments of the battle for the ford. His thoughts were grim, and without the vigour and vitality of children dancing around the flames, the Hymn of the Dead was a solemn sound and did nothing to raise his spirits. The warriors chanted the customary mantras, slow and deliberate, as their thoughts turned to those who were lost. Koren could name every one of the fifteen fallen men, but his thoughts were of Advisor Drenik. No one knew he was harbouring a mortal wound until he collapsed after the battle, blood flowing freely from his side. Kalac had cradled him in his arms long after the old advisor's last breath. A solitary tear trickled to the new king's chin, and, aware the men were watching, he resigned himself to his tent.

Koren sighed, feeling... what? Sorrow? Guilt? Had he misjudged Kalac? He could not say for sure, but everything he thought he knew about the young man was now hazy. Drenik had little input into the battle plans in the end, yet victory had been no less secure. Kalac had proven himself resourceful and his seer somewhat trustworthy, but the men knew little of this, and so the next battle would be crucial; if he could prove himself without Drenik, the men would begin to believe in him.

As the pyre died down, Koren remembered the last words of Kalac before he retired to his tent: 'The skull of the Great One is to be placed inside a padded canvas bag for safe transport back to Krem, for a man as wise as he should always have a place in the heart of the tribe.'

And Koren set about making sure those words were heeded.

Three hundred yards away and oblivious to Koren's actions, Kalac sat alone in the confines of his side of the tent. His scouts had returned word of the Talran emperor's decision to move further west into Eagle Talon territory, which had brought the briefest of smiles to his face, but on the inside, he was dying. For years he had witnessed Death snatch at men in battle, but never had it been those closest to him. Tears came again. Perhaps now you know, sneered his disloyal mind, how the loved ones felt of those you condemned to reckless tactics.

'I didn't want this war!' he said aloud. But of course, it changed nothing.

To distract himself from such thoughts, he pictured those one hundred warriors, apparently led by Speech, who had abandoned him three days ago now. He had heard no word from them despite Drenik's best efforts at diplomacy. Kalac wondered how they had faired with the decoy regiments. He would need to send a scout east to check on them and those positioned at the eastern border. Only now did he realise that he had had no messages from Neklic or Rhek since he had left almost two weeks ago…

A little way upriver and away from the men, Iskel sat on the cold earth, picking at the frosted white grass with her dirty fingernails, contemplating her choices.

You knew! She chided herself. You told no one, and you damn well knew! This timid leadership need not have arisen if only you had opened your mouth! You had ample opportunity! Ample! When Kalac came to your hut and asked, there should have been no hesitation! Would it not have been better to blabber and be dunked and drowned and found not to be a traitorous witch than to inadvertently be one? All you can think about is yourself!

Iskel sighed heavily; she had surprised herself at just how low she could go. How much longer could she hold this secret? How much more damage could she do? She wanted it to all be over. Well, she thought, clenching the grass into a tight fist, now it can be. She stood and made her way downriver, ignoring the hungry glances from a group of men returning from an unsuccessful hunt, and stepping through the goatskin flap into the tent she shared with Kalac. He was seated but not alone, and while she waited for his conversation to conclude with a warrior donned in long furred riding garments, she wondered if she was about to make a terrible mistake…

'Now leave us,' concluded Kalac to the warrior seated before him, motioning his hand towards the tent flap. He turned his red-rimmed eyes to Iskel. 'What do you have for me?'

The witch woman swallowed hard. 'The traitor, lord.' Kalac's stare became as unbreakable as a hawk's gaze on a fleeing hare. A harsh silence grew between them, whispering of the coming chaos. Iskel's head hung low. 'In a vision, I saw him before either of us met. Despite your suspicions, it was not I who sent your father to his death, nor I who twisted your words so that men would hate you, and who even now plots your downfall. Though in keeping this secret, I may have caused you more harm than both.'

Kalac stood methodically, his gaze unwavering, all of his other troubles forgotten. 'Enough with your riddles, woman! If you know something, say it! Who killed my father? Who seeks to ruin the White Fangs?'

'Neklic!'

The word burst from her lips as a magician conjures an ugly toad. Kalac's blood boiled, and the savage, unshackled wrath in his eyes was enough to make Iskel turn on her heel, but the king grabbed her skinny wrist and dragged her back before him.

'You'd better not be telling me lies, witch! If I were to wrongfully act against one of the most respected men within the tribe, I would make sure it ended worse for you!'

'Think, Kalac!' she said, and like a cornered animal, she struggled to break free of his callous grip. 'Who else could have duped your father and sent him to the gods? Which other's word is above suspicion and treated as though Marek's own? How much influence does a slave need to possess to topple his master?'

'No!' Kalac tugged on Iskel's wrist to hold her still. 'Neklic's visions were impaired! He had no power before the end!'

'Neklic has no visions! He never had! Not in the entire three years he sat beside your father! If a seer collapsed after every vision, we'd spend most of our lives unconscious! Neklic fainted only so the king couldn't ask him questions to which he didn't have answers! He knew of the enemy's positions only when Reshmal told him! They were merely well-timed lies! And we've had a lull in tribal disputes since the Talran loomed, so he was never truly tested on anything else! It was a deceitful game which lured the master to his demise!'

Kalac's head spun as it unravelled the past. That ugly, hobbling fiend! That devious-handed bastard who had held the respect of his father and the envy of Kalac! When Marek had looked upon the man with more esteem than he did his own son, how could that man have asked for his head? To say Neklic was capable required no stretch of the mind, but something was still amiss.

'Why tell me now?'

The witch woman looked at him sidelong. 'When else would I have told you? When you were hungry for death in my hut? Ha! Any words of blame on another would have only enhanced my own guilt! Not that you were there to listen anyway; you had already made up your mind! No. Much better to say this now after a glorious battle where trust in me was paramount. Had I wanted to ruin you, could I not have done so countless times already?'

Kalac's grip tightened as the soothsayer

pulled away. 'No! It's more than that. Speak! You said you had caused me more harm than Neklic.'

'No, I didn't!' The unconvincing words were quickly spoken, and if the eyes were windows to the soul, then Kalac's was now burning in a rage hotter than Hell, with a gaze that suggested there was no longer a place for mockery and deception.

Iskel cracked. 'If I had told you sooner,' she said, 'this could have all been avoided.'

Kalac sighed and released his hold on her, allowing his misguided paranoia to ebb away. 'A war would have come either way.'

Iskel shook her head. 'No. I mean the burning of the palace! And the fall of Krem! I have seen it!'

Kalac's jaw dropped. 'What? How? We have beaten them back! And I have been gone little more than two weeks; no city that size could fall in such a short time.'

'Not from without, my king, but from within it has changed hands. Neklic has set the night on fire; he has killed your advisor and blames the burning palace upon you. You – who he claims has betrayed them all and has tried to kill him.'

'What about my guards?'

'They are yours no longer. They are loyal to Neklic now. His lies and deceit have been great.'

'And my brother?'

'He is dead. I am sorry.'

Kalac hefted his halberd and moved to the tent flap, purpose in every stride.

'No!' he said. 'What you see is the future. He can still be saved!'

Iskel followed, calling behind him. 'We're a four-day ride from the city. I'm sorry, Kalac, but this future cannot be changed.'

The realisation hit Kalac like two tonnes of bronze; he keeled over, such was his pain. To be back in Krem at this instant, his raging soul would have destroyed armies, toppled mountains, and swallowed seas. Yet his mortal body could do none of these things. Struggling up, he waved Iskel away bitterly. 'Then what use to me are you?'

And with that, he was gone.

Signalling his men to crouch within the bushes with a swift shake of his hand, Turesh stared hard into the still trees ahead. Keep following the bank of the Meir, the scout had said the day before, and it will take you perhaps two days to reach camp. His men had wanted nothing more than to return to their families in Krem now that their task was accomplished, and Turesh had difficulty persuading them otherwise. Every warrior would be needed to repel the Talran invasion, he reasoned, and therefore they would only be going home when someone much higher than himself deemed it time to do so. Hastily he had followed the scout's directions lest, given the time to think, the men began to change their minds. Quickly, but nothing so reckless as to put his men in danger, unlike those rushing through the woods now. Though Turesh saw nothing, the sound of broad leaves slapping on many running legs was as audible as the birdsong.

A quiet few moments passed as the runners approached the position of Turesh's poised group, and the beautiful face of the ageing hunter's soulmate filled his mind. He hoped that Resha would still love him after all these years, even if he was now much older and battle-scarred.

Then a wiry man burst through the undergrowth and ran straight into Turesh's outstretched arm, which pitched him from his feet, rendering him unconscious. When the man awoke, a score of warriors stared down at him.

'I am White Fang!' he shouted, raising his arms for protection. 'Neferian!'

A warrior pushed past Turesh and into the circle of glaring faces, recognising the voice.

'Speech?'

'Yes!' he said, desperate to make a friend.

Having lost some good men with nothing to show for it other than a couple of dozen rescued refugees and a blocked pass, Truesh's mood was low. He had little patience for pleasantries, and a side-glance told him his men had also spotted the danger lurking in the trees.

'Call out the rest of your men,' he said.

'Erm... s`okay, lads!' said the desperate man. 'They're on our side.'

At first, no one moved, but slowly, beaten and bruised faces came forward into the clearing. No more than twenty in all.

'Is this your whole group?' asked Turesh. 'Why so few? And which advisor is leading you?'

'No advisor... sir,' he added uncertainly. 'T'was Kalac.'

Turesh's eyes scanned the tree line. 'The king himself? Well, where is he?'

'Further west.' Speech seemed to mumble something, then he spoke quickly, '`e knows not what `e's doing. The lads an' me moved east an' repelled the crossin' of the Talran. Kalac ordered us west, but none o' us wished to follow a mad man into `ell.'

Desertion was punishable by death, but Turesh's face remained impassive. None knew his true feelings. He did not wish to chastise those who would act on an impulse that he, himself, felt and would pursue when the time was right.

'Turesh,' someone said.

Then the old hunter realised the man before him was shifting uncertainly from foot to foot under his stare.

'So you all deserted him?' he asked evenly, his eyes flicking to every downcast face.

'We were more,' said Speech. 'After the repel, we moved further east, suspectin' they may try to cross elsewhere. Well, we were right, but too late. A cavalry force set upon us as we kipped for the night. Many were dead afore they could wake an' in the mornin' fog our slings an' swords were useless. They attacked an' disappeared into the dark. We made for the trees but were scouted out on foot this mornin'.'

'They are still in the woods?' Turesh gazed beyond the men, and a few of his own loosened their weapons.

'We were runnin' for a while… We may 'ave lost 'em.'

'I see,' muttered Turesh, running through a mock fight with the Talran in his mind. Then he flicked his gaze back to the man some called Speech. 'Perhaps you would like to know I stopped a scout just yesterday heading east. He informed me that Kalac King had had a great victory in the west, and the Talran vanguard had been forced to stray onto Eagle Talon soil. It seems you were wrong to mistrust him.'

There came no reply, but questions about their future hung in the air like a winter night's fog and Turesh, once again, drifted into thought. The sensible option was to draft every able man into his group and press on downriver in search of the cavalry unit. The problem, however, was that his own group were now veterans and had proven their worth on more than one occasion. Deserters would not be welcome among them.

'Well? Be gone,' he said at last. 'The White Fangs have little use for men who can't follow orders. And to return is death.'

One of his own broke the silence beside him. 'Is it right to let them go without justice?'

Turesh whirled upon him. 'That is my order! Any man who disobeys can add his name to their list!'

The deserters skulked away, aware now only shame lay before them. Turesh took his men and advanced into the wood, cautiously studying the sandaled tracks of the Talran regiment as they doubled back to their mounts before heading south into White Fang territory. To pursue them any further without horses of their own was impractical as they would never catch the cavalry and would be left only to stumble over the corpses in their wake, unable to help them. Instead, Turesh and his men continued downriver to receive new orders from Kalac himself.

By late afternoon the following day, with his men rejoining old friends by the riverside, Turesh had located the king's tent, only to find it vacant. As he wandered across the White Fang camp in search of Kalac, he sighted the grizzled veteran, Koren, knelt by the water's edge. The ageing hunter knew of Koren's almost obsessive worship of Meira, the goddess of water, the Bringer of Life. All men had heard of the fabled giant warrior with an irrational fear of fire, and though many drunken jests were made of him around campfires, none were made by those who knew him.

'Ho, Koren!'

The giant turned his gaze towards the hunter. The yellow-orange rays of the setting sun cast a radiant glow across his crouched but nether-the-less enormous frame; his broad shoulders; his barrel chest; and his scarred, muscular arms. For a moment, Turesh could have believed he was staring at one of the many legendary demigods spawned by the water goddess herself over countless aeons. Then the big man spoke and the spell shattered.

'Ho, Turesh! Good to see you well.'

Turesh was surprised and humbled that Koren had remembered his name, for they had met only once before and briefly at that.

'Building your collection, I see.' The giant beamed as he gestured to the red scar extending down the hunter's cheek. 'Long way to go before you catch up with me, though.'

Turesh smiled and watched as Koren returned his attention to the placid waters, scooping up a handful of wet silt before plastering the cold gloop over his left forearm. Turesh caught sight of the half-healed burn on his other arm before that, too, was covered. With his task done, the giant turned back to Turesh.

'Did you want help with something?'

'Have you seen Kalac King?' asked the hunter. 'I have urgent news.'

Koren extended a burly finger towards a hill on the far side of the camp. Turesh could just make out a small figure seated upon its top. 'He sits up there alone and has done for days,' said the giant. 'Only the seer goes up to offer him food. He will not say what is on his mind, but the men worry about his leadership as it is; this can't go on much longer. I hope your news is good.'

'Indeed it is, Koren. Kardek has been

blocked. Reshmal will be receiving no reinforcements anytime soon.'

The giant grinned. 'That gladdens my soul to hear. And I hope it will be enough to shake Kalac from his untimely depression.'

Thanking Koren, Turesh set off through the camp and found Kalac high on the hillock, idly watching the sunset. He approached without caution, a smile and a jest on his lips, remembering the easy-going conversation when last they met before the gates of Krem. Kalac did not seem to notice him at first, lost in his own world of thought. He looked worse for wear: tired, exhausted, his face a ghastly white, his eyes red-rimmed, his shoulders slumped like the world was upon them. Then suddenly, and without warning, he struck like a viper in the long grass. Turesh caught a straight right full in the face, and he fell. Rolling from a vicious boot, he leapt to his feet and circled cautiously.

'My lord, are you well?'

The question only seemed to fuel Kalac's rage. A right hook was his reply. Turesh misjudged the block, taking the blow with his forearm. He intercepted a left jab but missed the stomach-churning uppercut, which doubled him over. Kalac's knee swept up, and Turesh's palms smashed against it. Feigning the blow, Turesh hit the floor.

'My lord?'

Kalac's rage was great, but his weariness was overpowering him. Reaching to his waist, he pulled forth a soggy envelope and threw it at him. Turesh recognised the writing instantly.

'Lord, those are love letters.'

'From a lone rider galloping through a thicket?'

Turesh pushed his hands beneath him. 'I can explain!'

'Oh!' said Kalac. 'My brother is dead, and you can explain!' He lunged like a black panther, boot digging into the earth as Turesh dragged himself clear. Then Turesh countered with a shoulder charge before Kalac could recover his balance. Both men tumbled to the ground, tussling with each other for a short time. Eventually, Turesh saw his chance and kicked Kalac in the chest. A weak, weary kick, but it gave him enough space to clamber to his feet.

'I am no traitor.' His voice came more forcefully now.

Kalac was still seated, his energy all but spent. 'Why the secrecy then?'

Turesh sighed. He had hoped this would come to light under better circumstances. 'I wanted to run away.'

'Ha! The White Fangs too man enough for

you?'

Turesh shook his head, not rising to the challenge. Truth be told, he did not think he could win. Kalac had been bone weary and grey before the fight, yet the king still managed to beat him black and blue. Turesh would best him, if not with fists, then with words. 'Some of my best memories are in the White Fang capital. I have made enough friends to last a lifetime, but home is where my heart is.'

Kalac dragged himself to his feet. 'So, you would desert me too?'

Turesh felt his anger rise. 'I am not like those cowards!' He pointed in the direction he had seen Speech and the other deserters. 'I would never abandon my people, *my friends*, in a time of war!'

Now it was Kalac's turn to look sheepish. 'So you saw them then.'

'Aye,' he said. 'What was left of them. A cavalry regiment must have crossed further upriver. Eighty strong if the tracks are anything to go by.'

Kalac nodded but said nothing, his eyes suggesting his mind was elsewhere.

As the silence lengthened, Turesh found himself wondering why the men had lost faith in their king. Was he really as bad as the rumours back in Krem would have men believe?

Then Kalac said: 'I'll do you a deal, Turesh. You fight for the White Fangs, and I'll see you get back to your tribe when all this is over.'

Turesh nodded. 'I would have it no other way, my king. Now, what's all this talk about the young prince?'

9

Neklic stared down into the old advisor's shaving bowl; the still waters had quickly taken on the crimson of his hands. Strange, he mused. Somehow he imagined this day to be more upsetting, but he had felt no remorse for Rhek. The wretched years spent with that old fool could not have come to an end sooner! Leaning down, he dried his hands on the serving maid's torn dress. He had no idea Rhek had ordered a bath, so when the maid unexpectedly arrived, he had been forced to strangle the wench. Taking a great gulp of breath, Neklic composed himself and stepped into the corridor, closing the door behind him. Only a child now stood in the way of his plans. How simple it had been, he thought, to lie his way into power and watch as Marek's thirst for knowledge got the better of his judgement. Even the hateful Kalac had believed in his lies! Remembering the task at hand, he stalked down the stone stairs and moved silently through the corridor until he was met with Lekta's chamber door. Without announcing himself, he eased the door open and sidled in. A low candle flickered in the recess of a wall and then threatened to go out as a figure darted across the room. Neklic was startled by the speed of the young child, who now lay wrapped inside a vast expanse of rugs, a regretful look on his face.

'Sorry, Neklic. It won't happen again. I promise!' said the child. 'I just wanted to finish my picture. I'll go to sleep now though.'

Neklic did not force the smile which followed. His burnt and puss-filled face commonly attracted looks of disgust from the adults and terror from the children, but not Lekta. He was of the age where anyone was his friend, provided they helped him with his drawings. And Neklic had frequently done so. Taking the candle holder from the wall, Neklic lifted the tatty parchment from the floor and moved to sit on the outer reaches of the rugs.

'Let's see what you have drawn this time then.' He heard the child scramble from the rugs and smiled.

'What do you think, Neklic? What do you think?' Lekta bounded with excitement before sitting down next to him, the eyes of youthful hope clear to see.

'Well,' he began, twisting the image this way and that, 'it's a remarkable drawing of-'

'A horse?' said the child, to whom suspense felt like a lifetime.

'Yes!' said Neklic, with a smile. 'That's exactly what I was about to say! A horse.'

Lekta beamed, and Neklic saw within those eyes the dying dream of having children of his own. A dream lost on the eve of the brazier incident, for no woman could love such a hideous disfigurement.

Lowering the candle to the flagstones, he picked up a black charcoal stub and began to alter the image slightly. 'And if we add a shabby mane and a longer tail, it will look like a White Fang grey.'

'And a saddle for the rider!' said Lekta in the full swing of enthusiasm.

'But of course.'

With a keen eye, Neklic set about sketching a stirrup and harness for the side-on creature. All the while, the child smiled beside him as the picture became more and more horse-like.

'Do you think Kalac will want to see it?'

Neklic's blood froze in his veins, the name of his enemy bringing an unwelcome realisation. Lekta could never be his child. Not when his elder brother was Neklic's sworn enemy. What would happen when he discovered the lies that would be wrought this very night? Could an inquisitive boy be hidden from the truth forever? The smile fell from his face and the last remnants of his dream sundered against the rocks of reality.

'It is time you were asleep, Lekta.'

The child cocked his head at the sudden change in Neklic, but then, there were so many things Lekta did not yet know about adults, and he tottered obediently off to bed. Neklic followed and knelt beside Lekta, who was cocooning himself in the warmth of the rugs. Taking the child's feathered pillow, he fluffed it up, staring long into the recesses of the goatskin casing. A tear flowed freely down his blistered cheek before he pressed the soft pillow firmly onto the child's face. After the flailing had ceased, he smothered the candle flame and left the room.

Hours later, Neklic stood in a recess of the main hall on the ground floor. He coughed as acrid black smoke filled the great room. The upper floors: the study, his own rooms, the princes' and advisors' chambers, all were blazing well. Neklic had seen to that. Tapestries, books, furniture, everything that could be used as fuel went up in smoke; even the bodies which would allow him an unshakable alibi. The smoke was causing his eyes to water, and he tore at his dark fur robe, which saddened him, for it had been a good robe, but the fires of change were already ablaze, and he needed to look the part. A shocked cry reached his ears from outside, and he knew it would not be long before men dared the blaze to save their leaders.

Heaving open a single grand door, he took a great breath of fresh air and ran as fast as an ageing body would allow. Servants and slaves were already fleeing the building in maddened haste, but none knew of how the fire had begun. Neklic had strangled any servant who had seen him in his hours of preparation – *casualties of the fire* as they would later be known.

The crowd outside, lit in the wavering orange light of the blaze, was growing, and although shock and fear reflected on Neklic's face, deep down, there was a smile, for a performer loved an audience. As his exaggerated break for freedom wore on, however, a pang of doubt entered his mind, but the expected question was finally voiced to him by a nervous man at the front of the crowd. 'Where is the king, seer?'

'He has tried to kill me!' he said, choking on smoke and the effort of his run.

'Who, Kalac?'

Neklic nodded sadly. 'He left unannounced a couple of weeks ago. I was unsure why. I tried to stop him.' He choked, though secretly, he paused for dramatic emphasis.

'And?'

The soothsayer cleared his throat. 'The advisor he left with me came into my dormitory and tried to kill me, having already killed the young prince. As he was about to strike the final blow, he said Kalac had no more use for me. No more use for anyone. The pause in his actions gave me a chance. I fought him off and made a break for it, but he's still inside.'

A concerned warrior nodded to a small group that circled the building to cut off the murderer's escape.

'Why would he commit such a crime?' someone else said. 'And to kill his own brother?'

The soothsayer coughed to clear the smoke from his lungs. 'I don't know. Perhaps he felt we couldn't win. Maybe our lack of faith in him has bore within hateful seeds. One thing is clear: he is no longer White Fang.'

A witless warrior turned to another with the white gleam of fear in his eyes. 'Who leads the tribe?'

Neklic licked his lips. 'Sort that out amongst yourselves later,' he said. 'We have two enemies outside our walls now and no idea how many men Kalac has managed to defect with him, perhaps even unknowingly. Both must be defeated so the tribe can live on.'

The soothsayer watched his lies sink in. The warriors approached the revelation with indifference, shrugging it off as they formed a chain from the nearby Meir to the burning palace and began systematically passing water filled pots and jugs up the line. To them, it was merely another lost leader and a poor one at that, but for the women, it was harder to accept. Mothers, daughters, and wives all had men out there defending the tribe and no way of knowing if they had been deceived by Kalac. The seer smiled inside. He was in the clear as long as people directed their hatred towards that one man.

The dupe had been easier than Neklic had imagined. It seemed there was no love lost between a troubled populous seeking someone to blame and their ill-gotten king, who had never truly been able to break free from his father's shadow.

Kalac sat in the gloom of his newly erected tent, clasping his shaking hands together, his body was wrought with exhaustion, but he could not sleep. Feeling the cold, wet tears begin anew, he shut his eyes tight and wiped them away. Lekta had been far closer to him than his father had ever been. Young Lekta, little brother, even the gods must have loved you, he thought, for they have taken you already...

Outside, the night wind howled, and the nearly horizontal rain slashed against the hide walls. Tears of the gods? He doubted it, but tonight was not a good night to be out, and he wondered how the camp guards were coping, soaked to the bone in their leathers, their fur cloaks providing little protection in such torrential conditions. Perhaps, he thought, twice the changeovers were necessary tonight to keep a fresh and uncomplacent mind on the job.

Kalac sighed as he recalled the events from earlier that day. After his tussle with Turesh on the hilltop, he sat and described to him in detail what the seer had shared of Krem's fate. He had hoped to relieve himself from some of his grief... and his guilt. For it was their own king who had destroyed the White Fangs and singlehandedly brought Drenik's fears to fruition. He had not voiced his feelings of incompetence to the older warrior, presuming they were clear for all to see. Yet when Turesh began talking about his own leadership experiences, Kalac felt even more inadequate. He began to envy the ageing hunter, to whom leadership seemed to come effortlessly. Then came the news the pass had been blocked. A sign from the gods that the tribe was not yet defeated.

Perhaps they could still be saved….

The tent flap folded, and water dripped from its wet surface and splattered onto the rugs inside, announcing the arrival of Koren, who kicked off his muddy boots as he entered.

Kalac glanced up at him; his usual snide comments were lacklustre. 'Come to try your luck again, have you? You'll find my life is not worth taking at the minute.'

Only the seer had been close to Kalac since he heard of the terrible happenings in Krem and as the giant gazed upon the hunched, distraught figure of his king, a moment of pity reflected in his eyes.

Kalac's voice came strained and horse. 'Why are you here, Koren?'

The giant pointed to the simmering brazier. 'I saw you were still up and thought I had better relay to you the concerns of the quartermaster.'

Kalac sighed. 'Can this not wait till morning?'

'We have barely enough food for the morning, my lord.'

'What?'

'As you well know, we have received no food supplies from the city within the last week, and we cannot expect hundreds of warriors to hunt and feed themselves every day; besides, we would clear out every wood within a five-mile radius. The quartermaster needs to know when to expect Krem's wagons.'

Kalac looked away, shamefaced. 'There will not be any. We'll need supplies from the nearby settlements.'

Confusion spread across Koren's face. 'What on earth do you mean, my king?'

'You and the rest of the men will find out in the morning. Just send riders to lease wagons and take whatever the nearby settlements have to offer.'

The veteran warrior knew better than to let his curiosity get the better of him. 'Yes, my lord.'

The giant fell silent but did not move, and Kalac glanced up at him. 'Was there anything else?'

'Kalac, whatever has gone on, you need your rest. This isn't doing you any favours. The men need you strong.'

Kalac's voice came cold. 'Thank you, Koren. Your advice is duly noted.'

'Yes, lord.' The giant tugged his boots back on and prepared himself for the onslaught of the weather. Kalac called out to him before he left.

'Double the changeovers tonight. I want a

fresh pair of eyes on guard every few hours.'

Koren gave a sharp nod, and then he was gone.

Kalac slumped sideways until he was lying curled up on the rugs, his mind travelling back to the deathbed of his stepmother, Lynaea. She had been the only mother he had ever known, for his own had died in childbirth. Lynaea had caught a terrible illness and had been bedbound for one month before she passed away, her usually beautiful face becoming gaunt and grey. On the final night, Kalac knew she was dying and had crouched beside her.

'Mother, don't die….' He had said. 'I need you... Father needs you.'

She reached out with a bony arm and took his hand. 'Be strong, my young prince. Your baby brother will need you when I am gone.'

He had been close to tears then. 'I'm afraid. Please stay with me... Please.'

'Kalac,' her voice came as a whisper. 'You must let me go. No one lives forever, and when you are strong and wise and king of all of the White Fangs, I will be naught but a faded memory.'

'Not to me,' he said, pulling her close. 'I'll never forget.'

Kalac looked down into her glassy eyes.

'Promise me something,' she said.

'Anything.'

'Look after your brother. Protect my son.'

Kalac King buried his face in the rugs, and before more sadness could take hold, he succumbed to exhaustion and slept.

Koren stepped out into the rain. He had gone to Kalac hoping for some reconciliation; he had received none, and his mood was grim. What kind of mess was unfolding now? *There will not be any. We'll need supplies from the nearby settlements.* Koren shook his head. How did Kalac expect to win a war without supply lines from the capital? He had lost the one significant advantage the White Fangs had over the enemy. How had this happened?

After relaying the grim news and the king's temporary solution to the quartermaster, he helped pick the riders and issue the orders before returning to his tent, soaked to the bone.

He halted short of the tent flap. At first, it appeared as though one of the flaps had been blown open by the howling gale, but the peg which held the flap shut was still firmly embedded in the earth. For the knotted tassel to have come undone by sheer force of wind seemed unlikely, which meant someone had untied it and left it billowing in the wind, someone who wanted their presence known to Koren before he entered the darkness of his tent.

The giant approached cautiously and peered inside.

A voice said: 'You're getting wet, Koren.' The sound was distinctly feminine, and Koren recognised it immediately.

The grizzled giant grunted, his face hardening as he stepped in, drawing the point of his curved hunting knife from the earth beside the flap.

'Why are you here?'

The seer looked nonchalantly at the blade in his hand. 'You don't need to fear me, Koren. I'm not here to wish you ill omen.'

'Don't presume to know anything about me. State your business and be gone.'

Forced laughter pealed from the seer's throat. 'Who, pray tell, is presuming what of whom?' She leaned forward so that even in the ill light, Koren could see the parallel scars across her lips. 'These,' she said, indicating them, 'were given to me by someone I trusted long ago, who believed the same as you: That no single being should possess the mighty power of a seer. Such power breeds concern and distrust.' She leaned back. 'Do you trust Kalac?'

'I thought I did,' said Koren, who sat where he stood and placed the blade on his lap, 'but if we are talking truths tonight, seer, then I'm not sure who I trust.'

'Good. Then without any prejudgements, let me tell you of Neklic.'

Koren raised a suspicious eyebrow. 'Marek's seer?'

The witch woman nodded. 'The very same.'

And so, Iskel explained all that had happened in Krem: Neklic's lies and deceit, the fall of Kalac's rule, and the death of the young prince. 'Now Neklic has refused us aid.' she concluded.

'And what of the warriors' families?' asked Koren. 'They've agreed to this?'

Iskel shook her head. 'He hasn't told them.'

A sudden thought came to the giant. 'How do you know so much about Neklic? An outcast like you wouldn't have been allowed inside the palace. How did you get in?'

'I didn't need to. I began to suspect him months ago when I overheard some servants out on an errand discussing his bizarre ritual behaviour. Of course, I was curious. So I delved into his future and saw the liar that he was.'

'And you told no one.'

The seer's stare dropped to the floor. 'I couldn't. Nobody would believe' – her gaze flicked up – '*an outcast like me.*'

The giant sat in silence for a moment. If this was all true, then Kalac no longer ruled the White Fangs, and leadership was in disarray.

The words of Kalac came back to him: *You and the rest of the men will find out in the morning.* So the king planned to tell them. In his mind's eye, Koren saw the disgruntled chaos of the rebellion against the former King of the White Fangs and the inevitable tussle for leadership which would follow. He shivered. Who would lead them? Who *could* lead them? Turesh? He certainly had the beginnings of a leader, but he was far too inexperienced and did not yet hold the respect of the warriors. Only those who were with him at Kardek would likely support him. Akron? Experienced without question but arrogant and foul. Would the warriors truly fight for such a man? Himself? No. The giant had always preferred to lead as an exemplar warrior leaving the true responsibility for decisions on someone else's head, much like Kalac had done before his father's untimely death.

No. Kalac had produced a victory while at the same time battling the hostility of his men. A show of true fortitude. After Drenik's death, the one real choice of leader was the man currently at the helm. Of course, that was assuming all of this was true. The meandering fog of his thoughts cleared as the seer spoke.

'I'm sure you realise the importance of tomorrow. The men respect you, and therefore your voice holds a lot of weight. Use it wisely.'

Koren snorted. 'So you would have the warriors turn on Neklic who would be, had circumstances been slightly different, standing beside Kalac now in your stead?'

The witch woman's eyes grew cold. 'This isn't some petty rivalry! Neklic is far from here! Look at the facts, Koren! The future of the tribe may hang in the balance!' She took a deep breath and exhaled slowly. 'I'm sorry, but you must understand the importance of the part you play. I shall leave you to your thoughts.'

The seer rose and moved smoothly towards the open flap.

'I suppose,' said Koren, 'you already know if I will believe you come tomorrow?'

'Of course, but you must convince yourself to take that path.' Iskel paused before the storm consumed her and glanced back. 'Tonight, you have found reason for your distrust in seers. I pray you do not brand us all with such malice.'

Koren stood and moved to the tent flap to watch her go. What was she really about?

'A peculiar sight for sure,' came a voice strangled by the wind, and the giant saw Turesh striding towards him, eyeing the soothsayer. 'Made all the more strange since when last I saw Kalac in Krem, he was calling for her guts. Can she be trusted?'

Koren shrugged. 'I'm not sure, but she has proven herself on at least one occasion.'

'What's in it for her, I wonder?'

'That question, my friend, has scarcely been out of my mind.'

Kalac awoke to a commotion in the camp. His words to the giant the night before had obviously made the rounds. The wagons leased from the nearby settlements had arrived loaded with salted meats, which, until last night, had intended to be traded to the city, confirming to the warriors the trouble back home. All this Kalac realised as he emerged from the tent to the cold morning sun and an air edged with nervous tension.

The fear was too much for one such warrior, and he rounded on Kalac with cold hate in his eyes. An accusing finger jutted out from his clenched fist.

'What has happened in Krem? Why are they not supplying us? If your stupidity has caused harm to my family, you will wish you were never born!'

His friends and fellow warriors held him back, trying to calm him. Such an outburst was inexcusable, but Kalac's heart was filled only with sorrow and regret.

'Your families are fine,' said Kalac, though

bile rose in his throat at the thought of his own, 'but a traitor has risen among them. The soothsayer, Neklic, now has temporary control of the city and refuses us aid. He has sullied our names and declared us outcasts from the tribe along with anyone he believes knows the truth.'

The crowd stood for a moment in disbelief, then one of them said: 'So you expect us to believe Neklic is in league with the Talran?'

'He is.' said a voice from the front of the throng, and all eyes gazed upon Iskel as she moved to stand beside her king. 'At least, he was. Now he is a force unto his own. Though Emperor Reshmal has offered him much to leave the city open to the Talran, Neklic seeks a bigger prize, one which would leave him to rule over all of the White Fangs.'

'Impossible!' said one of the warriors. 'With what support?'

'Neklic's deceit has led him to rule in Krem,' said Iskel. 'Is he not already king in all but name?'

A stout, bald man pushed himself forward to stand before the masses, an open look of defiance on his face. 'Enough!' His finger struck out at Kalac. 'If this is true, then you, Kalac, have been deposed! You're no longer King of the White Fangs, and its warriors no longer serve you!' He turned his back on his king and addressed the crowd, hands raised in an open gesture. 'So who is to lead the White Fangs?'

Kalac's stomach twisted in his loathing for the conniving Akron, who had long ago held his respect. The warriors had fallen silent, each to their own thoughts, and Kalac hoped they had enough wit to see through whatever Akron no doubt had planned.

Then a voice rolled like thunder through the crowd.

'The man standing behind you, Akron.'

The bald man recognised the voice, for he faulted, his tone becoming strained. 'Come now, Koren. Think about what you're saying....'

'I have been thinking.'

Akron's jaw dropped. 'This is the man who embodies everything you hate about leadership! A man with very little tactical prowess; a man who so very recently ordered men to wade across the Meir to their deaths!'

During the debate, Kalac had ignored the words and focused solely on the curious eye contact between the giant and the old hunter, Turesh, who had managed to free himself from the throng. The hunter said, 'Have you heard nothing of recent events, Akron? Or only as much as you wanted to hear?'

The stout man before Kalac suddenly

seemed to shrink as he turned to face his new adversary. An uneasy demeanour settled upon him; this clearly was not part of his master plan.

'Come then,' said the old hunter with a dagger gaze, 'which *stout leader* would you have at the head of the White Fangs?'

Even from behind, Kalac could tell Akron's tongue was slithering around his mouth. Whatever was about to be ejected from the lizard's lips would be nothing short of a compromise.

'I would choose Kalac.'

The former King of the White Fangs was dumbfounded only for a second. If Akron needed to bide his time, he would need someone leading who he could oust when the time was right, someone who did not hold the warriors' total confidence.

He needed Kalac.

Akron walked away without a backward glance, and Turesh stepped before the men, his voice bellowing out, lifted by the breeze. 'Deceit has befallen the capital, but we know better! Kalac may not be king in Krem, but he is still king of its warriors!'

Kalac cast his gaze across the men; each held an undisguised look of uncertainty – their futures were far from clear.

Koren leaned into Kalac's ear. 'Addressing

the men like that was reckless, especially given our current situation. Warriors at war without a leader are like children thrust into the world without a parent. Lie, Kalac. It might just save your skin.'

Someone else called out from the crowd. 'What now then, warrior king? We return home?'

The question was inevitable, and he knew the men, thinking only of their loved ones, would not like the answer. Kalac flicked his gaze towards Koren, who solemnly shook his head.

Kalac stepped forward, his voice radiating a firmness he did not feel. 'To return is to die. Neklic will never open the gates to us. Sandwiched between our own walls and the Talran, we'll struggle to last a night. We need to press forwards and destroy the foreign invaders, to fight on as only a Neferian knows how!' He took a deep, consolidating breath. Rage, as ever, never too far from the surface. 'I stand before you now as an exile in my own kingdom, the only living son of Marek, with nothing to my name besides a weapon and a burning hunger to right those who have wronged me – wronged us all! And even if I'm to lose, they will know they have fought a White Fang before I die!'

He stood for the briefest of moments,

seeking to quell the anguish escaping from within. Then, as the tears began anew, Kalac stormed away.

Koren felt a nudge on his elbow and looked down at the stocky warrior beside him.

'What do you make of him?' said the shorter warrior. 'A man with nothing has naught to fight for, right?'

The giant nodded grimly. 'True, but a man who has *lost* everything is very dangerous indeed, my friend. Be as cautious as you would a pack of rabid wolves.'

Iskel had returned to the gloom of her tent. Kalac's position was precarious, and for a moment, as he stood before the warriors, opening his heart to them, she saw that he was vulnerable. Iskel's heart had almost broke; in that instant, he looked as he did all those years ago as a boy, protected by his mother. She remembered the soft touch of his lips on hers.

She shook her head, banishing the thoughts from her mind. The past would not help here; the future could.

The witch-woman swiftly lit a candle before scattering her various stones and crystals about her. She closed her eyes, and her mind floated through time and space, pulled by the child-like hand of Kayla, her spirit guide, towards the event for which she searched. The streams of time widened and split into events made possible only by the decisions of men. Then, like many boulders amidst a broad river, the flow of time rejoined again into circumstances which would always occur no matter what man did. It was here where her guide stopped, floating above the events below, which played out like the dreams of a mime, noiseless and distant. For distinguishing sounds from the stream had felt like an impossible task to her child-self, and she was too impatient to learn now. Unconcerned by this fleeting thought, Iskel watched as flames engulfed a village and men in the bright plumes of the Eagle Talon were driven to extinction by the might of the Talran war machine. Women fled with their children through the frozen fields only to be chased down by horsemen. Then a mighty figure astride a grey charged into them with the spear tip of his halberd.

The spirit guide pulled her further along the streams of time until they pooled once again. Judging by the distance they had travelled, Iskel guessed it was a few days after the previous event and what she saw almost froze her heart. The Talran were crossing the Meir without resistance.

Iskel glanced at the spirit. Though the seer had aged, her childhood friend had not.

'I have seen enough, Kayla.'

The spirit tugged on her hand and flew back to the tiny light of the flickering flame. Iskel's eyes revolved in their sockets, and the candle snuffed out, but the darkness had already been lost, for the tent flap was open, and someone stood in the opening, silhouetted by the sun. Iskel relit the candle, and as the figure moved closer to its light, she saw his red-ringed eyes and wondered how long he had been standing there, afraid to enter.

'What ails you, my king?'

Kalac sat cross-legged opposite the candle flame. 'Much ails me, Iskel.'

The seer was silent for a moment. She could not recall a time before when Kalac had used her name. The young warrior's eyes never wavered from the flame; his silence indicated the turmoil in his mind.

Iskel broke it. 'What worries you the most, my lord?'

'Betrayal.' Iskel sat patiently, and eventually, Kalac continued, his eyes fixed on the flame. 'I don't think I could manage another. I find it difficult to trust anyone, and yet I cannot do this alone. Tell me, Iskel, what is it you fear?'

The seer shuddered. 'Death.'

'Ah.' Kalac risked a glance at her. 'Then that is where we differ.'

Iskel's eyes widened. 'You do not fear death?'

Kalac's focus returned to the fire, and he spoke as though reciting from an ancient script. '*No one lives forever.*'

Suddenly the tent flap folded, and shafts of blinding light announced the arrival of two figures. The giant was undoubtedly Koren, and as the tent flap fell back into place, she saw the other was Turesh.

'You summoned us, Kalac King,' said the hunter.

Kalac gestured for them to sit beside Iskel as he, himself, stood.

'My father had a score of advisors around him at any one time; old men who knew how to win the old wars. Well, I need experienced warriors, ones who have faced our new enemy, ones with tactics which will work now, and, perhaps most importantly, ones who the men trust. I saw what you did for me today, and I thank you. I wish you both to be my advisors.'

'It would be an honour, my king,' said Turesh without hesitation, and all eyes turned to the reserved giant, who gave a respectful nod.

Kalac turned his attention to the soothsayer before taking a deep breath as what he was about to say went against everything he had ever known. 'I also want a seer. Do not let me down.'

Iskel smiled. 'Ever your guide.'

'So,' said Koren, 'what do we know?'

Kalac sat before them. 'A scout informs me that the Eagle Talon are taking heavy casualties. They run headlong to individual glory and are mercilessly swept aside by the interlocked shields and swords of the Talran. Our enemy is unlike anything we have ever seen before; they sweep through this land caring not for heroism but victory at any cost. Even my father, the great Marek, misjudged them. We cannot make that same mistake.'

He glanced over at Iskel, and she feigned to clear her throat. Her mind raced to decide how much she should trust the other two. As little as possible, she concluded. 'Reshmal's forces will ford further down river at an artificial wash area constructed of stone.'

Koren raised a surprised eyebrow. 'Will?'

'Yes.'

'So what hope do we have?' asked Kalac.

'I can only see what is certain to happen,' said Iskel. 'Reshmal will cross the Meir into White Fang territory. What we do about it is yet undecided. That's why we are here. Make no mistake though! The river of time flows through many events, and regardless of which come to pass, they all end with Reshmal crossing that river.'

'And we're to believe everything you say?' said Turesh.

'She has proven her worth to me,' said Kalac.

'And if I was your father,' said Koren, 'I would say: So had Neklic.'

Iskel's stomach tightened. 'Don't seek to compare me to him!'

'Enough!' said Kalac. 'What would you have me do, Koren?'

'Follow their path of destruction along the river and be there when they try to ford.' The giant waved his hand dismissively. 'Even if we cannot stop them, we'll make Reshmal pay for each step in blood.'

The tent fell silent, all eyes trained on Kalac as he contemplated his choices. Finally, he nodded. 'We can do naught from here. We will draw up better plans once we see this ford. Thank you all for your counsel.'

The three men left the tent, leaving Iskel again to her thoughts. Kalac clearly did not recognise her. And why should he? she thought. They had both been so young, and much had happened since then. She smiled suddenly. Kalac had defended her in that last conversation, an indication he was beginning to overcome his irrational fear of seers. A fear he had held since he was a child, for Iskel knew the source. She instinctively felt the hideous scars gouged across her lips – a parting gift from Lynaea.

10

Nostel, King of the Eagle Talon, tried hard to ignore the repressive silence of his capital. Most of the men were away at war, and the remaining women skulked about lost and alone, their thoughts only on the safe return of their loved ones. Nostel buried the grim thoughts in his mind and stared hard at the chequered board. Five of his sixteen ivory pieces had already been removed, and the remaining eleven were in precarious positions. Only three of the ebony pieces had fallen. The western world called it chess, and since no one seemed to know the rules, it was up to Nostel to make them up, usually when he was losing. He was about to create one now when he heard the familiar drumming of horse hooves on the half-frozen earth.

Nostel looked over his shoulder to see a distant figure, donned in battle leathers, his arm heavily bandaged and resting uselessly in his lap, galloping through the myriad of stone huts which formed the barely beating heart of the tribe's capital. As the figure rode closer, Nostel saw the long, unkempt hair beneath the man's feathered plume and the jutting chin which described Felas, one of his greatest warriors and oldest friends. The king stood from the board and swallowed hard; for Felas to report directly from the battle himself meant grave news indeed.

The chestnut gelding's hooves churned up the ground as it halted before the king, its ragged breaths like wisps of mist in the cold air.

'My king, it is lost,' said the solemn voice of the veteran warrior. 'The Talran march as though we do nothing but throw ourselves onto their swords. I have never seen the like. It's no surprise the other settlements have fallen.'

Nostel's outward appearance remained calm in front of the warrior and the advisor, who still sat at the chess board but had been listening intently, for his mouth was agape. Inwardly though, Nostel was panicking.

'How many of you remain?'

'Only two hundred and eighty-three, my lord. Many carrying wounds.'

Nostel's jaw finally dropped. He had sent almost eight hundred warriors, never before had he conjured such a fighting force, but his seer had advised throwing everything he had at them. Now he understood why.

'Have we made no dent at all?'

Felas shook his head. 'They lost, perhaps, a hundred and fifty men at most.'

Nostel fell silent for a moment. His men had outnumbered the enemy by almost two hundred, which meant Reshmal still had a fighting force of around five hundred men. He did a quick calculation of what he had left to muster. It was not enough.

'I have forty men here, maybe sixty horses, and three hundred women,' Nostel's voice suddenly hardened with pride, 'but Neferia is a harsh mother and breeds no weak.' He glanced at his advisor. 'Concentrate! Get up! Give weapons to any who are able. Send the children and the pregnant women south to the village by the Meir. It's the only haven left.' And not for long, said a treacherous thought. He turned back to the broad warrior. 'How long do we have, my friend?'

Felas shrugged. 'I can't be certain how Reshmal thinks, but if he's to keep his men fresh, we might have until sunset.'

'Then there's still time to prepare. Go and get that arm seen too.'

'I have. It's broken under the shoulder; the healers can do nothing.'

Nostel cast his gaze to the dreary sky and sighed. 'This is our last stand, old friend. Only the Gods can save us now.'

Lightning flashed in the sky as Felas staggered through the empty paddock, a gushing wound to his temple forcing his left eye closed. Even from the far outer reaches of the capital, he could still hear the moans of the dying. The cries of the women hurt him most; they were no longer battle cries but death throes.

Disorientated and half blind, Felas lurched from wall to wall, gripping his useless arm with his one good hand. Only his mission kept him going. Then he tripped on something in the dark and fell head-first into a bale of hay. He could not feel his broken arm now; everything was wet and numb with cold. His body told him to rest, his eyelids drooping, his mind wandering back to the moment of the Talran attack.

Reshmal had ordered his archers to light arrows tied with oiled cloths before shooting them into the straw roofs of the huts. Within a dozen heartbeats, everywhere seemed to be in flames forcing Nostel to move his warriors out from the protection of the huts and into the barren farming fields. His old friend had understood the dangers of this move even before Felas did and had commanded his sixty horsemen to skirt around the town into flanking position. Reshmal's archers were excellent marksmen out in the fields, even hidden from the Talon's slingers behind a wall of shields. Nostel acted swiftly. Hammering on his drum, he instigated the charge. War cries ripped from hundreds of lips as they charged across the field and onto the enemy shields.

Rains lashed down, and lightning forked the sky as it all fell apart. Nostel watched as his horsemen galloped into the unprotected bowmen. The archers dropped their bows and hauled up spikes half sunk into the ground. The horses smashed against them and writhed in pain, halting the charge immediately. Felas had never before seen such a tactic, and dread began in the pit of his stomach. The warriors were fairing little better. He watched as a thickset woman slammed her club against a soldier's shield. The man gave ground, and the shield wall buckled only for an instant as the soldier beside him dispatched the woman.

Now, observing the battle from a distance, Felas could see the problem. The warriors' weapons needed room to swing, which meant every one of them stood more than an arm's length apart. Reshmal's fighting formation was so close that each Neferian effectively fought one against two.

Felas leaned over to Nostel then so he could hear him over the torrential rain. 'Order a retreat! We have lost!'

Nostel did not respond. He was facing the other way. In his eyes were the flames of his beloved village crumbling into ruin.

'Nostel!' shouted Felas as he grabbed the percussion mallet. Only then did he follow his old friend's gaze. He dropped the mallet. Behind them was a wall of horsemen, lances levelled, cantering towards them.

Retreat was impossible.

Nostel grabbed Felas' good shoulder. 'The day is done. Sneak back through the village, my friend. Spread the word to the other tribes. Let them not make the mistakes we did.'

The king turned round and drew his favourite long knife.

'Where are you going?' asked Felas, grabbing his king's arm.

'I wasn't good enough to lead them, Felas. It's only right that I share their fate.' Nostel shook his arm loose and burst into a charge, and with him went the pride of the tribe.

Quickly Felas tore off his headdress and ducked back into the burning village. The Talran horsemen burst into a gallop and sealed the fate of the Talon.

Felas kept on running. The bandages

holding his broken arm tightly against his chest were beginning to unravel, but he dare not slow, for he knew he would be followed. The thick smoke made it hard to breathe and even harder to navigate. A few times, he slipped in the mud. Eventually, he stumbled upon the granary, and he stopped. All around him, the huts still stood untouched. Then he remembered the farmers' barns were untouched too. The answer was obvious to Felas.

The food!

In the winter, food was scarce, but an army needed it in abundance. Felas stumbled back the way he had come looking for something to light the granary, but in the pouring rain, it was hard to see. He approached a blazing hut with a caved roof and grabbed a bunch of straw already alight at one end. He turned back to the granary and a spear sliced open his temple. He threw the burning straw as he fell, and the horse before him reared. The rider was thrown clear, the horse bolting. Felas righted himself with his one good hand. He drew a dagger from his belt and leapt at the stricken soldier like a rabid dog. Adrenalin lending him strength, he hacked at his disorientated foe until he was sure the soldier was dead.

Felas dropped the crimson knife and stood slowly, his legs unsteady. The world seemed to be spinning. Blood flowed freely over his eye, forcing it closed. Carefully, he stooped to pick up the straw and staggered back to the granary. The side of his face felt as though it was melting off. His mind conjured an image of the sliced flesh hanging loose to his chin, but he did not check for fear that it was. Tossing the burning straw onto the granary thatch, Felas stumbled on. The paddock was not far, and a horse meant freedom...

Felas took a huge gulp of breath as though emerging from a pool. He was on the paddock floor. The room was completely dark, save for the orange glow from the village, and the rain had stopped. He had no idea how long he had been there. A sudden and searing pain enveloped his arm, and he cried out. Using his good arm, he lifted himself off his broken one and slumped against the wall. His head throbbed, but his vision was clearing, though he still could not open his left eye.

In the darkness to his right, a horse snorted. Felas had thought himself alone, and the knowledge of a companion made him laugh aloud.

The Gods had favoured him.

Koren sat with his mighty frame against the bough of a tree, listening to the soft sounds of the Meir flowing by. Guard duty had always bored him, and bored men were left to their own thoughts. Koren's were ones of embarrassment and shame. Since the torment of his childhood, he had been afraid of fire. 'Fire burns,' his friends had said. 'It's only natural to be wary.' But Koren was not just wary of it. He remembered the night Kalac halted the advance of the Talran on the frozen ford, and shame rekindled inside him. He had been a savage on the ice; men had fallen to his greatsword or been thrown aside by his strength. His fellow warriors had stood transfixed, watching him accomplish what a lesser man could not. He was a demon made flesh. An unstoppable juggernaut.

Then the slingers ignited the animal fat.

The plan, in part, was his own creation; yet, as his fellow warriors rushed forward to seal the fate of those not caught in the flames, Koren had leapt back. Fear overcoming all sense of reason. He had slammed into the warriors behind, his massive weight forcing them to move aside as he slipped back through the lines. They had said nothing, but Koren knew what they thought from the sheer astonishment in their eyes.

Koren was a fool, and behind his back, they laughed and jeered. He was the elephant afraid of the mouse.

The giant pushed himself to his feet and

walked to the river's edge. Dipping his fingers below the surface, he let the ice-cold water spray over his hand. Airc, the malevolent fire god, had but one weakness. Despite all of his destructive power, he could not stand against Meira, the goddess of water, the Bringer of Life. Koren had clung to that fact all his life. Of all the gods he worshipped, it was Meira to which he devoted himself. She who soothed his soul; she who healed his burns, but she could not heal the guilt he felt inside. He remembered standing away from the pyre in the funeral following the battle in which the Great Advisor had fallen, knowing that, had he continued his onslaught, many of them would have still been here.

Shame and fear had played a significant part in Koren's life. He had been running from the flames since childhood when he stumbled upon a dark secret which threatened the world. A secret he swore he would take to his grave.

Five days had passed since Kalac employed his new advisors, and they had agreed to move the men west downriver. Finally, they set up camp where the Meir widened and seeped slowly through a mound of large rocks: a man-made dam. A shallow, serene wash area had been created beyond before the river narrowed and dipped into a small valley speeding back into White Fang territory. Kalac eyed the surrounding lands carefully from his camp atop a large knoll. No one had strolled down to break the ice formed over the river in the days since their arrival, and Kalac had guessed why. In the middle distance, on the opposite side of the Meir and beyond the rye fields, he could see a small silent settlement nestled between two hills. Beyond this, as the ground rose before Mt. Kryan, charnel smoke billowed from several destroyed settlements, which announced Reshmal's movements. It seemed the silent settlement was all that was left of the Eagle Talon, and fear had halted all activity.

Their grim fate may yet affect us all, he thought. Hearing a momentary drop in the hubbub and the sounds of a troop of horses, he turned to watch his eastern scout, led by the small group he had left behind to direct him, dismount and tether his horse before crossing the camp. The warriors had made their own entertainment by wrestling and gambling on the outcomes, and items traded hands as fast as they would in the wine huts of Krem. A few of the men pointed the scout in Kalac's direction, and he watched as the scout threaded his way through the jeering maelstrom. Kalac knew that some of his men would not even own a weapon come the next battle.

'It's good to see you, my lord,' said the young scout, and Kalac was glad to see the exhausted, dark-eyed expression of a man who took as few stops as possible.

'What news?'

'The east has suffered a few battles, my king, but the Talran are contained. In the south, most of the men have yet to see the enemy.'

'How many warriors cover the southern border?'

'Nearly four hundred, lord.'

'Then rest today and start the ride back tomorrow with word for three hundred to come to me.'

The scout gave a sharp nod. 'Yes, my king. Err… my lord?'

'What is it?' The man's eyes were staring beyond him, and Kalac saw the charnel smoke reflected in his sad eyes.

'Will we ever stop them, lord? The Talran, I mean.'

Kalac smiled, but it was hollow. 'Of course. Why would I be waiting for Reshmal to try his luck with us again if I thought we could not halt him?'

The scout looked away. 'Because history has a habit of remembering final stands: brave warriors who fight to the last against a stronger foe. The White Fang way, right, my lord?'

Kalac's mood darkened. 'What's your name, warrior?'

The scout straightened. 'Flek, lord.'

'Well, Flek, I suggest keeping your opinions to yourself. Now be gone.'

Kalac turned back to his observations, but his mind was distracted by the scout's words. Rubbish! He concluded. Any country on any continent would defend itself in the same way.

When the world remembers your name, I will be but a faded memory. Had he subconsciously travelled out here so swiftly to make his mother right? He thought once more of Iskel's warning. *Reshmal will cross the Meir.* Sorrow touched Kalac then as he thought of the futility of his actions. Maybe the gods did not intend for the White Fangs to prosper. Images of his family flashed before his mind's eye. Maybe they never had.

But if gods willed it, then what could be done about it? So to draw himself from such solemn thoughts, Kalac ordered a wagon load of mead from a nearby vassal tribe. It took two days to arrive and was the most pungent thing he had ever tasted, nothing like the sweet stuff back in Krem, but after half a dozen tankards, he no longer cared. The men enjoyed the welcome release too, and the mood in camp rose to an almost celebratory level. Mild conversation and laughter rang out, and then someone stretched a goatskin across an empty wine barrel and began to play. The sound of the drum was embraced all across the camp, and moments later, other makeshift instruments joined the ensemble. As the music took up its own beat, it grabbed the drunken warriors, rejuvenated their dreary souls and taught them how to dance.

With the ensemble in full swing, the party lasted long after Kalac had retired to his tent. And though the noise from outside was great, the joyous sounds lifted his spirits, and he slept soundly for the first night in days. No dreams, no thoughts, just an endless peaceful black…

The once semi-great palace of Krem had been gutted; piles of undisturbed ash sat on the ruined floors, and singed tapestries draped down the soot-blackened walls. At first, Neklic feared the worst, but the warriors had acted swiftly that night. Some of the rooms had been saved: the throne room, its solid oak doors managing to hold the flames at bay, some of the lower dungeons, and the king's chambers which had apparently survived only out of sheer luck, though Neklic knew otherwise. What family would share their home with such a bedraggled, ugly, old man?

And so, with nowhere else to go, Neklic moved what little had survived of his false-trade possessions into the chambers of the King of the White Fangs.

Now he heaved open one of the blackened double doors to the palace hall, which had also survived due, in part to the impenetrable thickness of its doors but also because Neklic had not found anything inside worth setting fire to. He stepped in and closed the door behind him to suppress the thudding racket of the slaves' miserable restoration methods. The rest of the congress hushed as he entered, unnerving the old man. Ten men stood around a weathered old stone table, raided by warriors with an eye for decorative items long ago when the palace was young. Neklic noted the gleam of ambition in each pair of eyes and smiled inwardly. He stood at the head of the table, for in all their rush to steal the table, they had neglected to steal the chairs.

'As you all know, as acting leader of the White Fangs, I cannot make decisions for the tribe without support from my would-be successors. Hence why you're all here. I propose to increase the city's defence against the Talran and any potential return of the traitor, Kalac.'

'Kalac has no support here in the city!' said a young man from the table's far side. 'He had little support to begin with. Once the warriors with him begin to see through his lies, they'll surely turn against him. The warriors will be handing us his head for absolution.'

'The warriors have loved ones here,' said an older man, a tanner by trade. 'They wouldn't see their families hurt. For them to attack the city would be absurd.'

Neklic eyed the men before him. Their hatred for Kalac seemed to surpass his own, and he knew how ambition clouded the mind. His face remained impassive. 'Kalac has a talent for excuses. Who is to say he has not already convinced his men that we are the traitors? Perhaps he could persuade them to merely dispatch this congress; cut off the traitorous head of the snake, so to speak. Desperate men do desperate things, and, make no mistake, they will all be desperate.'

Neklic fell into silence and listened to the congress argue about how best to deal with Kalac. Tempers became frayed, and then, inevitably, insults and blame followed. Neklic smiled inwardly. None of them raised the question of why he would attack them, assuming instead that their hatred for the former prince was mutually reciprocated. The old hobble began to eye each man in turn. Disgracing them would not be an effort.

'Enough!' said a voice to his right, and the

meaty fist of Tumlek, master fisherman, hammered the table. 'Perhaps you need reminding of Reshmal's army beyond our gates. What if they arrive first? What if Kalac has already faced them and failed?' He turned his gaze towards the false seer. 'What is it you plan, Neklic?'

The soothsayer, whose half-burnt face was already difficult to decipher, took on an impassive expression. 'With such a dwindled force, we could not stand against the Talran. Word must be sent to the other settlements, and migration to the capital must begin. This will reduce unnecessary deaths and bolster Krem's defences when the time comes to crush Reshmal and sweep his bones from our lands.'

Tumlek nodded. 'I agree. First, we defend the tribe.' He cast a harsh gaze over the rest of the men. 'Squabbling can come later.'

A couple of the older men caught Tumlek's gaze and nodded in agreement. This was all the support Neklic required. Swiftly the seer bid them farewell and left the room, returning to the king's chambers on the floors above. Tumlek had shone like a beacon before the rest of the rabble, and it had unnerved the soothsayer. The others he could humiliate and belittle, but Tumlek needed to be removed altogether.

With the other leaders set for ruin, was it not only a moral right but also a civil duty for the current caretaker to continue ruling? Who could deny it?

Neklic smirked, but before he got carried away, he scrawled a brief note detailing a meeting place and the untimely demise of an old fisherman. The letter was swiftly dispatched via a slave girl to his formidable ally in the wild city outskirts, home to the deprived, the diseased, and, on this occasion, the deadly...

Lake Ryker, a large body of water south of Krem, named after the fabled giant who had once thrown a boulder from the mountains to form it. The boulder had shattered on impact and was carried away by the river Talich, eventually to the sea. Tumlek contemplated this as he waited at the shoreline. The lake's surface was strangely circular, so it was unsurprising that such a myth had formed. The fisherman had initially heard it when his father bought him here for the first time, which was more than thirty years ago.

As the light began to drain from the sky, Tumlek waded into the water and hauled at a fishnet, his hands numb with the chill of the lake and his back feeling all of its forty-six years. The winter had been kind to him this year, far milder than the previous ones. Last year he had needed an axe to hack a hole in the ice large enough for his nets, and even then, the fish had dispersed at the noise, and he had come home with a measly haul. He had brought the pick axe with him every day this year too, just in case, but it seemed his winter fortune was finally changing. The net breached the water's surface, and he nodded his approval at the fish flailing tightly within, a healthy final catch for the day. Transferring them to his large wicker baskets, he waded out into the icy waters and hauled at his second net.

As he did so, his mind wandered to the untimely deaths of Marek and Girak, the latter the man who had challenged Kalac the night he had announced his succession. To fight over leadership whilst the Fangs were at war was beyond stupidity. In fact, it was unacceptable. Tumlek had been in the crowd and had called for the leatherworker to sit down. Marek's entourage of advisors, including his seer, were still around to ensure everything ran smoothly, but some people blindly hated Kalac. Girak was no exception; his son had been killed under the former prince's command. Anger had been what had spurred them on, and Tumlek had taken his youngest sons away at the first sign of a fight.

He had no idea who the winner was until later when the event was described to him by his wife, though he had little doubt that Kalac would triumph. He was a man turned legend through battle.

And now, even he had taken an untimely departure from the throne. That left the fisherman in a prime position when the war ended, and candidates could garner support for a challenge once again. Though handy with an axe, it was his knowledge of food sources which would ultimately benefit his people. Having seen the rabble he was up against, he was confident the White Fangs were his.

A noise caused him to look over his shoulder, his hands tight around the net so it would not slip back into the waters. A slim man was moping about in the shadows, examining the wicker baskets and their contents.

'I should be a fisherman,' said the man nonchalantly.

'Then get your own spot. This one's mine!' said Tumlek defensively. He turned his attention to hauling in his net. He did not wish to be caught in his wet clothes long after dark when the temperature dropped.

'You misunderstand me,' said the man. 'I've never wished to fish....'

A sharp pain stabbed at Tumlek's back.

Thinking his back had gone, he let out only a subtle groan lest the younger man laugh at him, but the pain grew, and suddenly the net began to slip through his hands back into the Meir, despite his best efforts.

'… but I will be needing your clothes.'

Tumlek no longer felt cold or pain. He no longer felt anything. He tried to move, but his legs would not respond. Exhaustion ebbed and flowed across him, and his eyelids grew as heavy as the biggest catch that day. He heard the slim man wade into the water beside him and saw the forced smile on his foreign features.

'No hard feelings though, eh?'

Tumlek closed his eyes and fell into eternity.

Neklic moved between the shadows of the huts like the hideous creature he was. The night was still, the air cold. As he entered the wine hut, men turned to see who had brought the chill wind in with them, then immediately looked away. The warmth of the brazier came as a stark contrast to the winter air, and he shivered as he glanced around. At the edge of the hut, shadowed by a large group of merry men, sat a lone stranger, apparently a fisherman, but his body was far too lean for such a task.

Without pouring himself a drink, Neklic

moved across the hut and sat cross-legged before him. The man was dressed in ragged furs of brown, turned green over time with algae, and roughly concealed beneath were his hard waterproof leathers. A low fur hat cast deep shadows across his harsh foreign face, mostly hidden from the light.

'Where is he?' asked the stranger. 'Be swift, so I can get out of these wet clothes and be gone.'

The accent was surprisingly akin to Neferia's own, and Neklic curiously gazed into the gloom under the hat. Instantly, he wished he had not. Eyes like frosted stars glinted back. The eyes of a hunter. A hunter of men.

Neklic swallowed. 'My reports place him five days out on a high bank overlooking the Meir and the soil of Eagle Talon beyond. Head north, then follow the river west, and you should have no trouble.'

The voice came indifferent. 'No man has ever caused me trouble. How reliable are your reports?'

'They were given to me by Talran scouts, so you'd know better than I.'

The slim man turned his nose up and grunted before downing the rest of his wine with a cough. 'I'm not sure if this terrible red is getting to me or the smoke from that brazier.

Honestly, I don't know how you can live with it.' He stood up sharply. 'It's probably like smoking a pipe back home.' He smiled. 'But with none of the benefits.'

Neklic was about to reply when the stranger pushed himself into a throng of men waiting to refill their tankards, and, though the crowd parted quickly, the Talran assassin was gone.

Only now did Neklic see the slightly soggy letter which lay where the stranger had sat. Lifting it from the floor and unfolding it, he was not surprised to find it addressed to him.

You have until Kalac dies to bring the city to its knees or my assassin will be back for you.

The scrawl that was Reshmal's signature followed. Neklic sat silently, rolling the parchment over in his hands. He agreed to aid the Talran emperor in return for civilised riches that would have made him wealthier than any of the Neferian royalty. Still, it was a dream come true when Kalac left, and the city fell under his command. Why play at royalty when you can live it? He hoped that when the White Fangs triumphed over the invaders, they would look upon the man who had led them with as much respect as they had the late Marek. The throne would be his! Neklic's eyes flashed with greed and then, as always, the dream shattered. Unlike they did for Marek, the city would not weep at the death of its soothsayer. He shivered and suddenly hoped that Kalac was as tough as others thought him, for a man wielding a halberd against you in daylight was preferred to an unexpected dagger in the back from the shadows.

Kalac had spent the last couple of days watching over the frozen ford for any sign of Reshmal's forces. Now he stood, with halberd in hand, horrified as the screams rang out from the burning settlement across the river. He cast a glance at the ashen-faced Koren beside him and remembered their discussion by the river only the day before.

Kalac had watched Koren crouch and take a pickaxe to the ice of the Meir before plastering his arms with the cool silt; the burns had mostly healed, leaving vivid red scars which would one day match the rest. Kalac walked down to the water's edge and stood beside the squatted giant.

'Ho, Koren.'

The giant ignored him, but Kalac had expected as much, so he waited for him to finish. He was not about to interrupt the ritual of one of Goddess Meira's most devoted disciples. Of all of the Gods, the goddess of water was most inclined to help mortal souls, so he did not wish to offend her.

Eventually, Koren turned his head to face him. 'Ho, Kalac.'

Now it came to it, Kalac was unsure whether this was the time or the place to say what he wanted to say. He shifted uneasily, and the giant read the look of indecision on his face.

'You're wondering what to do about the Eagle Talon, right?' said Koren. 'I've been thinking of it too.'

Kalac nodded. 'I think any seeking refuge should be welcome here.'

The giant raised an eyebrow. 'That decision may not do your reputation any favours. As I am sure you are aware, our tribe has had a blood feud with the Eagle Talon for longer than your lifespan, and many of the warriors will have fought against them in battles past. I know I have.'

'I also have. But look at them, Koren!' Kalac gestured to the ruins in the distance. 'Our blood feud has ended! They have no tribe left!'

The thought made him shiver. The two tribes had been rivals for more than thirty years. What hope did the White Fangs truly have if the Talran could wipe them out in a single week?

The giant turned his attention back to the soothing waters and splashed his face. 'I didn't say it was the wrong decision.'

Now, as women and children began to flee through the frosted rye fields of the war-ravaged settlement, some with small babes in their arms, Kalac turned to his men watching from the bank. 'We must help them! And any who don't wish to be slayers of women and children should follow!'

Kalac sprinted through the camp, halberd in hand, and leapt onto his steed. Only now did he see Turesh and Koren had followed, bringing with them a score of men, but there were only twelve horses. Kalac kicked his heels, and the grey hurtled through the camp and across the Meir. Many of the warriors had crossed the frozen river and were already helping the quicker children to traverse the ice.

Kalac galloped through the rye fields, orange in the setting sun, and spun the grey around, offering his hand down to a woman carrying her child. The woman gratefully accepted, but Kalac heard someone shout a warning. Before he pulled her up, his gaze turned to the settlement. A dozen riders had emerged from the village, their lances levelled. Kalac released the woman's hand.

'Run!' he shouted, spinning the grey towards the settlement.

Instinctively, the warrior king levelled his halberd and charged the first rider. The rider lunged early. Kalac swayed in the saddle, hammering his blade into the soldier's armour, pitching the Talran from the horse. The king pressed on, lunging at the rider behind. He missed, and the enemy's lance lodged in his grey's chest. As the horse collapsed, Kalac jumped clear and hit the ground hard. He rolled, pain searing through his shoulder as he righted himself. Another rider drew rein, taking a downward thrust at Kalac. The warrior king stepped in and parried the blade overhead before reversing his halberd. As the rider turned in the saddle for a second thrust, Kalac hooked the soldier's cuirass and wrenched him from the horse. The king swiftly pounced on the Talran, but he was already dead, his neck savagely twisted.

Suddenly out of immediate danger, Kalac became aware of what was around him; steel on steel, baying horses, cries of pain, but those not making the noise had suffered the most. Kalac turned his head to not see the still child in his peripheral vision. *Why was Reshmal doing this? To make us cower? To make us break? How could he justify butchering women and children? Where was the honour in such an act? Is that what being civilised entailed?* Kalac stabbed his halberd into the earth and levered himself to his full height. *The harder he tries, the taller I will stand.*

Then came the thunderous war drums, and

two dozen more soldiers rode out from the settlement. He had given the refugees all of the time he could.

'Fall back!' he shouted, and those within earshot repeated the command.

A grey slid to a halt before him, and Kalac accepted the outstretched hand, though he did not recognise the rider's face. 'Not many men would have come back for me,' said Kalac as he straddled the saddle behind the man. 'What's your name, warrior?'

'Jeshar, my lord,' said the rider as he heeled the grey into a gallop for the crossing.

'I shall remember it.'

Kalac looked back over his shoulder at the enemy horsemen. They were not chasing with any real vigour, nor did he expect them to be; with every step towards the White Fang camp, they were losing numerical supremacy. Eventually, they fell back, and Kalac was left gazing at the black harbingers circling above.

Turesh rode up alongside him, his arm cupped around a heavily pregnant woman who sat side saddle in front of him. He wore a wide sardonic smile.

'Ho, Jeshar! My, you've picked up an ugly one!'

The riders laughed aloud, easing the tension in them. This would be the last Kalac remembered, for when the hooves of the last half dozen laden greys hit the ford, the ice cracked, and a huge slab shifted. The horses toppled into the river, hurling their riders. Kalac's head cracked onto a sheet of ice before he was dragged under.

Turesh opened his eyes and choked, his face half buried in the silt of the bank. Sore bruises and cuts covered his back and legs from his attempts to shield himself from the submerged rocks and flailing horses. His arms were heavy, his body exhausted, but he still clung with white knuckles to a clump of horse mane as though it had somehow saved him. He smiled at the thought, but a twinge in his back turned it into a grimace. Then he remembered the woman who had been riding with him. Dragging his head from the mud, he struggled onto his elbows and saw a cart bouncing its way over the frozen ground, a dozen warriors alongside it, and the giant, Koren, leading the workhorse. Turesh cast his gaze around, and he grimaced again. Men and women lay on the bank in no better state than he, but more lay face down in the water or tangled in the riverbed, their eyes wide with a fear they no longer felt.

The cart trundled to a halt, and Koren loomed above him for a moment. Another warrior moved past him, and together they hoisted Turesh onto the cart, where he cursed at the solid board and the lingering stench of its previous occupant: dried meats.

He grabbed Koren's arm before he could move away. 'A pregnant woman rode with me….'

The giant patted him on the shoulder. 'Rest. We will look.'

As the cart was filled with more injured, Turesh was left with thoughts of remorse. The Talon warriors had fought themselves to extinction for their families; for many, it had made no difference at all.

In the following few hours, the cart was hauled back and forth many times, carrying the injured to the makeshift healing house: the royal tent, since it was the largest. They did not have to worry about Kalac's wrath because, in all the hours of searching, his body remained unfound.

11

The chill of the blast knocked the wind from his lungs, and a flailing hoof cracked against his ribs, sending him spiralling through the water. Under went Turesh, without a hope or a prayer on his lips, for it all happened so fast. The rushing waters bubbled around him, making it impossible to see. He tried to curl up as he swirled and spun, his back and legs gashing on the rocks. His lungs burned, screaming for air. The torment seemed to last forever, though he knew it could only have been moments.

Then the chaos settled. Turesh saw the bodies tangled in the reeds and floating lifeless in the water; great gashes marred their heads. One such man was facing him as he drifted through the carnage. His heart sank as he recognised his old friend Jeshar; his eyes were closed, his mouth wide, his face grey. Like all warriors, he had wanted to die in battle, not here in the river's depths. The waters bubbled around the dead warrior, and his eyes flicked open, staring straight at Turesh. Turesh opened his mouth to scream and took a huge gulp of water. Choking now, he flailed his arms, trying to reach for the surface….

He sat bolt-upright inside the dim tent. Two women he recognised as healers had grabbed his convulsing arms and had desperately tried to wake him. Once he had awakened, they checked his temperature before scurrying off to deal with more urgent patients. Turesh lay back on the soft rug beneath him, cringing against the throbbing pain of his recent bruising. A few people in the tent were suffering from a sickness – brought on by the chill waters, he guessed. The low moaning of those in perpetual agony was frequently punctuated by splutters of coughing. Though Turesh believed in the far western idea that coughing somehow spread disease, he was oblivious to the sounds of the sick, his mind lost in the avenues of thought. He was being haunted. Of that, he had no doubt. First in his fever-induced dreams over a month ago, then after he assaulted the captured settlement, and now this. He could not escape it, and the prospect of being haunted for the rest of his life filled him with dread. But who could he tell? The healers here would think him mad, as would his fellow warriors, which would put pay to any leadership prospects he may have had. No. He could think of only one person who might be able to help him now, and though he did not believe in any of the powers she claimed to have, he would go anyway. Such was the fear in his heart.

Iskel cursed at the sight of the stacked funeral pyre. There would be no hero's welcome in Krem for these men. None of their skulls would sit proudly in her walls. The city had lost faith in them, branded them traitors, and yet still they fought for her, even died for her. Though Iskel had no family, she guessed that this was the reason why men would willingly die for a people that had cast them out.

As the pyre was ignited and the flames began to lick at the darkening sky, solemn hymns drifted up towards the stars, and Iskel's thoughts grew ever more inconsolable, so she returned to her tent. A night of celebratory drinking would begin in earnest, but Iskel sat in secluded darkness with nothing but her own misery.

Kalac was dead, and she had not foreseen it. After the steady changes in Kalac's perception of her, Iskel had begun to cling to a vain hope of rekindling their long-forgotten flame. Now that hope lay shattered. You were a fool, Iskel, she chided herself. So many years had passed he did not even remember you. Besides, he was a king. He would not wish to be shackled to a lowly witch-woman.

She sighed. None of it mattered now. He was gone, and Death would not be cheated. Though even as she thought it, she knew this was not true; she had been doing it for the past twelve years. Ever since she had watched her own death…

Scattering the crystals and lighting the candle, she sat cross-legged in the centre of the room. Her eyes revolved in their sockets, and time, once again, began to have no meaning.

A call brought her abruptly back to the present and drew her eyes to the tent flap. She watched it fold back. A silhouette was momentarily illuminated in the opening by the torches outside before the flap unfurled and blocked out the light once again.

Iskel could see now that it was Turesh. He stood uneasily for a moment and then whispered: 'It's very dark in here.'

Iskel smirked. 'Your eyes will adjust. Sit.' The warrior hesitated before he did so, and Iskel continued, 'Why are you here?'

Turesh shrugged his shoulders and gave a weary sigh. 'I'm having nightmares.'

At any other time, Iskel would have shrieked with laughter, but in her grim mood, she held it in check. There was more to this than there first appeared, she knew, for a man would never openly admit to such weakness. She waited, and eventually, the warrior continued.

'Always I am in a recent battle, and as it ends and I look upon the dead, I see some of them are people I was fond of.' He hung his head. 'And then... they're not dead. I mean, they *are* dead... but they awaken.'

'And what is it they do when they awaken?' she said in what she hoped was an even tone.

'Nothing. Just look at me or start to talk. Their faces are ripped open, and they talk to me!'

Iskel did not utter a word, and the place fell into a deathly silence. Turesh fidgeted uncomfortably, like a man who has said too much. Nightmares after a battle were nothing uncommon, she knew, though only the brave or the stupid dare voice it, but this...

'What is it you do when you see these undying?' she asked.

'I...' The warrior paused to steel himself. 'I run, wench! What do you expect me to do?'

Iskel felt her blood boil. What was it with men? Everything had to be a damn competition! They could never admit to weakness, no matter how obvious it was, lest other men laugh. Ridiculous! She wanted to retort: 'Perhaps next time you should stand your ground as a man should!' but she allowed herself a few moments of composure and rephrased the sentence.

'Perhaps you should listen. The spirits may have useful insights for you.'

'Or maybe they want me dead.'

'They cannot harm you, Turesh,' she said firmly. 'It's a dream. Nothing can physically hurt you. Besides, you said it yourself: you were fond of them. I'm willing to bet they also respected you.'

'So I am to just stand there whilst these things shuffle and crawl towards me?'

'Why do men find relationships so easy to cast aside? They are not *things*, Turesh. They were once human too.' The slight seemed to go unnoticed. 'Just don't travel too far, or you may forget the way back. A light would be good.'

Turesh raised a questioning eyebrow. 'What does that mean?'

Iskel shook her head. 'Never mind. Just take it as all the other dreams. No matter how horrifying; no matter how violent; they cannot do you harm.'

The warrior nodded slowly, clearly trying hard to convince himself. 'I was hoping for something more resolute,' he said at length, 'for I'm not swayed by any of this....'

'What other's word do you have to go on?'

Turesh was less than happy with the response, but he stood to leave regardless. As an afterthought, he nodded his thanks. Then he was gone.

'Perhaps fear is necessary to keep the likes of us in check,' said Iskel.

Barely an hour later, Iskel drew Akron's tent flap back and stepped into the ill-lit room. The occupants of the small tent stilled their tongues and cast their eyes upon the witch-woman with an unhealthy mixture of scorn and surprise. Iskel stood defiant in their gazes, remembering exactly how she stood in the vision in which she had seen herself no more than half an hour before.

'Care to explain why you've just barged into my tent?' came the irritated voice of Akron from across the room. The flickering brazier before him made deep, dark crevices of his frown lines. The other orange faces around the fire were looking at her, expecting an answer. She recognised Kalac's two advisors; the others had been handpicked by them for leadership qualities. All had anticipated a night of hot debate, she thought as she smirked. None had been expecting this.

'Well?' said the stout bald man.

'You must postpone this leadership debate for a few nights,' mimicked Iskel from the vision, 'and then you shall see it will not be necessary.'

The men glanced accusingly at each other, wondering who it was that leaked the information about their private meeting. Then the spell was broken.

'What are you talking about, stupid wench!' said one of them. 'Of course we need this meeting. The men cannot go leaderless!'

Others grunted their approval as Iskel knew they would.

'The men have a leader,' she said nonchalantly.

'Who?' asked another, his voice raised. 'Poor Kalac?'

'Poor? Ha! None of you truly believe that!' she said. 'You're all here for your own endeavours.'

At this, the men grew irritated.

'I don't care who you think you are, woman,' said Akron, 'but this is no place for you and your nonsense.'

'You *must* heed me,' she said.

The bald warrior leapt to his feet. 'Enough with your babble!'

But Iskel was staring at Turesh. She knew he held a pact to prove his worth to the king in order to be pardoned, allowing him to spend the remainder of his days back in his home tribe with his soulmate; it was in his best interest to hear what she had to say for there was no guarantee of a similar agreement with the next king.

Turesh understood this almost instantly.

'Let her speak!' His voice demanded the silence it received, and every man looked upon him with the knowledge that Turesh was probably the favourite to lead.

'This is madness, Turesh,' said the bald warrior in a more even tone.

'Be that as it may, Akron. Kalac King believed it.'

'He was insane as well! And I would have told him to his face had he not died beforehand. Don't tell me you believe in this drivel too, Turesh?'

Turesh snorted. Iskel knew that whatever he said now would be used against him in upcoming debates, and every man there knew it too.

'I don't know what to believe,' he said conservatively.

'Then allow me to spell out the facts for you, my friend,' said Akron. 'The king's body has not been found! The men are celebrating *his* death as well as the others tonight.'

'They would!' said Iskel. 'Such is their fickle faith in kings. They hope to somehow gain more for themselves from the next. No doubt most of you do too!'

Suddenly the silent giant, Koren, perked up. 'If you are keeping something from us, lass, you had best keep it no longer.'

Iskel smiled. When you were riding the chariots of fate, only a great haul on the reins could stop the mighty beasts, and for that, you needed to know what it was you were changing.

The fire crackled, and a sudden sputter cast an orange glow over the witch woman's face.

'Kalac still lives.'

Kalac awoke to an overcast sky and thunder in his skull, his body ached, and he could see the lacerations on one of his sprawled arms lying beside his head. He rolled his eyes and scanned the river bank where he lay before tilting his head up to look at the wooded tree line. He had no idea where he was. The Meir had obviously dragged him downstream, which placed him either further into Eagle Talon territory than he had been or swept beyond that and thrown back into his own borders. Were he not wary of every god in existence, he would have prayed for the latter. Instead, he painfully hauled himself out of the drying mud and up onto his elbows. His head spun, and his vision became hazy for a moment, his brain unused to the world the right way up. Using his elbows, he turned around and dragged himself to the water's edge to quench his thirst and wash his face. The cold water stung a two inch cut on his forehead and came away crimson with blood. He grunted as he rose, his ears straining for any sounds other than the plopping of the river rushing over the pebbles at its edges. Upon hearing nothing, he wandered into the undergrowth in a hopeful attempt to find something which would convey his whereabouts.

He must have wandered for over an hour. The sky had darkened, and it had begun to rain before he stumbled upon a small wooden shack nestled within the wood. A yellow glow flickered between the closed shutters as Kalac rapped on the door. He stood for a few moments in the pouring rain, then, with no answer forthcoming, he navigated his way through a row of fir trees to the rear of the building. Here the door was ajar, and Kalac peered inside. An old man sat in a wicker chair, a woollen blanket pulled tightly around his thin frame as he watched the fire spit embers from the glowing hearth.

'Ho, Stranger,' said Kalac through the doorway.

The old man craned his head round, further

than one usually would, suggesting he was blind in one eye.

'Who is it?'

The warrior slowly pushed the door open and stepped in. 'I am Kalac. I seek....'

The old man laughed without mirth. As he spoke, a grim recollection glinted in his eye. 'Once I would have given my right arm to slay a son of Marek, but now I'm old and know there's no point to it all. Tell me, son of Marek, why are you here?'

Kalac was caught off guard. 'Where is here?'

The old man raised an inquisitive eyebrow. 'Interesting. How does a prince become lost in an unknown land?' When no answer was forthcoming, he continued, 'These are the Woods of Woe, a battleground throughout the decades between our two tribes, and until recently, I would have called this Talon land, but now I think it belongs to neither of us.'

The old man's eyes flicked towards the backdoor, and Kalac's gaze followed. A rain-sodden middle-aged man stood in the doorway, his hair clumped together with mud, an ugly gash on his forehead was swollen and distended, forcing his left eye closed, and in one hand he held a round of wood; his other lay strapped to his chest. Kalac recognised him instantly. In times gone by, many a White Fang had fallen to this revered warrior's blades.

The old man stirred. 'Felas, this man is….'

'I know who it is, Uncle,' said the middle-aged warrior. 'The question is: what are his intentions?'

Kalac noted the slight shift of the warrior's hand on the round, steadying it for a blow. Kalac's hands came up slowly, palms open. 'I don't wish to fight you, Felas. It appears as though you've done enough of that already.'

'You know nothing of what I've done! Of what I've seen!' The burly man was clearly fighting some inward battle. For a moment only, his moist eyes reflected the horror he had witnessed. 'Everybody I respected, everybody I ever cared for is gone! I watched my entire tribe decimated in a day! Do you have any idea how that feels?'

Kalac shook his head. 'But I feel I might still. Tell me, Felas. You were at the front; you've seen their impregnable shield walls first-hand?'

Felas shivered. 'I've seen this and more besides. How Reshmal burns people out of their villages, destroys their horsemen in heartbeats, and leads them into a trap. Reshmal cares not for personal glory or heroic deeds; his is a battle of wits, and he has proven that wisdom is the sharpest sword in the armoury, for the Talon are no more.' He gestured to the old man, 'For all I know, we're the only ones left.'

'Not true,' said Kalac. 'Just....' He paused. He had no idea how long he had been on the bank but conceded, 'yesterday, the White Fangs rescued some of your women and children as they fled to our border. Our blood feud is over, Felas. Neferia protects her own.'

The warrior's eyes misted up, and he turned away, his voice breaking. 'We are in your debt.'

Kalac's heart was heavy. If Reshmal had succeeded in breaking this legendary warrior, what hope was there for the rest of them?

'Tell me of these tactics,' he said.

So the fire was stoked, and the three of them sat long into the night, exchanging battle stories of their invaders. Kalac shared the Fangs' small victory at the ford and the blocking of the pass before Felas recalled in detail his horrific ordeal. The revered warrior had fought in four doomed ventures – leading two of them – and Kalac sat in terrible silence as the story unfolded, culminating in the destruction of the Talon and Felas' escape from the flaming capital.

'I stole a horse and spared it none,' said Felas, 'but I was too weak. I fell unconscious and dropped from the saddle. My Uncle found me a couple of days later whilst gathering wood. Lucky he did, for I was struck with fever and would have surely died.' Felas stared hard into the fire. 'They have but one weakness, Kalac. In the capital, they had burned everything but the food stores.'

Kalac sighed. 'If we cannot defend our villages, then they can take all the food they need.'

Felas flicked his gaze at the warrior king. 'It is worse still. Reshmal hordes the food and carries it behind his marching army in carts; with portable grain stores, he can march his army anywhere.'

Their stories continued with half-baked plans of retaliation, which would never see the light of day but gave them hope at the time of conception. By the time the fire crackled and died, all three had long since fallen asleep.

Hours later, Kalac awoke to a boot. Instantly awake as the wild demands, Kalac gazed at Felas towering above him. For a moment, he had forgotten where he was.

'Help me fetch the firewood,' said the crippled warrior, 'before the old man wakes. He gets grouchy in the morning, and I'd rather not have him in one of those moods.'

Kalac sat up. The old man had been gracious enough to share his home with a White Fang. The least he could do was collect some wood. 'Lead the way.'

As the pair left the hut, Felas hefted the felling axe propped up beside the door – a long-handled, sturdy affair, perfect for cutting the bony fingers which clawed their way out of the frozen ground.

'Come,' said Felas. 'There's something you must see.'

At that moment, Kalac realised he had no fear of Felas. The legendary Talon was a warrior of honour and would not cut the White Fang down without warning. Kalac, too, would honour that unspoken pact.

The overgrown path through the wood was arduous. The rain from the night before had caused the ground to become a cold, sucking bog, the wet ferns in the undergrowth slapping at their legs. Eventually, they reached a small clearing of hewn trees, the dead stumps like warts growing from a witch's face. A few trunks lay half embedded in the mud, and rounds of wood had already been stacked by one stump.

Why would Felas come all the way out here just to fell a tree when there were plenty growing beside the house? He opened his mouth to speak but caught the warrior's gaze and followed it between the thin screen of trees. Then he understood why the warrior came out here. Through the trees and across the frozen rye fields, a small village jutted out like the fin of a shark. Kalac recognised it instantly, but no women and children were running from it this time.

Felas stared hard and grew agitated, as if his injuries were the only thing stopping him from charging headlong into the village. 'They arrived the other day. Five hundred strong. The force that wiped the Talon off the map, and now they set their sights on the Meir.' He sighed. 'Only divine intervention can stop them now. I would give my one good arm for the Gods to smash them to pieces this instant.'

'That would be nice,' said Kalac, turning away and gathering a few rounds, for they could do nothing about the Talran from here.

'Why do you think they allow it?' said Felas.

Kalac half turned. 'Who?'

'The Gods. Why do they allow these followers of foreign deities into their lands?'

Kalac snorted. 'Now that I can answer. Think about it. The freezing perils and starvation of winter; the blazing forest fires of summer; those traitorous thoughts that turn tribes against one another; everything the Gods have ever done, they've done to make us tougher, to allow us to survive in this bleak land. This is just another test, Felas. One I intend to win.'

'I wish I shared your confidence, but once you have seen what I've seen, you begin to doubt.'

Felas took one last look at the village before returning to the task at hand. Half swinging the axe, he lodged it into a round of wood, careful not to split it, then hefted it up with the handle. Kalac saw him glance over at the three rounds hugged tightly to his chest. 'That all you can manage?'

The White Fang smirked. 'I was about to ask you the very same.'

The veteran smiled, but it did not reach his eyes. 'I'm not up to the challenge anymore.' His smile faded. 'Truth be told. I'm done for. This arm will never heal properly, and a warrior with one arm is about as useful as a handful of dung.'

Kalac shook his head. 'Fight with me, Felas. You've seen them in battle. Your knowledge is what's important to us now.'

'No. I've shared my knowledge. For me, the war is over.'

'...And so I said, "I'll gut any of you swine that touch it,"' said the middle-aged man, in full swing of his exaggerated tale. The two soldiers beside him listened intently as though, at some point, there would be a test. Suddenly he halted short and scratched his bearded chin in contemplation. The others had seen it too. Nestled in the trees ahead was a small hut. A light flickered from within, and smoke drifted lazily out of a crude hole in the roof before being swept away by the wind. The middle-aged soldier gestured with his hands towards the hut. His two subordinates loosed their shields from their backs, swords snaking into their hands. They approached the hut in close formation. The senior soldier checked his stance, and the door caved in under his mighty boot. Inward they burst, tower shields raised, snarls on their spit-flecked lips.

They faltered.

Before them sat a frail old man in a wicker chair, his back facing them; he made no attempt to move as if he had not heard the door cave in. The trio hesitated for a moment, and then the middle-aged man gave a slit grin. Raising his sword, it glinted in the light of the open backdoor. He took one step forward. Something rolled across the floor from behind the chair. At first, the soldier thought it to be a copper bowl, but curiously, it was a round of wood.

'You can blame the loud mouth for what follows.' The old man had not looked round, but his voice came edged with defiance. 'All the good it'll do you.'

A thunderous roar rent the air. The senior soldier whirled to the noise. One of his juniors pitched forward, a wood axe embedded in his neck. The other had blocked the doorway with his tower shield. Whirling back round, the ageing soldier's nose exploded in a headbutt from a one-armed giant. He pitched backwards into his underling, and both fell through the doorway.

The senior stumbled to his feet, trying to give himself some distance between himself and his assailants. He strained to see through the blood of his shattered nose. The soldier he had fallen into had landed on his own sword and was writhing in agony. The one-armed giant had wrenched the axe free of the other soldier and moved through the doorway to stand beside another giant. This one was slightly shorter, his bunched sinews reminiscent of a lion – lithe and strong. The middle-aged man wiped the blood from his eyes. He had less than an even chance, he figured.

Then the taller one spoke in a broken Talran dialect.

'Where is your honour?' He gestured to the old man still seated within the hut. 'An elder?'

The senior soldier grew red in the face, his anger fuelled by the pain of his mangled nose. How did a mangy barbarian have the audacity to lecture him?

'You're savages!' he shouted. 'The world will be all the better without you!' He raised his shield and struck it with his sword. 'Here's my honour! Come and take it!'

The tall one made to pass the felling axe, but the warrior beside him shook his head and mumbled something in his backward language, leaving the cripple to fight alone. The soldier's heart lifted. Perhaps he would survive this after all.

Felas eyed the senior soldier before him and approached with the caution of experience. The soldier burst forward. Raising his tower shield, he thrust his sword at the warrior's guts. The Neferian moved with the speed of a jackal. He dropped to his haunches and arced the axe under the shield. Bones shattered, and the soldier fell, right foot almost severed at the ankle. The axe swept up and then down in a savage stroke, stopped only by the tower shield. Splitting the shield, it wedged solid, and the senior struck from beneath it. Hampered by his reach, the short sword gashed the giant's leg. Felas stamped on the outstretched arm and followed it with a boot, smashing open the soldier's face. Using the axe's handle, the giant wrenched the shield aside with his one good arm and stomped again, twisting as he did so. *Crack*. The soldier's neck snapped, his tongue lolled, and all was still.

Felas breathed a mighty sigh of relief before checking the cut on his leg. The leathers had done a good job – the wound was merely superficial. Kalac clapped him on the back.

'I knew you had it in you.' He grinned. 'A revered warrior never falls without a fight!'

Felas grunted. 'He was less than average and underestimated me; a poor combination. Had he been skilled, your little charade would've cost me my life.'

'What life? You had all but given up. I was showing you the strength that still remained within. And you can speak their language! Where did you learn that?'

Felas shrugged. 'Only a basic understanding. One of Nostel's palace slaves was Talran born. He was a plucky man. I liked him. In return for some extra rations, he taught me the language of his people.'

'That could prove useful to our cause.'

Felas turned to eye the young White Fang. 'Still insistent?'

'Absolutely.' Kalac beamed. 'If someone were to offer me the best warriors from all of the tribes of Neferia, I would accept. Of course I would!'

The middle-aged Talon adjusted the strap about his chest, pulling his useless arm into a more comfortable position. 'Even someone like me?'

'*Especially* a leader like you.'

Kalac fell silent, clearly lost in some thought, then looked up at the cold blue sky; tendrils of white clouds were drifting lazily, the sun fast approaching its zenith.

'I should get moving,' he said. 'The tribe will only lead itself to ruin without me.'

Felas raised an eyebrow. Was this truly the White Fang leader collecting rounds for a dying hearth in some lost wood?

'I had heard the rumours. Are they true? Your father has fallen?'

Kalac nodded slowly.

Felas solemnly returned the nod. 'Well then, my lord, it appears I'm living long enough to serve two kings.'

For half the day, Kalac and Felas had wandered through the wood, skirting the village the Talran currently occupied. They had talked at length about family and honour and how at thirteen, Felas had thought he would have found his soulmate, settled down and bore a couple of children by the time he was twenty-eight. Now at thirty-three, he was still yet to find that special someone, his life having been consumed by his ambition to aid Nostel and improve the quality of life for the tribe. All that seemed hopeless now.

'Life never turns out the way you expect,'

said Kalac. 'At thirteen, I was just learning to hold a sword. I wanted to be a famous warrior.'

'You got your wish,' said Felas.

'Did I? For I cared not for leading the tribe; battle strategies, food supplies, heeding counsels, none of this was for me. And now… My father, my mother, my brother. I have lost everything truly important to me. We are much alike, Felas. Perhaps that is why I like you.'

The conversation rambled on, reminiscing of less responsible times in their childhood years. Finally, they reached the edge of the wood. The rye fields where he had ridden to save the women and children a day or so before extended all of the way to the Meir a mile distant. The three-foot high crop would provide little cover from the watching eyes of the enemy, and so the pair had set up camp to wait until sunset, creating a small fire behind a natural screen of undergrowth. Felas had brought a small sack containing various cuts of dried meat and vegetables that his uncle had gifted them. Kalac wolfed it down, having not eaten properly for some time and then stretched out, enjoying the freedom and lack of responsibility whilst he could. Soon he would be in over his head again, but for now, he could put his mind to other uses.

He hefted the felling axe and examined the

work tool closely. A weighty affair, the axe head small but incredibly sharp, the long haft, made entirely of wood, gave the tool good leverage when swung, but in the heat of battle, a sweating hand would slip down the shaft with each impact. Kalac glanced around the rocky undergrowth of the wood, eyeing the materials at his disposal. He lifted a large round stone and nodded his approval as he examined its bulbous side. Tool in hand, he moved to the face of a small overhang and struck the corner of some slate jutting from under a giant fern. After a few attempts, a sharp piece of slate was sheered from the mound. Lifting this, Kalac struck the piece again, this time softer, the emphasis on precision. The slate split again, and Kalac dropped the round stone, picking up the sharp flake of slate. Returning to the fire, he began whittling a series of notches and grooves in the haft of the felling axe.

As the day grew old, Felas stirred from his slumber and looked at the reddening sky. 'Almost time. If we leave it too long, we will not be able to see where we are heading.' He looked at the axe resting in Kalac's lap. 'You've been busy.' He held out his hand, and Kalac passed him the felling axe. Felas cast a scrutinising gaze over the handiwork before nodding his approval. He gave the axe back and stood. 'I need to urinate. Be back shortly. Get ready.'

As Felas wandered off through the bushes, Kalac fed the haft of the axe through the top loop in the back of his leather jerkin. The weapon hung low, for it was much shorter than the halberd, and it would take several heartbeats to draw if called upon, but there was no other solution other than carrying it all the way.

'Kalac!' The hissing voice of Felas came from the bushes as loud as it dared. 'Come here.'

The young king followed in the general direction of the voice. He leapt lightly through the thicket and what he saw caught the breath in his throat. Felas was crouched on the ground in a slight clearing about ten paces ahead. Strewn around him lay half a dozen dead. Blood had long since stopped flowing from their mortal wounds. All were women and children wearing the brightly coloured markings of the Talon. Kalac's fists clenched until his knuckles were white. Why was Reshmal doing this?

'Here,' said Felas, snapping Kalac out of his trance.

The former prince moved to stand beside the revered warrior who was crouched over the body of a young woman. Her round, flat features were covered in mud and blood. An open wound in her side had stained her clothes crimson. Kalac was about to ask if Felas knew her when the woman's eyelids flicked open, and she convulsed, blood dribbling down one side of her mouth.

The crippled warrior laid a gentle hand on her shoulder before he gestured towards Kalac, clearly continuing some previous conversation.

'See!'

Kalac knelt beside the woman, and she swivelled her bloodshot eyes to encompass him in her narrow window of vision.

Felas continued. 'He has come to save us! He's already sheltering many of the Talon. I'm sure your son is among them.'

The woman uttered her child's name and stared at Kalac with imploring eyes.

The young king did not recognise the name and bit his bottom lip. A small boy lay not more than ten feet from her, killed with a blow so savage, his little head was almost sheered from his shoulders. Felas would have undoubtedly seen this too. Of course, the pair had no idea if this was the boy, but there were no other survivors, so Kalac feared the worst, for the child would surely not have abandoned his mother. Even so, the king had seen enough suffering for this once proud parent.

Sometimes a lie was merciful….

'I recognise the name,' he said, reassuring her by squeezing her hand. 'We rescued many fleeing women and children. I'm almost sure he is safely among them.'

The woman seemed to relax, the blood dribbling from her mouth ceased, and finally, the light went from her eyes as though she had held to life only to uncover her son's fate. Now Kalac felt the tremendous weight of guilt, for he knew she had died listening to a lie. Anger surged through him, granting his tired, hungry frame renewed life. Why should I feel so bad? I did not invade Neferia, he thought; I did not slaughter these people! And yet he could not shake the stigma that perhaps a more apt leader would have made a difference. What would his father have done?

Felas must have sensed his dark mood, for he stood and placed a warm hand on his shoulder.

'Nothing more could've been done. We should move.'

Glancing up at the setting sun, Kalac knew very few hours of the winter day remained but concluded that, provided the camp had not moved, they would arrive by nightfall. Unfortunately, the enemy lay between him and his men on the opposite side of the Meir. He knew the odds of avoiding the scouts and patrols of the Talran were bleak, but today, with rage fuelling him as it always had, Kalac was a gambling man.

12

Garn clenched his fists into tight balls to stop his hands from shaking. The young supply officer had given his emperor nothing but bad news since the onset of his campaign, and he knew Reshmal was beginning to take it personally. The emperor rose from his lacquered work desk, his hands clasped behind his back.

'I hope you are competent enough not to fail me again.' The tone was even, but Garn had come to know the underlying threat in the words. A threat that not only meant the end of an otherwise successful career but potentially his life as well.

'I am, Your Grace.' The response was automatic, and Garn kept his head low, never meeting his emperor's gaze; such was regulation.

'I severely hope so,' said the emperor. 'You will strip whatever supplies you can from this backward settlement and issue me with a full report within the hour. Dismissed.'

Garn bowed low and left the mud hut turned headquarters as fast as respectfully possible. The young emperor was nothing like his late father, he thought. He would not expect miracles from the supply depot when delays and setbacks occurred. When the barbarians had blocked Kardek Pass, crushing any hopes of valuable reinforcements or supplies, Reshmal had found the opportunity to drop the blame squarely into Garn's hands rather than accepting his own inept mistake of not posting enough defenders to keep the pass open. And now that old bastard, Neklic, had betrayed the emperor's word, it fell to the supply officer again to make good the setback and keep the soldiers fuelled for more days of fighting. The men were already on emergency rations. What more could he do? The emperor had obviously misjudged the ease of the whole affair, even without the largest tribe's great tactician. He had to hand it to the Neferians. The animal fat and fire arrows had been a mark of pure genius and just went to show how forward-thinking these barbarian races were when it came to killing one another.

Garn strode quickly through the apparently random scattering of huts and tents, so unlike the streets and roads of home, towards the supply depot on the settlement's far side. He took the long route giving the makeshift hospital a wide birth. A handful of men had died over the past few days from a strange illness caught from being in this god-forsaken land. Garn sighed. Not for the first time, his mind wandered back to his fiancée and seven-year-old son on their farm just outside the Grand City. The weather had been fine on that late summer's day when he had left to rejoin the military again for his fourth year of service. It had made it so hard to leave. The day had become an immortal dream, reliving it on rare occasions when he slept; he yearned to be with them on that joyous day forever.

A jostle drew him from thought, and a junior orderly turned to him as he hurried by loaded with bags.

'Sorry, sir.'

Garn bit back his anger at being interrupted from such longing thoughts and weaved his way through the milling workers into the hastily erected yard area for the supply convoy. A quick scan of the wagons confirmed the grim message he would convey to the emperor. Food provisions were only good for another two weeks, and it would take months for supplies to reach them from the mountains. He cursed that ugly, old hobble in the White Fang capital. If he had played his part, a supply line could have been set up from Krem, and victory would have been assured. He cursed again. Leaving the frenzied activity of the yard, he picked his way through to the calm outskirts of the settlement in an attempt to shake his foul mood.

Perhaps it would all be over soon anyway, he thought as he stared out over the plains towards Kalac's camp beyond the river. It was too far to see any specific details, merely a brown smudge where the tents stood, but the scouts had reported only a moderate force. This morning though, news that another three hundred warriors had entered the camp, including a hundred horsemen, had put an urgent wind in Reshmal's sails. With the threat of more barbarians arriving with each passing day, Garn knew Reshmal would strike tomorrow, even before the sun rose to catch them off guard; such was the new emperor's way.

The new emperor's way…

Garn shivered at the horrific memory of the massacre some two days previous. The women and children had been unarmed and frightened for their lives. They had every right to be. Solemnly, Garn shook his head. He had not expected that when he re-enlisted, but Reshmal had made his orders perfectly clear. With the blockade of the pass, it was unlikely the emperor could annihilate all of his enemies in one crushing blow. Therefore, it was decreed that any conquered tribes needed an act of genocide to bring stability to the area, for even the barbarian women and children, it was reasoned, would raise arms against the emperor. Garn had felt sick. He had not taken part in the culling but had been in the camp some five hundred yards away. He had buried his head in his haversack to drown out the screams. They were nothing like their massive warrior men who had died some days before, snarling and cursing with even their last breath. There were no curses of defiance from the families they tried to save, only begging and pleading.

The young supply officer sighed. Sometimes evil needs to happen to make progress. The savages here, he figured, would not look back once civilisation and all of its majestic marvels had been given to them. He took one last glance at the smudge on the horizon, cursed it for the grim report he was about to make, and turned fully into the shadow of a giant. Garn was instantly paralysed with fear. The man had his arms raised. He recognised the stern face of Kalac, King of the White Fangs. Then the axe fell.

Garn's eyes flicked open. His head was groggy, and the sea ebbed and flowed in his ears. Blood smeared the long, flattened grass as he tried desperately to drag himself along the floor. He had to make his report to the emperor; he had to warn him the enemy was here; he had to….

The sky darkened, and the waves crashed over him. He saw his fiancée and son on that warm end of summer's day, three days before they were killed in the accidental barn fire. His son ran around the paddock chasing the horses while his mother watched gaily from the fence. She turned her head and smiled brightly at Garn, who ran as fast as he could to greet them.

Kalac lowered himself into the long grass. The killing of the guard had been a gamble. For the briefest moment, he would have been clear for all to see, but it had been necessary for the pair to travel undetected. He flicked his gaze between the men milling about amid the huts, looking for any sign that he had been witnessed. He heard Felas let out a sigh of relief as he crawled up beside the king.

'Quickly, before he's found.'

They were still more than half a mile from the White Fang camp, and though they could have made a run for it, any horsemen would have caught them in heartbeats.

The long grass parted and gave way to the rye field as Kalac moved through, crouching beneath the seeded yellow tips of the reed-like grain. After a while, the orange sun began to sink below the horizon, but the pair were only halfway across the plain. Hunkered down in the crop, they moved far slower than he thought they would. Kalac's stretched calves burned, the axe on his back feeling cumbersome. He started to move faster, more upright, his head bobbing in and out of the ryegrass. For a short while, he thought he had become too far away for them to notice and then, on a fleeting glance back, he saw three horsemen peel from the settlement and ride out towards him, their long spears glinting in the light of the setting sun.

Both warriors hesitated for only a heartbeat, then they were up and running. The waist-high crop stained Kalac's leathers as he whipped through the countless blades. A swift glance over his shoulder told him they were rapidly gaining. He judged the distance he still had to cover and realised he would not make it – not running anyway. Slowing to conserve energy, he drew the felling axe and adjusted his palm to cover the new grip. The horses bore down on him at a relentless rate. Then the thunder of their hooves sounded all around him, the snorting of their nostrils in his ears. Kalac glanced back at the levelled spears of the first two riders. Then he dived to the ground, the spears hissing through the rye as the horses roared past. The third rider had waited. Now he pulled his gelding alongside Kalac and thrust down with his spear. The warrior leapt aside with the litheness of a panther, the weapon grounding in the dirt. Before the rider could drag it free, Kalac hauled on his outstretched arm and flung him from the saddle. The rider hit the ground hard and was still. Kalac jerked the spear free and turned to the remaining riders who had circled for another charge. The warrior king threw the weapon like a javelin, skewering one of the horses through the chest. No sooner had it fallen, Kalac had swept up his axe and ran roaring at the final horse. The unintimidated gelding came head-on, his rider grinning savagely, heeling the beast on. Kalac swung the axe high over his shoulder and sidestepped the beast, swinging out. The rider's spear deflected from Kalac's leather jerkin and ripped a gash in his side before the king's axe knocked him from the saddle. The rider struggled to his feet, sword drawn, his cuirass having taken the blow. But Kalac was upon him with the speed of a tiger, his axe cleaving the Talran's head.

Ripping the blade free, Kalac spun back to the impaled horse. Felas stood beside it, the horse rider's spear in his hand, the body lost to the reeds. He pointed the tip towards the settlement, and Kalac glanced back as a score more horsemen rode out to aid their comrades. The warrior king wasted no time and vaulted into the saddle of the nearest gelding, hauled Felas up behind him and heeled the beast into a gallop for the river. The task ahead of the Talran horsemen was impossible. Kalac would reach the camp long before the riders could catch him and the horsemen knew it too, drawing rein as they did upon arriving at the three beaten riders.

Kalac slowed the horse and dismounted as they reached the river. All three drank from her precious waters. The king's mouth was dry, and the fresh water was a welcome relief, but it brought back his feeling of hunger. Pain lanced under his left arm where the spearhead had caught a rib.

Supporting the wound with one hand, he dropped into the half-frozen water and wadded swiftly, the previous day's events replaying in his mind. Felas followed as a man entering unknown territory. Kalac left the horse standing on the bank. Had the gelding been unruly, he would have killed it so the Talran could not reclaim it. However, he liked the plucky beast so standing it was left, for he could not ride into the White Fang camp flashing the bright blue colours on its barding, especially when followed by the most hated and revered warrior in White Fang history.

By the time the pair arrived at the camp, the sun had disappeared over the horizon casting a fire of pink gold over the nearby tents. The first guard he approached was so surprised to see not only his formally dead king but also the Talon's very own reaper that he forgot to welcome his king. A mistake Kalac was quick to condemn in his grim hunger-fuelled mood, and as the guard bowed low, apologising profusely, both men wandered by. Kalac's fight for survival was evident in the briefest of glances; mud encrusted his weary body, his leathers were torn from his battle with the jagged rocks of the Meir, and fresh blood oozed over his hand from the wound in his side. Yet his blood-smeared axe told all who saw him that his enemies had come off far worse. Of course, those still awake would be eyeing the second incongruous figure, also battle-worn with a strapped up arm and a fresh gash from cheek to chin.

They climbed the hillock and passed the ash-ridden earth where he knew a great pyre had stood not many nights before to honour those warriors lost to the river's anger and those sons and daughters who would have been rivals only nights before. His mind wandered again to the dying woman in the wood.

Always reactive, never proactive; perhaps if you had put aside your differences sooner, the Talran would have already been driven from Neferian soil. He cursed his accusing thoughts as he weaved through the scattered tents, the last of the sunlight fading from the day leaving only the waxing moon. Then he spotted some seventy mountain horses grazing on the pastures to one side of the camp, their rumps white in the moonlight, and knew then his reinforcements had arrived from the south. A small blessing in an otherwise dreadful week, he considered. The pair walked on through the empty ground between the tents. Most of the warriors had retired early to their bedding on orders, Kalac guessed, of which he would need to be informed.

When Kalac eventually approached his tent, his eyes narrowed at the sight of flickering lights within. Nobody had even bothered to search for him, yet someone had obviously taken his place – *certainly taken his tent!* The warrior king drew the felling axe, adding his second hand to the long haft. Well, thought Kalac, this premature bastard will get a premature burial! Before Felas could stop him, he leapt through the flap, almost bringing down the tent, a grim expression on his face, a snarl on his lips. Then he stood stock as he eyed the many wounded that littered the floor.

The healers, caked in their patients' blood, froze in fright, and the place fell silent for the briefest of moments. Then the spell was broken.

'What in the gods has happened to my tent?' shouted Kalac.

'My lord, Kalac,' came the nervous rattle of a healer woman. 'We were told you were dead. Our orders were to use your tent as a healing house.'

Felas stepped inside and smiled at the reddening embarrassment on Kalac's face.

'Who gave such an order?' asked Kalac.

'Akron, my king,' said the healer casting a critical gaze over his cuts. 'Your wounds look infectious, my lord.'

Kalac sighed. 'I have issues that need attending to, but I shall return.'

Another healer felt Felas' strapped arm as he was heading for the tent flap.

The veteran warrior smiled. 'Nothing can be done about that, lass.'

With that, they left and trod the short distance to the tent of the loudmouth, Akron. Fingers of frost were creeping over the ground; the mild nights of the previous week were coming to an end, and the chill ached his tired body. He ordered the nearest passing warrior to fetch them some food before he pushed aside the goatskin tent flap and entered.

Inside it was warm, the air thick with the smoke from the brazier. Six orange faces turned towards Kalac in the firelight. A few mouths opened, but their words caught in their throat.

'Kalac!' The king recognised the awed voice of Turesh, though his face was indistinct in the flickering glow of the flames. 'So the witch woman was right....' His voice trailed off into thought, but Kalac ignored it.

'Who turned my tent into a healing hut?' he said, his tone as sharp as knives.

'I did, lord,' said Akron defensively from the fire's far side. 'In your absence, decisions still had to be made. The men needed orders.'

Kalac nodded slowly. With his best gambling face on, he scanned the other four figures that had yet to speak. Now that his eyes had adjusted to the glow, he could make out the faces of the veteran leaders his warriors thought of highly. So he had not been totally wrong about his replacement then, he thought. One of these men would challenge him once the war was over. Of that, he had no doubt. How else would Krem allow them back into her walls? Not with a traitor king, that was certain.

'I am taking this tent,' he said. 'You will sleep elsewhere tonight, Akron.'

The bald man almost choked. 'Where, my

lord?'

Kalac shook his head. 'Not my problem. Sleep with the wounded if you must. You won't be sleeping long. What is my concern are the orders issued in my absence. Care to inform me of what you plan?'

Akron fell silent as Kalac seated himself, taking care not to knock his arm against his ribs. Koren was left to answer.

'We've decided to fall back to the nearest settlement, Kalac King, to bolster our food supplies and better fortify ourselves for a long defensive slog.'

Kalac eyed the giant seated before him. However Koren felt towards Kalac, he would not let his people suffer, and for that, Kalac respected him. 'What are these defensive positions of which you speak, and how do you suppose to make the Talran attack us once we move back from the river? Why won't they simply encircle us and watch us starve?'

'We were just discussing that very notion as you entered, Kalac King.'

Then the tent flap swept back, and a man entered, proffering a crude copper bowl filled with dry meats to his king. All the occupants of the tent fell quiet. Kalac took the bowl and thanked the man before dismissing him, then he loudly scoffed his face in the hushed silence that followed. As the silence lengthened, he looked up into the ghost-white face of Koren and tracked his hawk gaze to the tent flap. In the flickering light of the brazier stood a legend, a harbinger of death, a warrior whose name had transcended his own tribe and whose death would have decorated any White Fang who slew him. In his burly hand was a copper bowl filled with fruit.

'I'll be damned if that man walks into this camp and still draws breath,' said the giant. 'Many a great warrior has fallen to his hands. Good men. With children. Some of them I would have even called friends. Even now, I'd give my final breath to make it his last.'

'It was just war, Koren,' said Kalac sympathetically. 'Nothing personal. My father spent the latter part of his life integrating defeated tribes into our own and allowing them to self-govern their lands.' He gestured to the ageing hunter. 'Turesh is one such example. I don't see you baying for his blood.'

The giant stood and, without saying a word, made his way to the flap, his gaze never wavering from the revered Talon.

'For what it's worth,' said Felas calmly, 'I'm sorry we had to meet this way.'

Koren snorted, and with that, he was gone.

Kalac gestured to the now vacant spot beside the fire. 'Come. Sit. You're needed at this counsel.'

The tent's other occupants had still not uttered a word, as though they were waiting to wake up from a daydream. Turesh was not originally a Fang and therefore held the least respect for the honour of the tribe, so it came as no surprise to Kalac that he spoke first.

He chose to ignore the newcomer.

'Our scouts report a smaller force than our own across the river, my lord. But given how they fight, retreating to a nearby settlement is a must, even if it's only temporary.'

Kalac looked up from his food bowl. 'I agree. I've seen this enemy fight, and for those of you that have not, they do so as a collective and are worth far more than their numbers suggest. We must not underestimate them lest we share the same fate as the Talon.' He gestured to Felas. 'This man can tell you more.'

Felas cleared his throat. 'Everything the king has said is true. Reshmal possesses techniques that are ahead of his time. The Talran fight not as warriors seeking glory but as a single entity, a machine with only one mind and goal. The sky will turn dark with arrows, and, honour bound, we shall run at them. Then a wall of shields will halt us, a wall of swords will stab us, and finally, a wall of boots will trample us like ants as they advance. If we don't plan for this, Neferia will fall to the Talran.'

'You paint a bleak picture,' said the bald warrior.

'It gets worse,' said Kalac, flicking his gaze towards him. 'We will have to leave this camp tonight.'

'What? Why?'

'I passed the Talran camp this evening, Akron. Bar a minimal guard and men raiding supplies, I saw no one. Meaning either Reshmal sent his *entire* army to search for supplies, which is far too impractical for such a military mind, *or* they're all cooped up in bed.'

'So?'

Kalac sighed. 'So why give your warriors an order to sleep through the day?'

Those amongst the group who were quicker thinkers than the others cursed.

'How long do you think we have, my lord?' asked Turesh.

Kalac shrugged. 'Who can say for sure? But I want the men up and out well before sunrise, for I don't wish to risk facing them on open ground. That would be disastrous.'

Akron cursed. 'We barely have a half-cooked plan, and we're expected to act upon it shortly?'

'Got any better ideas?' said Kalac.

The king eyed the bald warrior he called his

sword brother back in his youth. Time has made you bitter and twisted, he thought. With no response forthcoming, the warrior king returned his attention to the last scraps of his meal bowl.

'If the Talran were raiding the village, as you say, Kalac King,' said Turesh on a new train of thought, 'then perhaps they're less well equipped than we've given them credit for.'

Kalac glanced up into the fire-lit eyes of the scheming warrior. 'I'm listening.'

'When my group returned to Kardek Pass, we saw their supplies trundle past in a long line of wagons. It's guarded by regiments at the front and rear but only lightly at the sides. Suppose we can take this out. Reshmal will be forced to attack us no matter where we stand.'

'What's stopping him from raiding another village?' asked Felas. 'For I have also seen the supply wagons and know it to be one of Reshmal's few weaknesses.'

Turesh gave a wry smile. 'We'll send our horsemen to evacuate the settlements before we arrive, take what food we can and burn the rest, keeping Reshmal out of reach of his precious supplies.'

Akron nodded. 'And how do we attack *him* exactly?'

Turesh shrugged and threw a handful of

small sticks into the brazier. 'I didn't say I knew the answer to everything.'

With no more headway being made, the council was adjourned, and Kalac told Felas to remain behind once everyone else had left.

'You should go and see the Talon women and children in the healing hut,' said Kalac. 'It'll raise their spirits to see you.'

Felas smiled. 'I shall. It'll do me well also.' He offered the king the last from his fruit bowl, but Kalac raised his hand in grateful decline, so he placed the bowl beside the brazier.

'I'll not keep you much longer, Felas. The nearest village lies southeast, and we'll be gone before dawn, but I'm sending your people to a settlement a few days southwest of here with a small warrior escort. They've been through enough, and risking their lives further is senseless. At the last count, we had a dozen carts. They can have five to carry their wounded, but we'll need the rest for the days ahead. They'll have to manage the best they can. Before you get some sleep, could you relay that message to them? I feel it might sound better coming from you.'

'Of course, my lord,' said Felas.

Kalac smiled and gestured to the tent flap with an open hand. 'Then don't let me keep you from your audience.'

The revered Talon stood and hefted the

goatskin flap. An icy wind swept in, carrying with it Felas' departing words. 'From one honourable warrior to another, thank you for all you have done.'

Reshmal was gently rocked back and forth as he sat astride his gelding, glancing up at the frosty, twinkling stars. Somewhere up there, the gods were playing dice, he knew, deciding the fates of millions in a game where no mortal knew the rules. But Reshmal knew the odds were always stacked in favour of those who helped themselves. So he had. He had helped himself to his father's kingdom, helped himself to other kingdoms, and now he was here, helping himself to Neferia. With such good odds, how could victory slip from him tonight?

Deception had been the answer, of course. Reshmal struck his saddle in his rage, frightening the horse beneath him. He had been a confident man when his ten regiments had crossed the river earlier in the night. Even when his scouts had reported a lack of guards around the perimeter of the barbarian encampment, he had not been shaken, thinking the foreign savages as inferior, foolish and reckless. Indeed they were, he knew, but tonight when his regiments had stalked into the enemy's silent camp, it had been he who was all of these things. The camp had been empty, the tents bare, and though no man dared speak it, they all thought the same thing so loudly that the emperor could hear it inside his own head: Reshmal had failed again. Anger had touched him then, and he thought of the mutilated body of the useless supply officer found outside the settlement in the late evening and the slaughter of the three horsemen assigned to chase down the savage they believed responsible. He concluded that the enemy scouts must have been far closer than he realised. A failure, therefore, of the eyes which should have been watching. He had made a show of this and charged fifteen men with a week on latrine duty.

Now Reshmal rode the perimeter of the camp, which up until a few hours ago had belonged to the White Fang, eyeing the large clumps of trees in every direction. At least he was finally across the river, he thought, and his enemies were running before his might.

'Sir.'

Reshmal spurred his horse around and stared at the mounted scout he had sent barely an hour ago to locate Kalac and his rabble army. To be back so swiftly meant the news could only be good. 'You have found them?'

'Less than a mile southeast, sir.' The soldier suddenly smiled. 'I think they need to be reminded how to run.'

'You are not paid to think,' said Reshmal, and the smile fell from the scout's face. 'Are you sure they're not just empty tents this time?'

'Yes, sir,' said the scout, his confidence fading with every passing moment.

'Good. Keep an eye on them. Report any changes in position. Dismissed.'

The emperor glanced back at the woods and called for another three scouts. Somewhere out there was a cavalry force that had been separated from him in the last failed river crossing, and he needed to get an order to them urgently. They could swing round and stop the Neferians from retreating further if they were far enough south.

13

Chaos exploded in Calderkash. Men, women and children filled bags, pots, and anything they could with food and personal possessions before slinging them onto the back of wagons, piling them high. A hundred people jostled for a chance to cram their possessions onto the overflowing carts and be gone before the Talran arrived.

Not so for one such man.

'So much chaos,' he whispered calmly as he weaved his way through the crowd. He was dressed in a long leather apron burnt and stained by hazardous solutions. An assortment of skinning knives hung about his waist, and all bar two were discoloured by years of bloodied hide and matted hair. The other knives were noticeably different: longer, slender blades that had been oiled and well cared for. He sidestepped a woman emerging from a hut with her meagre possessions and threaded his way through some baggage carts, a jar of dark liquid in his hand. Entering a nearby dwelling, he shut the wicker door to muffle the noise from outside.

The assassin held the jar to the low flickering flame.

'Tannin.' He smiled at the room's only other occupant. 'Can be made in a bunch of different ways but back home, we use the acid from the wood ant.'

He broke the seal on the lid, and the pungent fumes escaped into the room.

'Unfortunately, it appears this doesn't belong to you.'

The White Fang warrior, curled up on the floor, groaned. His hands and feet were bound with long lengths of rope, and his face was swollen and bloody; who he had been before was indistinguishable. The false tanner hauled on the warrior's long matted hair, dragging him to a seated position. Keeping one hand tight around the big man's locks, he hefted the tannin jug high in the other.

'You'd better tell me everything again because I'm quite the forgetful type,' said the assassin, mockery and threat rolling from his tongue like treacle.

'I've… told you,' said the warrior, 'everything… I know.'

The assassin clicked his tongue. 'Are you

sure Kalac sleeps alone and not with a woman? I know all you hairy barbarians look the same, but surely you are capable of basic numeracy.' His voice rose, and he jerked the warrior's head back. 'Does he sleep alone?'

'I… said yes.'

'Good. When does he usually change the night guards?'

The Neferian clenched his teeth, his pride fighting for control. 'Never…'

Deciphering the savage's slurred words was difficult for the assassin. 'When?'

'Tell… you.'

The tannin dripped from the tilted jug and splashed onto the warrior's open-toed sandals. Instantly a bestial roar escaped his shredded lips as the acid ate away at his skin. The assassin wiped it off with his apron, and as the last drops hissed on the blistered foot, he asked again: 'When do the guards change?'

'Depends…'

'On?' said the false tanner, sloshing around the liquid contents of the jug.

A knock on the door shocked the assassin into silence. He yanked back the warrior's head and held the tannin over it.

'Say something.'

'Yes,' shouted the Neferian.

'You need to get moving,' shouted the muffled voice from behind the door, barely audible over the crowds outside. 'We're leaving soon.'

The assassin gave a piercing stare. 'Tell him you will be out in a moment.'

'Will I?' said the warrior, his eyes dull with the last ashes of hope.

'*If* you answer my question.'

The Neferian swallowed. 'I'll be... out... in... a moment.'

'Okay,' said the disembodied voice, 'but if you're struggling with something, you had better hurry or leave it!'

The assassin sighed and turned back to the question at hand. 'The night guards! When do they change?'

'Usually... only at... midnight.'

The false tanner nodded. 'And you say he carries but a single weapon?'

The warrior sighed as the last vestiges of pride melted away. 'Yes.'

'This is purely business, friend,' said the assassin, with a smile, 'so no hard feelings, eh?'

He pulled his captive's restraints loose and waited. Leaders always put men on guard for too long, he thought, especially at night. Towards the end of an uneventful watch, people tended to become tired and complacent, missing things they would have otherwise seen earlier.

When the bloodied man finally struggled to his feet, the assassin casually threw the dark liquid into the warrior's face and made for the door. The man who had interrupted him had not moved far from the hut, for he heard the screams of agony. The wicker door crashed inwards as a knife leapt into the assassin's hand. The burly figure on the other side had just enough time to register the weapon before he lay in a pool of his own blood. The assassin jumped the corpse and disappeared into the crowd as someone pointed past him. More people turned to the spectacle, and the crowd backed away, terrified by the screaming man staggering from the doorway, his face red with blistered burns.

Koren stood as one of the eleven warriors on the night watch, his gaze locked on the smouldering ruins of Calderkash, where the Talran now spent the night. The flames from the storehouse had spread to the thatched roofs of the nearby huts, and the whole place had gone to Hell long before Reshmal had arrived. The emperor had swiftly set about dousing the fire with a chain of men hauling huge buckets of water from a nearby stream to the blazing thatches. Of course, nothing had been left to save; the leftover food stores were the first to go up. In his mind's eye, Koren saw the ill-tempered emperor in a blackened, roofless hut bawling at one of his subordinates to fetch his pissing pot. He laughed aloud. The only thing missing was the rain. Then the silence settled again; the only sounds were the hooting of the owls in the trees and the rustling of nocturnal hunters on the prowl in the long grass. The stillness seemed to stretch into the darkness forever, and the man whose face had been horrifically burnt that very afternoon rampaged like a wildfire in his mind. He tried not to think about it. In truth, only ten warriors had been ordered to stand watch, but Koren could not sleep and had hoped for some suspicious activity from his foes to occupy his thoughts. None was forthcoming, and the more he tried not to think about it, the more he thought. Somewhere in his flayed subconscious, the burning, writhing warrior had unlocked the door he had run from all his life. A door surrounded by fear and flames. A door he had begged the goddess Meira never to allow open.

He saw himself as a wily child again, barely seven, using his size to bully the other boys and then running off to accuse them of something before they could tell his parents. Even at that age, he had found something alluring about the flames of a campfire: the intensity of its brightness, the power of its heat.

He would sit and watch as it devoured everything the adults threw into it. Then he discovered the explosive wonders of animal fat mixed with ground sugar beet and various combustible nuts and seeds. Lit inside a clay jug, it would burn for a while, the flames licking at the rim, but seal the top with a large stone, and the jar explodes, dousing everything within its blast radius in liquid fire. The trick was how to light it once the top was covered. Of course, no parents would allow their child access to such things, so he did it in secret, stealing to feed his curiosity and threatening the other boys to say nothing. The trick, after a year of failed attempts, was horsehair. Soaked in the fat and left to hang over the rim, it was the perfect liaison between fire and fuel. With the aid of hindsight, he knew now he should have left it at that. No man had meddled in such things, and no man had since, so his younger self did not know it was the key which unlocked the cage of a demon.

Such was the child Koren's fascination with the blast he began to hide capped jugs deep amongst the rounds of firewood stacked beside his parent's hut for the winter. On one particularly warm day, a freak forest fire had ignited in a copse, the southerly wind fanning the flames towards the settlement. The guards had been alerted and were swiftly trying to control the blaze. They did not succeed. And as the fires grew closer, a few embers must have touched the horsehair he had bundled and rigged to each of the stashed fuel jugs. He had been out foolishly collecting more animal fat when the demon awoke inside his hut – with his parents still inside. In those fleeting moments, he had witnessed the power of the imprisoned fire god, a power no man should ever possess the knowledge to beckon. The hut had been blown to pieces. Airc had taken his parents and belongings as a sacrifice just to be summoned for a few heartbeats from his eternal tormented abyss. He had felt the demon's melting breath, heard his thunderous roar, and felt the ground shudder as he rocked the gates of his prison.

And Koren had run; run so as not to be killed for meddling in such an affair; run so the demon-god could not take from him again; run, and never looked back at the dreaded flames.

Koren shivered as the cold night hung about him like a cloak. Something off to the far left caught his eye, a black shadow on a dark plain. One of the nearer watchers also saw it and stalked into the field to investigate. Then the guard tripped over, and it was only when Koren had almost reached the sentry that the guard recovered.

'What is going on?' asked the giant as the other waved his hand to say he was uninjured.

'Nothing unusual. Must have been a doe or something.' He pointed back over his shoulder, wafting a pungent smell of tannin from under his cloak. 'Ditch there though, so best avoid it in the dark.'

Koren cursed the other warrior's stupidity and turned away. A doe! Everyone knew deer migrated in the winter. His dark mood quickly turned sour as he thought once again of the predicament he was in. Kalac was searching for any means to conquer the invading army, and Koren had the means…. He just preyed Airc would be more forgiving to those who worshipped him.

Kalac rubbed his dark eyes; he could not remember the last time he had properly slept, but it felt like a lifetime ago. A quick snatch here and there was all he seemed to manage. As Turesh finished his pitch, Kalac stared at the burning brazier and yawned. 'I don't want too many risks. Hit and run. Are you confident this will work?'

Turesh nodded. 'I passed the supply train at Kardek. It has a rear guard, but its flanks are only lightly guarded. If we can soil some of their supplies, Reshmal will have no choice but to seek a swift victory. It will work, my king.'

'And you will lead?'

Turesh was briefly silent. For an instant, Kalac saw the gleam of power in his eyes, and then it was gone.

'Only if you wish me to, lord.'

The warrior king nodded. 'I do. Remember Turesh: no major risks.'

A cold wind whipped around the room, and their attention turned to the tent flap where a giant stood in the doorway.

'I understand, my lord,' said Turesh before he greeted the newcomer with a swift nod. 'Koren.'

The solemn giant rumbled a reply before turning to his king. 'I need to speak with you alone.'

Kalac nodded, sensing some unkempt dread in his voice. 'I think we're done here.' He glanced at Turesh, who concurred. 'Leave us then.'

The warrior king waited as one man left and the other sat down, his mood becoming more formal. He much rather enjoyed the company of Turesh than Koren; something frosty and distant about the giant made Kalac wary of him.

'What news, Koren?'

The warrior leaned towards him. 'I have a way to destroy the Talran, but the risks are high.'

'I'm listening….'

'When I was a child, I was fascinated by fire; it was in my home and in my head.' He paused for a moment. 'I found a way to summon Airc.'

Kalac's heart leapt into his throat, and he choked. '*The* Airc? From his hellish prison?' And Koren nodded. 'Then you must forget what you did and never speak of it again!'

'This could help us,' said the giant. 'Believe me, I despise the idea as much as you.'

'No, Koren!' shouted Kalac, thrusting his hand into his other palm. 'We would throw everything at the whim of a malicious god.'

'And yet throw it you must.'

All eyes turned towards the speaker of the last as she pushed her way through the tent flap.

'You have seen our defeat, should I not?' asked Kalac.

'It is one possible future.'

Kalac cursed. 'So you have come barging in here to demand we release Airc only to pray he doesn't destroy us all.'

'If we are to be destroyed anyway,' said Iskel, 'what difference will it make? I have seen the streams of the future, and this is the only chance you have. You must heed me, Kalac!'

The king sat silent for a moment, his face

contorted in his revulsion of choice. 'I'll consider it,' he said, 'but the men cannot know about this.'

The witch woman fled from the king's tent, her hands shaking, not from rage, she knew, but from the fear she had no wish to show. Fate had finally forced her into a corner. Now she had started along a path which would ultimately kill her.

Iskel walked swiftly to her tent to consolidate herself, the reddening moon mocking her every mortal step. Too long had she lived; too many were the people who had died in her stead, and yet even now, when the stakes were high, selfish acts were still weaving their way through her resolve. She gripped her hands together to stop them from shaking. Her life had meant little so far, she chided herself, but soon her actions would mean something – something every Neferian would remember. Her mind wandered back to Kalac's question as they rode through the woods on the way to the Meir all those weeks ago: 'Why are you helping me?'

She sighed. Once upon a time, nobody would have asked her such a question; she would have freely helped anyone in need. People had referred to Kalac's childhood sweetheart as a caring girl, fit for the prince.

Then Lynaea had struck out and banished her in her misguided fear of the young girl's gifts. That day the innocent girl had been lost to history. She had become so bitter over the years: cruel and unforgiving. But now, she could make amends.

Iskel sat in the silent dark, and slowly the shaking began to cease, but there was always the harrowing knowledge that death was coming for her in Bandlekin, and this time she would not run.

Koren left the king's tent, unsure of his actions. Had he just set in motion events that would lead to the end of the world? Would Airc be unleashed, and his hellfire scorch the Earth as he raged against the other Gods for imprisoning him? He hoped, demon or not, Airc would aid Neferia's plight.

'Koren!'

The giant halted mid-step. He recognised the voice. The man who had spoken stood in the shadow of a tent, using its wall as a windbreak.

'You need to watch your step around me, Talon. Blood runs deep where I'm from.'

'I understand. I'm not asking you to like me, Koren, but I need to know we can work together.'

Felas stepped from the shadows into the light of the almost full moon, and Koren saw for the first time just how gaunt and grey his old adversary had become. Once a man of legend, Felas would rise against impossible odds, destroying all those who would stand before him. Koren had never fought him on the battlefield, and although he yearned for the glory of killing him, locked deep in the recesses of his mind, a small part of Koren was glad of that.

He sighed. Perhaps worse than being killed as a legend was living as a cripple under the shadow of it.

'I serve the White Fangs, and Neferia.'

Felas nodded. 'As do I.'

'Then I will do you no harm, Felas. I swear this on my oath to the goddess Meira.'

'That is all I ask.'

'Good.' Koren shrugged. 'Then leave me be. I've much preparation to do.'

Emperor Reshmal glanced fleetingly at the tree lines on either side of the dirt track as the warning was issued.

'Keep the train moving!' he shouted as the supply wagons began to slow, conscious of his slipping distance from the fleeing Neferians. For days now, his supplies had been hounded from the trees by the charge and retreat tactics of a hundred horsemen. The first assault had come by surprise, and a few of the more empty wagons had been overturned, the food stores flung across the dirt track and trampled by the retreating horsemen before his own regiments could form a counterattack. He had ordered additional soldiers to flank the supply convoy, and since then, despite the powerful breed of the barbarian horses, the remaining wagons had only taken light damage.

Reshmal wheeled his horse at the head of the column and galloped down its side, bawling his steadfast order to keep moving. The wagon drivers whipped their oxen, knocking them from their fear-induced paralysis, as wild snorts and the clash of steel reverberated around them. The regiments stretched along the wagons, and Reshmal ordered those engaged to fall behind instead of awkwardly trying to move with the slow trundling carts. But the barbarians had disappeared back into the trees the moment they were faced with a wall of organised shields.

The emperor cursed at what his men had dubbed 'the mild annoyance tactic'. Whether he admitted it or not, his supplies were stretched thin. He could ill afford to lose another wagon, especially now that the barbarians had taken to burning their own food stores. But this tactic could not be used indefinitely; at this rate, the savages would run out of territory before his own army ran out of food. It was only delaying the inevitable, and Reshmal had all but ran out of patience. It would all be over by tomorrow. He quickly reminded himself. Scouts had communicated with the southern cavalry regiment who were riding to the next settlement, the locals called Bandlekin, only a day ahead, on orders to waylay the enemy upon their arrival. Added to this, he had received a report that his assassin had infiltrated the White Fang camp a few nights ago, though there was no news yet regarding Kalac's health.

Reshmal shrugged. The plan was beginning to come together, it would all end tomorrow, and after a decisive victory, the tribe could not hope to hold from him the city of Krem – his supply depot for the campaign's duration.

Kalac was bone weary. The heavy rain thundering on the goatskin roof drummed loudly in his ears. Who would have thought his father had done so much? First, there were the food supplies – sources, freshness, not too heavy on the stomach. Then the battle plans - positions, tactics, and logistics – before anyone had even swung a damn sword! Then there were the matters of the dead, the dying, and the injured, morale... The last forced a half smile. He had not figured everything out yet.

He stood with a scout's crudely sketched

map of the area, twisted into the yellow light of his tent brazier. The map had been smudged somewhat by the drawer's hand and the torrential rain, but he could make out the square huts representing the different settlements, the simple arrow tails for the woods, and the lines of small streams of fresh water. In certain places, the scout had noted things of interest about the area, but Kalac could not decipher the words; he guessed, however, it was associated with terrain levels. One thing he did know was that it would be another day before they reached Bandlekin and a further two days until they arrived at the hills of Hoelock. That gave Koren and his small team three days to prepare, for, at Hoelock, he would light a mountain of Koren's summoning jars and watch Airc rise and the whole world go to Hell….

He froze, mid-thought. A strange smell had reached his nostrils. Tannin. An odour carried by an unknown warrior who had hung around his tent as of late. Kalac had noticed his calculated, poised steps; he moved almost like a dancer, most unlike the warriors of Neferia. Once, he had even looked into his eyes and saw only himself reflected in them. No emotional upheaval, no burdens, no regrets, just an empty calm. A deadly calm.

'I figured Reshmal would eventually send

someone like you,' he said without turning. 'There's no need to linger in the shadows.' He thought he was being paranoid for a brief moment, but then he heard a boot scuff the rug as the assassin relaxed.

'I'm curious,' said the faux warrior conversationally, and Kalac was surprised by his grasp of the local dialect, 'from a business perspective, of course, what gave me away?'

Kalac rolled the map and half turned. 'Tannin.'

'Ah, yes.' The foreigner circled Kalac and warmed his wet hands with the brazier. 'It's frightfully difficult to get rid of the blasted smell.'

'You should try removing it from your face,' said Kalac evenly.

The assassin indulged him with a smile. 'I'm glad you can appreciate my handy work. Now, shall we get down to business? After this, I have an ugly, old hobble to kill, and then I shall be off somewhere warm.' He cracked his fingers. 'No hard feelings, eh?'

The next few heartbeats were a blur to Kalac. He would never know whether the assassin was genuinely that fast or if it was merely sleep deprivation. The one thing he did know was that if the rolled-up map had not been tightly in his grasp, he would have been dead before dawn. As it was, the throwing knife which flashed out glanced from the parchment and embedded itself in the rug. Even the assassin was surprised.

'Of all the luck,' he said before drawing a longer knife from his belt and advancing on Kalac, blocking the path to his axe.

When the assassin struck next, Kalac had been prepared and parried the dagger aside with his palm, pulling his smaller opponent into a savage headbutt. The blade slipped from the foreigner's hand. He crashed through a central tent pole, but a lithe roll righted him, and he hammered a left hook into Kalac's jaw. The warrior king had been hit by bigger men and absorbed the blow, lashing out with a straight right of his own. The assassin leapt back and charged at Kalac with a flying kick. Head snapping back, the king crumpled against the side of the tent. The Talran swept the long knife from the floor as Kalac hauled on the rugs beneath them. The assassin staggered. Then the king came up swinging the broken tent pole just as the Talran's knife hand flashed out. The blade was batted across the tent. Kalac whirled, the tent pole singing in a savage arc. The assassin ducked beneath it, sending a vicious kick to the warrior's knee. Kalac roared as his knee cap twisted, falling heavily onto his side. He reached out for the throwing knife, but the Talran stomped on his hand, and Kalac howled as he felt his fingers break. The foreigner must have known the wail was loud enough to be heard outside. Swiftly, he swept the dagger up and pushed Kalac onto his back, pinning him with one hand, knife raised in the other. Kalac felt something prick his leg, and in that instant, memories of the wine hut and Girak's death came flooding back.

The assassin's eyes were vacant, the dagger poised, and an emotionless voice said: 'It's just busine-'

His words cut off. Kalac guessed the assassin had expected his good hand to come up, vainly trying to push him away as the blade fell. He had not expected the ornate dagger the warrior king held in it. Crimson pumped from a slash which had opened his neck, and his body slumped onto Kalac's swollen knee just as Koren burst into the tent.

Kalac tried feebly to kick the corpse from him with his free leg, but the heady mixture of pain and exhaustion finally took hold, and everything went black.

The following day saw Kalac temporarily hand leadership to Koren. The camp retreated further south into White Fang territory, snaking its way around hills and across barren winter fields towards the next settlement. All the while, Kalac was carried on the wagon for the wounded, giving him some much needed respite. Fortunately, his knee had not been dislocated, and the healers' hands were refreshingly gentle, the various herbs and salves cool and soothing. By the time he was back in his own tent, he was walking normally and feeling more like his old self again, though his hand and knee were heavily bandaged.

Koren had found the king in his tent later that afternoon. Kalac had half expected it; he knew the giant was never one for the unrelenting pressures of leadership.

'I've set twenty guards on the perimeter, and we have no problems with our food stocks,' said Koren. 'I just wished this damn mist would lift so we could see where Reshmal's men are down on the plain. Anyway, I've relieved myself from your position. I'm under your command, Kalac King.'

Kalac was seated on the rug, revolving the ornate dagger in his hand, his eyes never wavering from it.

'Do you believe everything has a purpose, Koren?'

The giant raised an eyebrow. 'I know not what you mean, my lord.'

'This dagger,' said Kalac, proffering it to Koren so he could get a better look, 'I won on the roll of a bone die back in Krem. First, it helped me kill Girak when I had, perhaps naively, not taken my halberd to the Dance of the Dead when my father passed. Then I had forgotten about it until it helped me kill the assassin the other night. Had I not won it, things might have been very different, though, at the time, I couldn't have cared less, for I had lost my father's finest fur coat.'

Koren laughed as he returned the blade. 'It's a spare weapon, my king. It will always help you in a time of need.'

'You don't believe in any of that fate nonsense then?'

The giant shook his head. 'Do you, my lord?'

Kalac was silent for a moment. I had not, he thought. Throwing the dagger aside along with the subject of fate, he suddenly smiled. 'Whatever has come between us, Koren, know I don't hold it against you. You do more than I give you credit for. I realise that now.'

Koren was at first confused, then his laughter boomed out. 'It's not just your hand you need to worry about, my lord. You must have taken a knock to the head as well.'

Kalac smiled, and though the giant said nothing more, he could tell he had appreciated it. The king had left it at that, and with a word of, what Kalac considered genuine respect, Koren left, leaving the king to the solemn knowledge that in a couple of days, when Airc was released, none of this may even matter.

Then that evening, with Reshmal's troops bearing down upon them, they had hauled the evacuation carts into Bandlekin.

14

Kalac heaved a sack of possessions high up onto the cart with his one good hand and raised the buckler strapped to his other forearm to stop its owner from clambering up behind it.

'No. You walk. We need the space.'

The aged man scrunched his nose up in disgust before turning away, and Kalac glanced around to judge the progress. At the same time, the other warriors continued with the now standard evacuation procedure. The food store had been crammed with provisions which could not be carried, and still half the population had not yet left their huts. Bandlekin was the largest settlement so far, and though Kalac knew Turesh and some one hundred horsemen were trying their damnedest to slow the Talran, he began to doubt they had enough time to evacuate them all.

Suddenly cries erupted from the other side of the village. Kalac turned to a cloud of mud, dust and horses' hooves, bright blue colours flashing from their barding. Panicked villagers were trampled beneath the charging wedge of snorting beasts. The dying sun smeared the sky red as the warrior king ordered the carts to be unhooked from the workhorses and upturned. Sacks of food, pots, and jugs spilt out and smashed onto the hard ground as the wagons were rocked onto their sides, forming small walls of wood. Despite the desperate barricade, the cavalry manoeuvred between the wagons, lances lowered. Dozens of Neferians were trampled under hoof and a score more skewered on the ends of the cavalry's spears, but it quickly became apparent the attack had been overzealous. The carts had slowed the charge, and the sheer number of Neferians had halted it altogether, quickly turning it into a rout.

Kalac lowered the axe head to the earth and leant upon the haft, watching the horsemen fleeing towards their inexperienced leader who sat atop his steed, rallying his men to him with a thrust of his spear. The writhing injured crying on the ground beyond the wagons was suddenly audible to the warriors, and Kalac flicked his gaze to Koren, who shook his head. The king needed no confirmation; the open ground beyond their barricade would be the death of them, but while the horsemen lingered, his people had no chance of escaping. He could feel the weight of a thousand eyes upon him, waiting for his decision, knowing full well his inept ability to give them one.

Then, with Kalac feeling the day could not get any worse, it did. Fingers began to point back across the plain, and Kalac saw the red sheen of the dying day in hundreds of bronze helmets above a dark smear of shields and armour. The Talran were less than a half hour's march from the village, and he saw no sign of Turesh and the White Fang horsemen. Flee and be cut down by the cavalry, or stay and be slaughtered by an army, he mused. There was but one option left. The warrior king wore a grim face as he glanced at a set of nearby wagons hidden from the enemy's scouts between two large huts. They were only half full with the clay jugs of the animal fat concoction prescribed by Koren, but it would have to do. He bawled orders to fall back to a large, high fenced paddock on the outskirts of the settlement, long since relieved of its horses and cattle, before he spun to the giant.

'We stand, Koren!' he said defiantly, and then he pointed to the far side of the paddock the rest of the men were rushing to. 'Prepare the wagons in front of the field-side gates. We'll coax them into a trap!'

Koren stood in fear-filled silence, the order echoing inside his mind. He had been steadily building up the courage to face such a thing once again, but now that it was thrust upon him so unexpectedly, his stomach tightened, and his hands began to shake. The giant turned from Kalac so as not to embarrass himself further and marched like a man approaching the executioner's block – slowly, deliberately – towards the warriors sitting upon the wagons. One of them dropped from the side of the first cart and nodded as he drew near.

'Ho, Koren.'

The giant straightened and pointed back from whence he came. 'Kalac King needs the jugs on the far side of the paddock.'

Another warrior dropped from the second cart. 'He just wants the one wagon?'

Koren paused. All his life, he had been running from the dozen fire jugs which had taken everything from him. Now he was faced with fifty in each cart, and the thought filled him with dread. He jerked at the sound of the warrior clearing his throat to force an answer. Koren shook his head. 'Both.'

The giant watched the laden carts trundle through the maze of tipped wagons and on into the paddock. Every fibre in his body screamed out to run in the opposite direction, but he knew he could not outrun the cavalry which lay in wait. Reluctantly and at a distance, he followed.

As the wagons were positioned to flank the far gates, Koren eyed the nearby stables with its adjoining storage hut. It must have been at least partially filled with grain, he figured, as his eyes were drawn towards the solitary mare sniffing around the building.

And so it was that Koren saw his chance to escape. He vaulted into the mare's saddle and spun her towards the field gates. His eyes were fixed on the path ahead, the path of freedom from this twisted nightmare. He did not hear what was said behind him as the horse bolted through the open gates, but Koren felt as though Airc was behind him laughing.

The red sky turned dark as the sun finally guttered out, leaving the White Fangs alone to their fate. By the light of the full moon, Kalac watched the cavalry stand sentinel, clearly on orders to hold until the emperor's arrival. The rhythmic drumming of infantry feet grew until it pounded along with the heart in his chest, and as the Talran regiments halted within skirmishing range, the bright blue plume atop Emperor Reshmal's helm settled in the still air.

The king knew that without archers of his own, a skirmish would force him to charge at his enemies and give up the bottleneck of the paddock that so suited the Talran fighting style. Within a few heartbeats, he understood the emperor knew that too, and the enemy regiments reorganised themselves for an assault.

His fist clenched tight around the haft of his axe, Kalac glanced at the warriors beside him, their deep, calming breaths disguising the nervous turmoil inside. The Talran had made quite a name for themselves in the last couple of months, wiping out entire tribes, including their closest rivals, the Eagle Talon. The men had a right to be nervous. In truth, he was too.

'Hold your ground until my order,' he said. Glancing further around, he spotted the ashen faces of the farmers, tanners, and fishermen, wielding wooden hoes, pitchforks, mallets, and skinning knives. Fear gave them a gaunt look, but the White Fangs were bred on courage. Their tools would be useless against the armour of their opponents, Kalac knew, but even as king, he could not refute a man's right to fight for his life, especially when many still had family inside the village.

The sudden sharp sound of a horn pulled Kalac's attention back to the invading army. The first few regiments detached themselves and marched for the nearside gates, their shield wall an omen the other tribes had seen only hours before their extinction. The warrior king bent low and rose to smear a swirling pattern of mud across his face; the swirling fires of Airc, the greatest Neferian demon of all. Then, with a wordless war cry, he leapt at the Talran.

The battle was short, bloody, and one-sided. The shield wall was nigh on impenetrable, and Kalac used his entire prowess just to keep life in his lungs. Then a shield struck him a blow to the face, and he fell back. Up became down, mud churned up all around, someone stood on him, and then a strong arm dragged him from oblivion.

'Koren?' he said through ragged breaths, but as the world righted itself, he saw it to be the unknown face of a tanner. His gaze caught the wavering confidence of the bloodied warriors on the front. He knew it was time to call the retreat but the order lodged in his throat. The Talran cavalry regiment had blocked the far gates, and hundreds of soldiers circled the paddock to join them. Kalac bellowed out a warning. His eyes widened as the Talran cavalry burst into a sudden charge, longswords swinging in brutal arcs. The warriors were forced back under the onslaught to the farmers and fishermen, who stood dumbstruck and were hacked down. Kalac knew the battle was over. All that remained was the final stand. The White Fang way. He saw Flek, the scout who had doubted him all those days ago, standing nearby, and he called out to him. When Flek looked towards his king, he did not disguise the fear in his eyes. His doubt was now a certainty.

'No one lives forever,' whispered Kalac, and he pushed himself to the rear, raising his shield in stout defiance, his axe high above his head, daring the cavalry to attack him. Three scores of the more steadfast warriors joined him, and Kalac was surprised that Flek was among them.

The Talran cavalry drew rein. The paddock was only so big; to charge headlong into the fray would cause them heavy casualties.

Felas pushed his way alongside Kalac and gave a false smile.

'I see you have a handicap too!' He turned to the rest of the line and threw up his one good hand. 'Oh, come on, men! Look how puny they are. We have to give them a fighting chance!'

A few of the warriors on the line laughed, relieving some of their tension. This was precisely the response Felas was hoping for, Kalac knew. Wars were won or lost in moments like these.

The cavalry parted for the hundreds of organised soldiers who marched in their wake. And behind them, on a small knoll, mounted on a chestnut steed and flanked by two horsemen, was Emperor Reshmal II, heralding the death of Neferia.

The soldiers closed in, shields raised. Then a bright blur darted from the stables – a woman with a torch. Her outstretched form landed on several swords before falling headlong into the first jug-laden wagon. And time, as Kalac knew it, seemed to stop.

'Airc have mercy…' he said.

Iskel sat in the flickering gloom, her thoughts grim. Outside she heard a horse whine before galloping through the gates to a chorus of angry shouts and curses, and she knew it to be Koren. Everything was playing out as she had seen it. The small torch raged in her shaking hand, and by its dazzling glare, her mind was transported back through the years to the pivotal moment when her life had fallen apart. She touched her lips and felt her scars afresh. The rain had not stopped cascading from the sky when Lynaea cast her from the young Kalac's gaze and banished her and her mother from the safety of Krem. Outside the city walls in makeshift hovels barely able to withstand the bombardment of the freezing rain dwelt those deemed unsuited to society. Here, the young Iskel had experienced years of hardship like no other. An endless spiral of depravity from which there was no return.

Then had come the time she had first meant to die.

The frost-hardened ground announced the coming of winter, and bitter snow began to fall all around. With her mother away trying futilely to work them both back into society, the lonely Iskel sat under a ramshackle awning, snow intruding through the tears in the cover. She rocked on her haunches, mumbling to the spirits she could not see but whom, even then, she considered her only friends. They had shown her the bearded animal that would beat her to death in a drunken rage as she begged him to stop. In this vile act of deranged dominance, he would be caught by a passing warrior and brought before Marek himself. But what soul accepts such a cruel fate? Who in the gods' names would not change it if they could?

And so she had. The bearded man had gone on to kill three times before being caught. Three lives for hers. She had accepted it then, but these events had become far more frequent, as though her overdue death was a debt the Gods wished to acquire. The last time they had tried to collect what was owed was when

Kalac stormed her tent. She ran her fingers over her scarred lips again and thought of Lynaea. Kalac's mother harboured a great hatred of seers, which she had clearly instilled in her son. He had not recognised Iskel that day or any day since, but she accepted that now. She had to, for she now faced the most horrible choice yet. The destruction of the tribe hinged on her decision to finally accept her belated death.

The torch shook in her trembling hands as fear sought to overwhelm her, and anger touched her then. Oh, how the gods must be enjoying this! Poking her and prodding her, riddling her with guilt until finally she would break. Well, she could still show *them*! She would run and turn her back on the tyrannous gods who do not understand the true value a mortal holds to life!

Trampling hooves outside drew her attention to the slither of moonlight seeping through the stable door. A clashing of steel and cries of pain rent the air, and Iskel knew it was too late to escape. She clenched the torch haft like a boa seizing its prey and stood on unsteady legs. Vomit entered her mouth, but she swallowed it back. Placing one hand on the door, she breathed in the last of life in all its unsung glory and pushed out. Foreign eyes turned towards her as she charged them. At first, they were amused and bewildered, but a sword struck out as she approached the nearest wagon. A clumsy blow that took her breath, and she staggered. Another two pierced her, and for a moment, she stood, propped up by the Talran blades. Then the witch woman fell, a tear in her eye, the torch in her outstretched arm igniting the horsehair bundle.

'Come, Airc...,' she whispered. 'I release you!'

One irrefutable fact few people knew but which Kalac would never forget was this: dried horsehair burns quickly. He watched wide-eyed from across the paddock, anticipation bringing an air of stillness to the choking chaos. Then the wagons were swallowed by a second sun, and the cacophony of steel on steel was drowned out by a thousand peals of thunder. All within the Hellfire were disintegrated. And every man outside the fireball was blasted from his feet; they felt the rumble of Airc's earthly prison and cowered in his wake. Kalac hauled himself onto his knees as wood, steel, flesh, all were torn asunder before him, and his eyes gazed upon the demon's fury and the column of fire which threatened to reach the other gods in the stars. Airc's breath alone was hot enough to cause uncovered skin to blister, and

Kalac brought his arms up to shield his face. A charred roof beam came crashing down beside him. Kalac had no idea how long he had cowered, deafened by Airc's roar, but it felt like a lifetime until the Gods sealed away the demon once more. Charnel smoke was everywhere, and he could still feel the heat of flames as he clambered to his feet. The warrior beside him gazed up with dead eyes. A broad timber beam had plummeted from the air like an enormous club, smashing his neck and jaw to pulp and caving in the chest of the man alongside him.

As the ringing in his ears eased, he began to hear terrible screams of agony. He stumbled forwards through the smoke, avoiding burning bits of debris, and saw the wooden stable and grain store were no more. Even the paddock gates had gone. Blackened bodies in battered bronze lay scattered where they were thrown, and as the smoke began dissipating, Kalac wished it had not. On the opposite side of a giant crater, one Talran was on his knees, screaming in agony. His arms were bloody stumps at the elbow. Another, his legs a tangled gory mess, was desperately trying to drag himself away from the fires, leaving a crimson smear on the scorched grass. Those few soldiers that had survived with lesser injuries were urgently attending to their comrades.

Kalac averted his gaze from the horrors and returned to his men. Most had already hauled themselves up, and the king stepped over the dead, using his one good hand to help others to their feet. He glanced over his shoulder as the wind blew the smoke north, and in the middle distance atop his steed, illuminated by the light of the fires, sat Emperor Reshmal II, flanked by his guards. One of which raised a war horn to their lips.

Kalac cursed.

A gap had formed between the two armies on the village side as the remaining Talran pulled back in disarray, a mask of horror and confusion on every face. Never before had they witnessed the savage power of a malevolent god. Then the horn trumpeted, and their long years of training took over. They reformed into their rank and file and advanced on the dishevelled barbarians.

Koren reined in the mare high on the hillside and looked back down the slope at the burning village. He had refused to glance behind him as the thunder rose. The shadows of the trees changed direction and stretched out before him as the second sun ignited. He could feel Airc's breath on the back of his neck. And Koren had become as fearful as the horse, not wanting to stop until Bandlekin was nothing more than a smudge on the horizon.

It had taken all of his effort to rein in the horse. Now he gazed upon the enormous ring of charred earth around the smouldering crater where once stables and fences had stood, the air thick with black smoke and burnt flesh. At first, he thought Airc had taken everyone as blood tribute, but as the moments passed and the smoke drifted north, men had begun to stand up. They had bravely weathered the demon's wrath, and Airc had spared them. Koren felt instantly ashamed. He spotted Emperor Reshmal in the orange firelight perhaps two hundred paces back from the carnage. The giant imagined how the tactician's mind was whirling, trying to calculate what might be done with the remaining troops.

Then Koren saw something glinting far to the north and down across the plain. He raised his hand to shield his eyes from the fire's glare and gazed into the darkness. As his vision adjusted to the moonlight, he saw the silver sheen of stirrups and lances. The giant nodded. The smoke meant Reshmal could not see what was coming for him.

Then the horn blared and the Talran reformed, the battle for Neferia beginning again. The giant cursed. Heavy guilt pressed upon his shoulders. He should have been down there, standing beside the men in their time of need, not cowering on a hillside like some lowly sheep trying to avoid the farmer's sheers. Koren swore. Fires still burned within the settlement, wild and deadly. Then a new thought struck him. What if all the jugs had not exploded? Surely he should just stay here where it was safe? No, he knew. He *should* go back and aid those he considered friends. A long moment passed, and the shame turned inwards, becoming anger. He would not abandon them again. Unaccustomed to flashes of rage, Koren heeled the mare into a gallop down the hillside to cut off the emperor's escape.

The king had taken up an unwieldy spear as the fighting broke out. He gripped it halfway down the shaft, resting it on his injured hand and using the thumb for stability. Lunging out, he skewered a soldier in the leg as he stepped over the corpse of his comrade. All across the line, Talran shields had clashed with Neferian steel, and even now, Kalac knew the White Fangs might yet be beaten.

'Stand with me!' he shouted, using the shield strapped to his arm to hammer aside a sword thrust before dispatching its wielder.

Then it was that he caught the faint

drumbeat of horses over the cacophony of battle.

'Keep pressing!'

Soon the sound of horse hooves thundered in Kalac's ears. He glanced to the north as Turesh and his one hundred galloped into the village, forming a wedge. The greys foamed at the mouth as they smashed through the Talran lines to a chorus of shrieks and snapping bones.

Only now could Kalac afford to survey the battle. Some of the Talran rear ranks had fled into the fields before the horses arrived, and half of the remaining soldiers were scattered or punched off their feet as the horsemen ploughed through; their notorious shield wall was in disarray. The warrior king knew it was now or never. He raised his spear high. 'For my father! For the White Fangs!' And he jumped tip-first into the chaos. The bedraggled Talran lines gave back under the swell of barbarian broadswords. The soldiers were forced back to the southern side of the village, and the White Fang horsemen charged again, cleaving through the enemy lines. The soldiers' formation buckled, then broke, and within a heartbeat, the Talran routed. Chased by warriors and hounded by horsemen, they ran across the field, heading for the safety of the woods.

Another blow of the horn drew Kalac's attention to the Talran emperor and his horse guards who had rode amongst the fleeing men bellowing orders. Reshmal sat atop his gelding, a curved scimitar raised high above his head, shining like a beacon in the orange glow of the village. His elite guard carved a circle around him, cutting down any Neferians who ventured near.

Despite his injured knee, the king dashed towards a riderless grey. He noted the pommel of a longsword scabbarded to the saddle's side before jumping onto the horse and heeling the grey towards the Talran emperor, rage rising within. Reshmal had to die! Already, he had weakened the White Fangs; butchering countless tribesmen, including women and children; establishing a traitor king in Krem; slaying Kalac's father, and murdering innocent little Lekta! The warrior king heard his father's words burst through his clenched teeth. 'A pox on civilisation!'

He hauled the spear up over his shoulder.

Suddenly a raging giant bellowed a war cry from the darkness beyond Reshmal and bounded with almost inhuman speed at the horse guards, a greatsword flashing enormous arcs in the moonlight. The first guard fell, both rider and horse nearly severed in two. The second guard had just enough time to raise his shield, but the ferocity of the blow hammered him from the saddle.

Kalac took his opportunity. Fury lending him strength, he threw the spear, punching Reshmal from the gelding. Drawing on the reins, the king drew the longsword and leapt lightly to the ground. He saw Koren dispatch the second guard before turning his attention to Reshmal, who had scrambled to his feet, wielding his twin scimitars, a huge dent in his breastplate.

'Koren!' Kalac raised his hand to hold the giant at bay. The king saw the turmoil in the massive warrior's eyes as Koren glanced at him.

'I failed them,' said the giant. The rage faded from his face until only despair remained.

The king had no idea what he meant and was too preoccupied to ask. 'The warriors need your aid!'

Kalac's gaze flicked back to the emperor as Reshmal leapt a fallen horse, blades singing through the air. The King of the White Fangs stepped in. Batting one sword aside with his shield, he parried the other and struck an elbow into Reshmal's open face. The Talran's head snapped back, and he staggered, the plumed helmet falling to the grass.

The emperor's first attack had been

overzealous, and now he circled with caution. Kalac noticed him grimacing and trying to subtly adjust his breastplate. Then he attacked with blinding speed. Blocking and parrying, the king gave ground under the ferocious assault; his only counterthrust bounced harmlessly from Reshmal's armour. As the two circled again, the warrior could see the emperor's breathing was laboured. Perhaps, thought Kalac, he was used to his enemies falling quickly to his blades.

Then a lunge and a lightning flick of the Talran's wrist scored a crimson gash across the back of the king's forearm. Kalac blocked the second strike, his riposte opening the emperor's cheek. Reshmal did not let up, kicking out at the warrior's shin. The king's bandaged leg buckled. He fell onto his knee, raising his shield as the Talran struck again. The scimitar bit into the wood. Kalac swung his shield aside, dragging the blade with it, opening Reshmal's defence whilst shifting his balance onto his good leg. He sprung like a jackal, longsword thrusting out. The emperor's other scimitar arced a parry but the sheer weight of the king kept the blade true, and the longsword opened the Talran's throat. The warrior king rolled as he hit the grass and watched Reshmal step back, swaying like a tree in the breeze. The emperor's last scimitar thudded to the earth as he dropped to his knees before falling onto the frozen dirt.

Kalac drew himself onto his good knee. He removed the splintered shield from his arm and rolled the Talran over, feeling the blood trickle from under the emperor's breastplate. Reshmal's eyes were glazed and fixed. The war was over.

The king took a deep breath. As his adrenalin passed, the pain from his gashed forearm began to flare. He looked again at the emperor's breastplate. It had caved in on the left side of the sternum, no doubt cracking a few ribs and causing internal bleeding. Reshmal had been dying even before he fell from his horse.

Kalac stood and tested his knee; it would not hold much weight. He looked around the field and saw the last pockets of Talran resistance flee into the trees. This time the warriors did not follow. The king hobbled to the horse and untied the scabbard from the saddle. Returning the longsword to its sheath, he used it as a crutch and began the slow walk back to the village.

When he arrived, he saw Felas organising the men, helping to relocate the bodies of the honoured fallen in preparation for the funeral pyre and the song of the dead. Healers moved among the injured, seeing to their various ailments. Kalac limped into the paddock, where most of the fires had now either died or been extinguished. He saw the Talran injured lying on the far side; those with lesser wounds were trying to help their companions to see another sunrise. To see them still lying here just a few hundred feet from the White Fang warriors was no surprise to Kalac. There was no honour in killing them.

The king called Felas over. 'I need you to translate for me.'

He led the giant warrior over to the wounded Talran. Kalac had expected swords to be drawn as he neared, but the soldiers just watched him. Sadness touched the king as he surveyed the scene. The able Talran had merely made their fellow soldiers more comfortable. They had accepted their fates, he knew, and were simply waiting for their deaths.

He turned to Felas. 'Tell them they can have a couple of horses and carts for their wounded. It's a two-week walk, but no man should accost them between here and the border.'

He watched as Felas stepped forward and began to translate. The Talon warrior paused and stumbled over his pronunciation several times, relying on his one-handed gestures to assist his words. As the giant finished, one of the soldiers stepped forward, a tear forming in his eye. He looked as though he wanted to offer a gift in return, but with nothing appropriate, he settled for holding out his hand. A handshake was a widespread mark of respect in many countries, Kalac knew, but it was not something to which Neferians were accustomed. Felas, however, must have learnt their traditions and language, for he returned the gesture.

Kalac smiled, but it did not reach his eyes. He turned away and hobbled towards the crater. His thoughts were on the lone woman who had, by one action, turned the tide of the war. He knew without much doubt that it had been Iskel, for she had come to him the night before once Koren had left his tent. Her face had been ashen and grey, very much like the ghosts who had served her all those years. Kalac had been instantly fearful for the events of the coming days.

'Sit, Iskel,' he said, beckoning her to the rug beside him. 'What ails you?'

At first, the witch woman said nothing, and Kalac sat patiently, hoping the news would not destroy him as it had her. Eventually, she spoke. 'Airc requires one of us to give ourselves to the summoning.'

'And he has chosen you?' asked Kalac, but he did not need a reply. Iskel sat staring at the rug, the conflict of indecision and doubt raging in her eyes. At one point, he thought she would get up and run. The king knew such indecisiveness could yet be the death of Neferia, and he drew a great bolstering breath, his mind filling with the days of old. Kalac had been part of a family once. He had held a mother's love; felt jealous of the attention his newborn brother had received; felt joy when playing with his father, the indomitable figure that every child knows; and elation when Lekta had grown enough to join in. Yes, he had been part of a family once, and though he had not realised it then, they were all he had ever lived for. Now all that remained was an enormous hole, impossible to fill. 'I'll do it,' he said at last. 'If it saves the White Fangs, I'll do it.'

Iskel's sudden outburst startled him. 'But you cannot! You must lead the warriors, for there is no one else who can.' Her fearful eyes caught Kalac's then. 'I have thought long and hard about this. It has to be me. It was always meant to be me.'

Sadness touched the young king, for he saw the loneliness in her eyes. Perhaps it was better to have known a family's love and joy than to have never felt that joy at all. He reached out and placed a comforting arm around her shoulders. 'Whatever happens tomorrow, Iskel, you'll not be alone.'

The witch woman leaned in and kissed him on the cheek. A clumsy kiss.

'Yes, I will,' she whispered.

Kalac could still recall the roughness of the scars as her lips brushed his face, and his heart hung heavy. He had wondered why she had come to him if not to change anything, but now he realised she *had* changed something. She had not spent her last night as she had all the rest: alone, with her terrors. The kind that starts small but wakes you at midnight, having grown into a fully-fledged monster. She had sought the comfort and distraction which had vanquished her nightmares and stopped her from running as she had countless times before. She had sought solace in Kalac and had opened up to her fears. In turn, that night had brought a deep-rooted sense of familiarity in the king, as though he had known her from somewhere before. He sighed. Now he would probably never know, for the truth had died with her.

'Kalac King.'

Kalac was pulled from his sombre thoughts and turned towards the voice. 'Ho, Turesh,' he said with a nod. 'How are your men holding up?'

The warrior dismounted and fondly brushed down the grey. 'Twelve men were lost in an overzealous hit and run. A further twenty had been slowly whittled away throughout the skirmishes.' He gestured over his shoulder towards the village. 'And we lost a score more in that last battle. Sorry we couldn't have joined you sooner. Reshmal had overturned some of his carts and set up a defensive wall in the woods to waylay us.' He paused. 'I'm ready to be relieved, my king.'

The last comment shocked Kalac.

'Why in the Gods would I do that?'

Turesh said nothing, but his face had become crestfallen. Kalac did not know what was expected of him.

At last, Turesh said: 'The war is over, my lord.'

Kalac knew it was a hint and his mind wandered back to the pact they had made on the hillock overlooking the Meir.

'I'll do you a deal, Turesh. You fight for the White Fangs, and I'll see you get back to your tribe when all this is over.'

'Our war with the *Talran* is over,' said Kalac in what he hoped was his negotiating tone.

Turesh shook his head. 'Your tribal war doesn't interest me. My deal was to fight for the White Fangs, not against them.'

Kalac took a deep consolidating breath. He was disappointed. Turesh had been a loyal warrior; losing him would be a shame, but loyalty demanded loyalty.

Kalac gestured to the gelding. 'Take the grey.'

Turesh nodded, and his face brightened as he swung himself back into the saddle.

'I'll not forget this, my king.'

Before Kalac could reply, Turesh had heeled the grey and was gone.

The young king took one last glance at the smouldering crater and thought once more of Iskel. Strange, he thought, how you never knew who the true heroes were until they died. Perhaps it was the ultimate sacrifice which made them heroes in the first place? Had Iskel somehow lived, would her deed have been lessened because of it?

A cheer went up, and Kalac turned to see White Fang horsemen trotting into the settlement, lances high with pride and a victory cry on each of their lips. They joined the rest of the warriors in the ruckus of merriment which would continue long into the night. Kalac grinned with genuine relief. A tremendous burden had been eased from his shoulders. He watched the men in the full exaltation of their triumph, their bodies heady with the joy of life, every breath a gift from the gods. Someone turned and began to chant his king's name; others followed his lead. Kalac gave a cynical smile. They *must* be giddy, he thought. He knew the fickle ways of men, but today he did not care. The warriors were happy, and Kalac knew his father would have been proud.

Epilogue

Turesh rode the stout gelding long and hard, but the horse was battle bred and not built for endurance. As such, the animal tired quickly and jostled the rider around in the saddle as it galloped. Turesh, himself, was also weary from the day's events, but his urge to return home and embrace his soulmate far outweighed any other of his cares. Too long had they been separated. Too great had been the distance, but no more. The horse galloped on, and time rewound inside Turesh's mind to the days before the dreaded battle with the White Fangs, before he was taken to Krem and trained for war when all the young hunter's dreams revolved around Resha. These soothing thoughts spurred him on, and by daybreak, he was perhaps only a day from the Great Claw border and then only a few hours more from Greno, his home village. He was so exhausted now that he risked falling from the saddle and never arriving at all. Bringing the gelding to rest, he dismounted and tethered him to a tree, where he began to chew the long grass. Turesh sat deep inside the hollowed-out bough of a mighty oak, and within a few heartbeats, he was asleep...

... and back in Bandlekin. The ground thundered, and white flame exploded all around him, painlessly licking his skin but disintegrating everybody else. When the flames died away, leaving the blackened and broken bodies lying on the scorched grass, Turesh saw that someone else also stood, though only the gods knew how. The blackened body, removed of all skin, shambled towards him, its entrails tugging across the floor behind it. Turesh stood stock still, not trusting his legs to move. Every fibre in his body screamed out to run, for such a creature was never designed to grace the lives of man. But he understood now fleeing from the curse would never break it; it would always find him no matter where he tried to cower.

When the corpse grew near, the horrid smell of charred flesh hit Turesh's nostrils like airborne poison, and he retched. The blackened body gripped his shoulder, and he realised then that if he were to die now, he would never see Resha again. The thought caused him to step back but the corpse held to him with a death grip. A white glow seemed to emanate from the hunter, travelling down the rotting arm to the burnt body. He could feel his life force being dredged up from within and coursing into that mutilated figure. The corpse began to glow as though infused by his soul, becoming younger and fresher. Pink skin stretched out from the bright glow and wrapped itself around the burnt remains. Slowly, the figure of a young woman began to take shape, and then, like covering a glistening pearl in mud, a torn, ragged robe began to form upon her until, at last, the light faded, and Iskel stood before him, as scornful as ever.

'Finally grown some balls between those legs of yours, I see.'

Turesh's fear was replaced by anger.

'So this is it?' he said. 'I stood through all that just to be ridiculed by you.'

Iskel laughed with genuine humour. 'Not quite.' She moved her hand from his shoulder and touched two fingers to his forehead. Turesh inhaled deeply as the world fell away. His stomach twisted; it was as though falling in reverse. When he reached the misty clouds, he continued to rise, and gradually before him formed a hazy river that began narrow but in the middle distance started to spread like the branches of a tree, forming a delta that stretched on into an endless black.

'I've never seen this river before,' said Turesh.

'Few people have. This is the flow of time made hazy by the lost souls of the dead endlessly drifting across it without flesh nor bone to anchor themselves to any particular time or place.'

Turesh was both wide-eyed with awe and frightened to the pit of his stomach.

'Is this your destiny?' he asked.

'No.' Iskel moved her fingers from his forehead and took a clammy hand before returning a mocking smile. 'I have you, silly.'

Together they drifted through the surging river, and Iskel led him to a small hut where all of the streams of fate connected – no matter what happened, this would always come to pass. Turesh could tell it was Bandlekin from the layout of the huts and the recently scorched earth, though the mists refused to clear, and as they descended closer to the hut, he could hear two men talking within.

Iskel's face took on a surprised expression. 'I've never heard anything within a vision….' Her voice trailed off.

The pair passed through the straw roof as though it was air but even within the mists continued to choke the scene, though now he clearly understood the topic of conversation.

Turesh's frustration rose.

'Who are they? Why is it so damn misty?'

Iskel shrugged. 'Could be that you have not prepared with the correct stones, or perhaps we cannot see and hear a vision at the same time.'

'I haven't used *any* stones-'

'Shhh! We'll sort that out later,' said Iskel. 'Let us hear what they have to say for now.'

Turesh concentrated. The first voice seemed fired by ambition.

'It doesn't matter whether he has had a decisive victory! He has been branded a traitor in Krem. We need a new king.'

The second voice sounded withdrawn, as if the owner was weighing his options.

'And that would be you, would it?'

'What do you think?' said the first voice cynically. 'So will you help me or not?'

The second voice did not reply for a while, and the first came again. 'Well?'

Turesh opened his eyes, and the visions faded, returning to the bough of the tree where he slept. His mind remembered the last words spoken before he awoke: 'Yes, Akron,' the second voice had said, 'I'll help you.'

THE END

Printed in Great Britain
by Amazon